# ONCE UPON THE TRACKS OF MUMBAI

# ONCE UPON THE TRACKS OF MUMBAI

a novel

## Rishi Vohra

JAICO PUBLISHING HOUSE

Ahmedabad Bangalore Bhopal Bhubaneswar Chennai
Delhi Hyderabad Kolkata Lucknow Mumbai

Published by Jaico Publishing House
A-2 Jash Chambers, 7-A Sir Phirozshah Mehta Road
Fort, Mumbai - 400 001
jaicopub@jaicobooks.com
www.jaicobooks.com

ONCE UPON THE TRACKS OF MUMBAI
ISBN 978-81-8495-305-3

First Jaico Impression: 2012

Printed by
Repro India Limited
Plot No. 50/2, T.T.C. MIDC Industrial Area
Mahape, Navi Mumbai - 400 710

# DEDICATION

For my Mom
Late Mrs. Chandra Prabha Vohra

# PROLOGUE

I WOKE UP ALL OF A SUDDEN. DARKNESS RETURNED MY sleepy gaze. And the stillness that serves as a prelude to the morning was like a familiar friend waiting to greet me.

My name is Balwant Srivastav, my friends call me Babloo. But even the name Babloo sounds alien to my ears since I don't really have friends. Very few people know me. And contrary to the ways of the world, I am happy being unknown. The fewer people one knows, the less complicated the rollercoaster of life is. But somehow my simple life did get complicated. I didn't plan it. It just happened. Destiny took some surprise turns, which rendered me a stranger to my own life.

'They' said that I had psychiatric problems. That I was autistic. 'They' said that I was schizophrenic and psychotic. That I had a split personality disorder. 'They' said that I had no social skills and all my conversations were disjointed. 'They' said so many other things that I eventually stopped paying attention. By the way, 'they' also said I had Attention Deficit Disorder. But these so called experts who had the upper hand – 'they' didn't really know me.

My pride doesn't prevent me from admitting to my shortcomings. I admit that I'm a little slow in my responses. It is a fact that most of the time, I have nothing to offer to a conversation. But little do 'they' know that I understand everything.

However, no one ever understands me. And when that happens, one feels all alone in the world. Yes, I do feel alone but not lonely. There's a difference.

Nature was generous enough to give me a best friend within myself. Sometimes 'he' answered me, at other times, 'he' asked me questions and provided me with clarity of thought. In situations that demanded it, 'he' helped me recognize my inner strength and manifest it into physical force.

No one understood the dual existence of 'him' and me that made me the person I am. Only the railway tracks that ran along outside my bedroom window knew the both of us individually. The endless, idle wooden planks connected by durable steel had formed a fine segregation between my fantasy and reality.

I lie awake while my mind races and thoughts overlap each other, putting me in a state of confusion. My restless mind starts pulling me in different directions as I recall the uneventful chain of non-events that are my life and piece them together one by one. Soon I surrender to blissful sleep.

MY EYES OPENED SUDDENLY AT THE TREMOR OF THE FIRST local train shattering the silence of the dark winter morning. I grimaced and tried to retreat into my safe world of slumber. But within minutes, the rattling of the next train forced my eyes open, into the beginning of another unpredictable day.

Naturally, I scanned my surroundings. The first sight to catch my eyes was the familiar form of my brother who lay fast asleep, mouth half open to facilitate his daily snoring. This was one of those rare moments when I envied my brother Raghu. I wished I could sleep as peacefully, unperturbed by any form of noise.

26 long years had passed since my family moved to the railway quarters. And for 24 years now, I had been opening my eyes every morning to my unchanged world in this colony located next to the busy station of Bandra in the restless city of Mumbai. Ever since, aggressive train sounds of steel clanking on weary railway tracks had been a part of my daily life. And yet the cacophonous, rumbling noise aggravated my peace of mind and woke me up early every morning, obliterating any possibility of further sleep.

I considered myself a misfit in this fast-paced world. Deep down I hoped that the boredom synonymous with my life was temporary. The merciless Mumbai trains had made the first 24 years of my life unmemorable. I was determined not to let them control whatever time I had left on this earth. But I didn't know how.

The same random thoughts darted through my mind every single day as I woke up in the inky violet light of the early morning. First I cursed the trains and thought about my hopeless life. Then I consoled myself by imagining and pinning my hopes on promising turns I wished my life would take. And then, before getting out of bed in a fleeting, positive frame of mind, I cursed my luck again and resigned myself to my fate. This was Babloo Srivastav's daily routine, which lasted only a few minutes before I followed my unpredictable day in whichever direction it took me.

I kicked off the thin sheet, which was a poor substitute for a warm comforting blanket. The sheet had proved defenseless in the chilly January morning. I looked two feet across at the bed on which Raghu lay sprawled, wrapped comfortably in a woollen blanket. I secretly hoped that my brother's blanket caught static and electrocuted him, if that were possible.

I was the elder of the two by just nine months. I had once overheard my parents telling their relatives that Raghu was "a mistake". If that were the case, it always puzzled me as to why my parents were much fonder of my younger brother.

But no one considered me important enough to put even my slightest queries to rest. As a result, I usually found myself confused by all these unanswered questions, which gave rise to rapid Q & A sessions in my head.

Over the years, no brotherly bond was cultivated between Raghu and me. And besides, I was never made to feel like a part of the family. My parents were always proud of Raghu and made it obvious in every way possible – from his favourite food when he wanted it to directing the remote to his desired TV channel when he was at home. As a result, I grew up a neglected child.

Throughout my life, I tried my best to make my parents proud of me but could never win their approval. My inadequacies weren't my fault but I felt that my parents didn't seem to understand that. I tried hard at studies but my grasping power was very weak. Classroom learning didn't help much because if anyone spoke too fast, I had difficulty in understanding him or her.

In comparison, Raghu always did well in school and brought home good grades. He exceeded our parents' expectations by graduating with a Bachelors degree in Commerce with honours; it took me six years to secure a mere passing grade for the same three-year degree. I never gave up trying even though I had to give my exams again and again. But my parents never saw it that way.

The sun was beginning to rise, bringing in the heat with it. The sweat trickling down my face brought me back to the present, reminding me of the sweltering heat that was characteristic of Mumbai. Even though I loved the city because of the crowded familiarity and emotional security it offered, I hated everything else about the city – the heat, dust, excess population, pollution, traffic – the list went on. But it was the heat that topped my list.

The fan rotating lazily 10 feet above was barely successful in providing intermittent relief. It collected dust so rapidly that even a daily cleaning routine did not render it back to its original colour. It needed repair since even at its highest speed I could see each of its well-defined blades cutting through the faintly murky haze that seemed to be permanently suspended overhead, again courtesy the proximity to the dusty world of the train tracks right below my bedroom window. Sometimes to kill time, I would gaze at the blades and count the number of rotations each would make. Even though I was a bit slow mentally, I never lost count.

I contemplated going back under my sheets but then figured that if I didn't make it out of the bedraggled colony soon, I would be bogged down by the hopelessness of my life and would end up idling away my time at home all day. For me, leaving the house was not the routine event it was for most people, rather it was an escape.

I lazily kicked off the bed sheet, which dangled at my feet before settling into a slight heap on the floor. My feet groped and found the bare floor around it and with the support of my hands, I lifted my fit frame to full height. I stretched my strong arms above my head to ease the stiffness from sleeping cramped up in the bed that I had outgrown years ago. But instead, the stretch tightened my muscles further, reminding me that I was still tired.

I surveyed my small confines and once again the hopeless feeling of being trapped threatened to overwhelm me. A small window, seemingly held up by its rusted iron railings, appeared cleaved in the middle of the wall at one end, acting as a dividing line between the two identical, iron, single beds. The window had never seen any curtains as Ma explained that hanging curtains was useless, that they would always get dirty with the perpetually invasive dust and grime. However, the doorway, 10 feet away, was always curtained to conceal the palpable, dismal look of the bedroom from the main door.

I advanced to the full-length, unvarnished, wooden cupboard, which stood gloomily in one corner of the diminutive room. The cupboard was crammed, mostly with Raghu's clothes, with just one lone shelf relegated to me. I had to settle for the metal hooks on the timeworn bedroom door. It was a hierarchy that had been established ever since Raghu started work.

The bright blue walls had faded to a pale tone a long time ago. Now, with the paint peeling off, it looked like a different shade altogether and made the room feel even smaller. I wished my parents would do something about the appearance of the room and make it more tolerable. But whenever I tried to discuss the issue with them, they made it clear that they weren't interested.

I let out a huge, jaw-cracking yawn. Right at this moment, my parents felt like a distant memory. But in reality they were sleeping in the next room. When I had asked as to why they didn't sleep in the bedroom, my father replied that the trains disturbed them. His logic never made any sense to me because it was he who had chosen to live in the railway colony!

The bright sunlight found its way into the bedroom, engulfing everything in its harshness. I wiped away my thoughts along with the heavy beads of perspiration that had formed on my forehead. I expertly collected my sweat onto my palm and carefully let it trickle down to the tip of my fingers and flicked it on Raghu's face.

Instinctively, I dropped to the ground and commenced my daily push-ups. I was only five feet eight inches tall, but athletic and well built. My stomach was flat, mostly because I hardly ate, and my shoulders and chest were well defined which I attributed to my exercise. I felt it was important to stay strong and therefore made push-ups a part of my daily routine.

I finished my brief workout and headed towards the washbasin outside the tiny bathroom that formed a clear division between the bedroom and living room. As I soaked my face with handfuls of cool water, memories rapidly started flowing through my head. I thought of the days when I took walks down in the colony just to be able to pass Vandana every few minutes. She always smiled at me whenever I caught her eye and made it a point to talk to me, unlike the other colony residents who mostly pretended not to see me.

I had adored Vandana ever since I could remember. In fact, I knew I was in love with her. Just thinking about her brought a smile to my face, reminding me of facial muscles I had forgotten I had. I rarely had reason to smile in my otherwise desolate life.

My mother would soon wake up and hustle the household into instant activity. She would move noisily around the house because of which my father would wake up just five minutes after. But they would tiptoe around Raghu to ensure that he woke up later, only at his daily scheduled time of 8 a.m. My parents made it a point to be quiet around Raghu since, unlike me, he was the one with the job.

Raghu had recently been employed as an assistant to an eminent stockbroker. His bookish, yet sound knowledge of financial concepts was often mistaken for intelligence and masked his rather unimpressive personality. However, I had been unemployed for the past year, ever since I finished college. With some half-hearted help from Raghu, I had prepared a resume and sent it off to many companies for office manager positions. I had even managed to secure a few interviews. But the interviewers asked questions too rapidly for me to follow, and were very rude and humiliating when I couldn't answer.

To impress my father, I had appeared for the written exam to qualify for an Officer's position with the Mumbai railways. But even after intense preparation, I drew a blank by the time I reached the examination hall. Instead, I produced an illegible scrawl, my honest views on how the railway system could be improved. I recommended that a metro system be set up, similar to the ones in the western world. With trains running overhead or underground, it would not interfere with the city planning and would even curb noise pollution. As a result, I scored the lowest marks in the history of the railway exams.

I examined myself closely in the mirror. Even though my complexion was wheatish, it was still lighter than that of the rest of my family. I was no Riyaz Khan (Bollywood's best looking actor) but definitely better looking than the average Indian. My straight, silky black hair stopped just above my shoulders, giving me a wild, unkempt look. My face was long and chiseled and my jaw line well-defined, a characteristic feature in the North Indian population. However, the perpetual expressionless look on my face sometimes negated my positive physical attributes.

I decided against bathing, as the hissing sound of the tap would wake my parents. Instead, I would take a shower at night since the municipal water supply was consistent then. Most apartment buildings in Mumbai relied on tanker water to maintain a steady 24-hour water supply. But income disparities in the colony made this alternate source unaffordable. All too often, when anyone bought a new car in the colony, a jealous neighbour would put a deliberate scratch on it, a temporary satisfaction that somehow made up for his or her own financial inadequacies.

I quietly tiptoed across my parents' lifeless figures, sprawled on narrow mats on the bare living room floor, to the balcony where we all parked our footwear. The balcony faced the interiors of the colony overlooking all the other balconies of all the other apartment blocks. In the evenings, the gossipmongers would stand in their balconies to give them easier access to the activities in the other residents' quarters.

I moved back to my bedroom and quietly changed from my shorts into my favourite blue shirt and faded blue jeans. Since this was my favourite clothing combination, I wore it as often as possible in the hope that it would bring me good luck.

On my way to the door, I deliberately knocked over a steel glass on the bare floor and quickly dashed out. Only when I reached the end of the first flight of stairs did I hear my mother's high pitched voice shouting.

## 2

THE HUGE, EVENLY-SPACED PALM TREES IN THE railway colony had outgrown the six-storied buildings in the complex, giving it an appearance that bordered between an upwardly mobile chawl and an old, crumbling housing society. Sometimes in the middle of the night one would hear an occasional coconut falling on the terrace of one of the ten buildings that constituted the 60-year-old colony.

The long shadows cast by the trees were not very successful in hiding the dilapidated state of the buildings. The structures may have been made with the cement used in British times, but looked worn out, as if they were tired of being a part of the history of that area. They looked ready to give up but they must have had some sense of responsibility, which made them withstand the hard-hitting monsoon every year and still emerge triumphant, except for the fresh water leakages adding to the woes of their residents.

At first the leakages were confined to the insides of the buildings. But they gradually found their way to the outer walls, streaking across the entire surface of each building in lines shaped like tree branches. It was strange that all the buildings matched each other in appearance, not one of them was left unmarked.

The buildings formed an uneven semi-circle. Cars were parked in front of the buildings on a first come first served basis, between faded parking lines. The colony committee had come up with a designated plan to keep the parking organized. But at the end of the day, the senior railway officials parked where they pleased, inconveniencing the other residents. The senior officials were the only ones with cars, while the rest mostly had two-wheelers.

The saving grace of the colony was the central lawn that was tended by an old, shirtless gardener who unfailingly maintained the manicured green patch all year round. It was nothing great to look at but the fresh grass infused a sense of youth and hope in the otherwise aged colony.

Along the periphery of the lawn ran an iron railing which most of the youngsters stuck themselves to in the evenings. Across from the railing at equal intervals were concrete park benches where the elderly folk sat in the evenings, exchanging stories about their day and when they ran out of those, focusing on expressing their disapproval of the nearby youngsters. There was a considerable distance between the railing and the benches, enough to allow two lanes of cars to pass. As a rule, the cars only ran clockwise around the compound.

The morning heat hit me like a hard slap on the face as I stepped out of my building block. I took a moment to take in the early 'winter' morning and get a bit more acclimated to the muggy Mumbai weather before walking further.

As I walked away from my building, I tried to leave the sounds of the trains behind. But wherever I went, they seemed to follow, forming their own tracks in my head. I wished that my father had been allocated a house in one of the corner blocks or at least by the main gate facing the street. But the relatively peaceful quarters were reserved only for the senior officers.

I did a quick scan of the colony hoping to catch Vandana on her way to work. But she was nowhere to be seen, among the scurrying residents. I glanced at my wristwatch. It was already 7 a.m. Where could she be? She would usually emerge from her block around this time and head towards Bandra Station to catch the 7:20 a.m. train to Churchgate Station. I figured she must have left earlier than usual.

As I walked ahead, I saw an empty can of diet coke lying on the ground. I kicked it along the railing, happy that it gave me some temporary distraction. It was when I was going to make my third kick that her uniquely dulcet voice fell upon my ears.

"Hi Babloo!"

I quickly spun around. I saw Vandana running to catch up with me. I immediately abandoned my short-term companion and waited for her.

"Where are you going?" she asked, looking at me inquisitively.

I took in the light pink salwar kameez she was wearing which accentuated her perfect figure and silky-smooth, fair complexion. Her long, wavy hair, black with red highlights, left untied, was blowing wildly in the light morning breeze. She quickly confined it to a ponytail with a red hair band from her wrist, to reveal the beautiful contours of her soft face. Her big, beautiful, black eyes turned to gaze intently at me.

"How come you hardly reply to me when I talk to you? What do you keep thinking about?" Vandana asked, with a light smile.

I felt that Vandana was the only person who cared about me. She was the only person who seemed to want to know what I was thinking about. I wanted to tell her so much but every time I tried to get a hold on my thoughts, they just slipped away.

"Just about my day," I mumbled almost immediately.

"And what is it that you're going to do today?"

"Nothing."

Her smile broke into instant laughter. The aura of happiness that emanated from her brought an instant smile to my face.

"You're so strange," she said in between her laughter.

I didn't mind her being judgmental about me. She was the only person who could criticize me without getting me infuriated.

"Yes. Thank you," I said, with a blank expression.

She laughed again but stopped quickly, on seeing my face. My stolid expression broke into a smile. I knew I loved her very much. Every time I saw her, I imagined a beautiful life with her; the two of us living in our own apartment by the sea, married of course. We would spend the evenings sitting on a park bench and talking about beautiful things, things that she found beautiful.

"Hello! Is Babloo home?" Vandana was asking.

I immediately transported myself to reality.

"No. Babloo has stepped out of the house," I replied candidly.

Vandana's luscious lips gave way to a sudden laugh and this time I laughed too. I had no clue what the joke was but was happy that she seemed happy.

"You're so funny!" she chuckled.

Now I realized that maybe the joke was on me. My countenance immediately changed to a vacant expression. She noticed that and quickly simmered down to a smile.

"So will you walk me to the station?" she asked in a polite tone of voice, "that's if you're not busy."

I waited for these moments when we both were alone. These were the moments I wanted to retain as memories and I wished that they happened more often.

"No, I'm not busy. Don't worry. I'll come with you to the station."

We reached the perpetually open, unguarded, rusted gates of the colony and stepped out into the traffic-choked road that led to Bandra railway station. I hoped that one day we would step out together and never come back.

The road was lined with mostly Xerox and stationery shops, all eating into each other's space. Whatever was left of the disheveled footpath was occupied by vegetable vendors who were laying out their products either on a cart or on a dirty cloth spread out on the street. The women who came to buy their vegetables didn't mind the dirty cloth since they would wash the vegetables once they got home.

A *falooda* stall stood a little ahead on the right and the popular National Dhaba encroached on to the footpath on the left. Both complemented each other because after having a cheap, tasty meal at the *dhaba*, people would flock to the *falooda* stand for dessert. When I was a child, I thought that both the turbaned owners were related. It was only later on that I learned that one was a Sikh and the other was a Muslim.

As we dodged our way through the busy station road, I kept an eye on all the people we passed. In my mind, Vandana had entrusted me with the task of walking her to the station because she felt safe with me and so it was now my responsibility to protect her. I focused so intently on each face that passed us that Vandana had to jerk my arm to get my attention.

"Babloo, you are not even listening to me," she chided amiably.

"Yes," I replied.

"Yes what? Are you or are you not listening to me?"

"Yes."

She looked away in frustration and fell silent. I sensed that I needed to salvage the situation. I quickly said the first thing that came to mind.

"It's such a beautiful day."

"Yes," she smiled. Then she fell silent again and diverted her attention to a woman haggling with a vegetable vendor about the steep price he had quoted her for the *bhindi* she was inspecting. I felt the need to say something more to keep the conversation going but my mind offered nothing.

"Vandana," I said suddenly.

"Yes?"

"What time are you coming back home?"

"Why?" she asked, now focusing all her attention on me, looking a bit perplexed.

"Because maybe I can walk you back home from the station."

She smiled. "Thank you Babloo. That's so sweet. But I don't know what time I'll get back from the office. It all depends on my boss' mood. You know, it feels like a school. Even at the end of the day, I have to ask my boss whether I can leave. Isn't that ridiculous?"

I didn't understand what the word meant but nodded my head anyway. I knew that she didn't like her job much because she always wore an agitated expression on her face whenever she spoke about it. I remembered her mentioning that she worked at a private advertising agency in a position that I could never remember.

"Today the boss has asked us to stay back for a meeting," she continued eagerly. "He could have easily called for a meeting during office hours. But he needs to show his father, the founder, that he is totally dedicated to his job and so we have to suffer. And we don't even get paid overtime, just the same low monthly salary. Do you know that in America they get paid by the hour?"

I knew about America. With the advent of cable television, the West was no longer a mystery. I wished that I could go there, but even though I could travel for free by local train (courtesy my father's employee benefits), I knew that no local train would ever take me there. The local trains kept one trapped in the city.

"I'm dying to go to America. It's a land where dreams come true. There are so many opportunities there and the quality of life is amazing. Did you know that even a plumber there has his own car?"

I visualized Narayan, the plumber who visited the colony, driving a car through the colony gates. That would really knock the socks off of all the colony residents!

We stepped into the street to avoid an open gutter. Vandana covered her nose with her dupatta to avoid the overwhelming stench.

"I want to have a beautiful house there, a wonderful job and make lots of friends. Did you know that the people there are very friendly and women have lives of their own? Oh, how I wish I could go to America!"

I looked at the dreamlike expression in her eyes as she spoke. I imagined us taking residence in our own private home by the sea in America; and America did have many parks where I could lie down, with my head in her lap and talk about beautiful things.

We were immersed in our own thoughts when an *auto rickshaw* suddenly snipped us, pushing Vandana towards the gutter. I caught her arm just in time and pulled her back on her feet. My reflexes were good.

"Fuck you!" Vandana shouted at the speeding three-wheeler, disgust consuming her face.

Aghast, I looked at her. She saw my shocked expression and smiled as she regained her composure.

"You know Babloo, sometimes you have to talk back to people in their own language. Only then do they understand."

*Talk back to people in their own language, only then do they understand.* I decided that I would remember that. It made sense.

"Ok, I have to go now Babloo." I looked up to see that we were standing under the huge renovated signboard at the entrance to Bandra station.

"Thanks for walking me here," said Vandana.

"Can I walk you back in the evening?" I asked, with a glint of hope in my eyes.

"Thank you Babloo. But I don't know what time I'll be heading back. Besides, if I have to stay late at work tonight, I may get a ride back. Thanks though. That's very sweet."

She quickly adjusted her hair in the sideview mirror of a parked Hero Honda motorcycle. She turned towards my listless face and waved at me as she walked into the massive commanding architecture of Bandra Station. Within seconds she melted into the river of daily commuters who depended on the Mumbai railways to transport them from one harsh reality to the other. Long after she had disappeared, a slight snickering from a few people nearby made me realize that I was standing by myself, vacantly waving my hand at nothing.

# 3

I FOUND MYSELF A SHADY SPOT ON A BENCH ON THE Carter Road promenade that ran the entire length of the upscale residential road. The sun was at its brutal best. Within minutes, beads of perspiration formed on my face as I sat facing the vastness of the Arabian Sea. The seemingly endless body of water always gave me a sense of freedom and some days, I would sit thus, gazing at the murky waters for hours.

In the afternoons, the promenade was more or less empty except for some college students, either bunking classes or done for the day. They would mostly come in couples and find a spot well concealed by the tall, thick bushes lining the place at regular intervals. Their make-out sessions would be brief, as *paandus* on the lookout would dismiss them, forcing them to part with some of their pocket money. Even though the *paandus* were a constant here, the same couples would return the next day and resume from where they left off because this was probably the most convenient place for them to do so. In Mumbai, intimacy was a luxury as places where a couple could get cosy were tough to find and hotel rooms were too expensive. So unless one had a car with tinted windows or a generous friend's empty flat, one was at the mercy of greedy police constables.

The evening brought in a different kind of crowd. Young, old, fitness freaks, as well as gossiping aunties and retired uncles would throng the promenade, chatting excitedly, rehashing the events of the day. Hawkers selling bacteria-infested munchies would plant themselves at regular intervals. The college couples would come back, but this time sitting in groups of friends chatting the evening away, since they could be spotted by a passing family friend or gossiping neighbours if seen in their afternoon avataars. At this time, the making out happened beyond the promenade, on the rocks during low tide, and the participants were mostly servants and drivers who would conceal themselves under open umbrellas. I would sometimes descend on the rocks to try and get a closer look, but then soon get bored of seeing the same driver touching the same maid in the same way and hearing the same moans of pleasure from the maid and the same promises of a good future made by the driver as he moved his hands in deeper.

The popular open-aired Café Coffee Day was landmarked as the starting point of Carter Road. Hip youngsters would arrive at the joint as early as possible and occupy a table with just one coffee between them the entire evening. Cars and bikes whizzed up and down the street, drowning out the babel of evening chatter on the promenade and the loud music of the parked cars. It was always a huge party and everyone was welcome. But I knew I could never be a part of it – because I was different.

Making friends was never easy for me. In my first year at college, I found my peers using me merely for entertainment. My classmates kept changing with the years as I kept getting left behind. Each academic year, I tried to make new friends but the professors always openly reminded me in front of the whole class that I was "repeating the year" and this would always plant preconceived notions in the minds of the other students. Through my college years I was perceived by my peers to be a failure and the class clown.

Over the years I realized that I didn't really need friends. I believe that people should be friends for life and not just companions during a certain phase. Throughout college, I saw people changing groups and friends changing loyalties. That was not a world I belonged to.

I found my best friend in 'him'. So I never got bored alone. Sometimes I did wish that there were someone else I could talk to, who would make me feel happy. And I knew that that someone was only Vandana.

I found Vandana to be more beautiful and smarter than all the mini-skirted, fashionable women of Carter Road. I had overheard some of these women's insipid conversations, about movie stars, clothes or men. They didn't seem to foster any dream or have any goals. In that regard, I considered Vandana unique.

I didn't know what my own dreams were. But I was certain that whatever they were, they lay somewhere beyond the entrapping walls of my colony. And there was little that I could do to find them. They would have to find me.

Darkness started swallowing the sunset and the fashion parade began retreating from the buzz of Carter Road. By the time my watch struck nine, Carter Road was mostly populated by cars making their way home. The days of the sturdy Fiats and Ambassadors were over, replaced mostly by big flashy cars adapted to Indian roads by joint ventures with foreign companies. These expensive cars were driven by two categories of people. The first were the ones who wanted to flaunt their wealth. Their windows had no tint so that they could be seen and envied. The other category comprised of those oblivious to attention, who used their luxurious cars only as a means of transport. Their windows were always accompanied by a dark tint. I always noticed that the cars of new film stars were never tinted. But as they got richer and more comfortable with their star status, their windows darkened to the outside world as well.

I rose from the bench that I had occupied since afternoon. It was time to head home. The crowd on the promenade had thinned down to a handful of people, all walking with lowered energy levels, the exciting evening having come to an end. I crossed the street and set off in the direction of home.

As I reached familiar-looking Turner Road that connected Carter Road to the main Bandra Station road, I missed getting run down by a speeding car playing blaring music. By the time I decided to curse them the way Vandana had cursed the *auto rickshaw*, the car was long gone. I was too slow.

## 4

EACH DAY WAS AS EMPTY AS THE NEXT. NEITHER DID I have a Sunday to look forward to nor did I have a friend's birthday to dress up for. The only eventful part of my day was going to the cinema, where I was able to override my sense of self and get lost in the larger-than-life images on the silver screen. I was able to afford a movie now and then from the allowance my mother gave me for travelling, which I saved by either walking or running to my destination.

I preferred the masala films churned out by Bollywood, to other forms of entertainment, because they mostly ended on a note of justice. The bad guys rarely escaped moral punishment and the good guys always got the girl. I wished that this cinematic ideology of fairness would translate to my own life. But I was aware that there was a fine line between reel and real life. Outside the cinema hall, the so-called bad people literally got away with murder while good people lived a life of suffering.

I rarely had any meaningful conversations with anyone at home or in the outside world. School and college hadn't taught me much either. These visual elements and moral lessons of cinema were my only form of education. I analyzed the actions of the characters and created my own concepts and logic behind them. It was this powerful medium of communication that developed my own sense of right and wrong, rather than my upbringing.

I usually frequented the dingy, lackluster, single-screen Nandi theatre, cramped between businesses in the choked up lane opposite Bandra Station. Nandi suited me well since the tickets were very cheap – just 10 rupees a show. The main drawback was that the outside heat found its way into the fanned cinema hall and since mostly the lower class crowd frequented the theatre, one couldn't escape the aroma of sweaty armpits. The theatre was always dreggy and old *paan* stains adorned the achromatic walls, resembling splashes of orange-red paint, with fresh patterns after every show. Trails of cigarette smoke were apparent against gaudy, scratched prints on the screen. The theatre mostly screened C-grade Hindi films featuring cheap, tawdry, sleazy scenes. For the common crowd, it was a rare treat to see magnified women's breasts staring down at them from the screen. For me it was just a convenient way to pass time. Besides, the actors spoke so fast that at times I didn't understand the story of the film. Mostly, these kinds of films had no story.

When I was in a luxurious mood as I was today, I would shell out more from my pocket bank and treat myself to the comparatively posher Gaiety Galaxy multiplex, located down the road from the colony. The film I chose to watch featured my favourite actor Riyaz Khan in a comical role. The theatre hall was mostly empty, which was a bad sign during the second week of any film. But I was delighted to watch the easily understandable film with its slapstick comedy. By the time I left the cinema hall, I was in good spirits and felt it was 60 bucks well spent.

It was evening. The Bandra Station road was crowded with weary commuters finishing the last part of their day's journey from the station to their homes. As a result, there were people buzzing madly in all directions. Soon, after the swarm of people returning from day jobs receded, the true avataar of Mumbai would settle over Bandra Station. Prostitutes, pimps, drug addicts, transvestites, greedy cops – they would all come out and make their presence felt turning the station into a documentary filmmaker's project.

As I approached the colony gates, I heard a huge commotion in the direction of the station. The snake-mongoose fights were attractions that pulled a crowd only during the day so I knew that it had to be something else. I headed in the direction of the disturbance.

Vehicles were slowly inching past the commotion to get a glimpse of the action, creating a traffic jam in front of the station. There were two pot-bellied cops on the scene who seemed to be deriving entertainment from the episode, completely disinterested in clearing the gathered spectators and traffic jam caused by vehicles inching past slowly, so that they could have their own view of the vehicles. Mumbai was the Mecca of entertainment and the glamour world and yet people were always starved for more.

I used my powerful shoulders to shove through the crowd. I found my way to the clearing in the centre of the circle, amidst censures from the eager public. Two street prostitutes in cut rate sarees and cheap make-up were clawing at each other, hurling abuses while they were at it. The cops showed no signs of intervening and were grinning throughout the show. The fight became more intense, with one prostitute pulling at her adversary's saree. Judging by the low whispers circulating among the crowd, the fight had started when one poached the other's customer.

An elderly man appeared from nowhere and started reprimanding the cops. They laughed him off telling him to mind his own business. However, he quickly produced some sort of government identification, which led the cops to immediately disperse the crowd and haul the two contenders into a nearby police van. I walked away too but knew that within an hour both the prostitutes would be back on the streets after paying their bail in kind.

I understood how the system worked. But people assumed that I was dumb. And I could never understand why. As I entered the gates of the colony, a Q & A session started in my head.

"*You are smart, Babloo. One day they will all realize that!*"

"*But they think I'm dumb.*"

"*You're not dumb. I know that and I'm your best friend.*"

"*Then why don't these people see it? Why do they all treat me like I don't exist?*"

"*Because they don't exist themselves. They have no purpose in life.*"

"*What is my purpose?*"

"*You, Babloo, are made for bigger things. Time will…*"

My inner conversation was broken by a familiar, deep voice.

"Hey *Gaandu!*"

*Gaandu* was a common Mumbai cuss word, the literal meaning of which was homosexual. I didn't take offense immediately. I could only do one thing at a time and was trying to process why I was called that before figuring out how I should react. I took a moment to identify the familiar voices of Sikander, Mahesh, Madan and Pravin. I always recognized sounds and voices and was very sharp at tracing them.

I located them where I sensed they would be – on the southern side of the railing. This was a safe time for these bad boys of the colony to be hanging out. Some naive young girls, who didn't know better, were out on their balconies stealing Romeo-Juliet like glances at them. The girls' excuses to their parents were probably that they needed to gather the clothes hung out to dry or to water the plants. They would soon be called indoors by their mothers.

Sikander was the coolest and hippest looking of the lot. Standing tall at six feet, his wheatish complexion looked more like a tan, the kind that foreign male models sported. His straight black hair was middle-parted, and gelled, as always. With a toned body, designer clothes to accentuate it, and a flashy car, he always managed to make an impression on the opposite sex. Mahesh, Madan and Pravin, tried very hard but looked like cheap replicas of him.

The group of four was seen in the colony only during the later part of the evening when the rest of the colony had retired to their homes. Sikander owned the local cable network in the area and was the leader of the notorious group.

I couldn't fathom why women preferred guys with a 'bad boy' image. Maybe they weren't the decent kind of women. But then many girls from good families swooned over superstar Riyaz Khan even though he had been in and out of jail.

I didn't know where Sikander lived. He mostly hung out in the colony in the evenings with his modified Maruti Esteem parked close by, blasting loud remixed versions of popular film songs. The music though, was barely audible over the familiar din of popular soap operas issuing forth from multiple television sets all over the colony, so it rarely disturbed any of the residents. It was a show about some mothers-in-law and daughters-in-law and had become the talk of the nation. Even my mother religiously watched it. Previously, my family would dine at 8:30 p.m. But ever since the show went on air, dinner was served only at 9:30 after the show ended.

Sikander had literally grown up in the colony and was well-admired by all the residents. The women found him stylish and handsome while the men were dependent on him to grant their requests to air late-night pornographic films on the cable channel. I caught the films once in a while when my parents would travel up North to meet their extended family.

"Hey *Chutiya*! I'm talking to you. Come here."

My face convulsed with irritation. I dislike people calling me names. Everyone in the colony knew better than to insult me, especially after my infamous episode with the milkman. The milkman had spoken boorishly to my mother, in my presence. I hit the milkman hard causing him to fall down the stairs and sprain his ankle. My mother had to calm me down, explaining that it was not the milkman's fault but hers, as she had forgotten to pay the milkman for two months. From that day on, I came to realize that I had no control over my anger.

I walked purposefully towards Sikander but forgot my anger when his face broke into a smile. I hadn't spoken to anyone all day and in a way was glad that Sikander had called me over to talk to him. Sikander's overbearing presence didn't intimidate me but he didn't seem to know that. Since childhood, he was disdainful and occasionally mean towards me.

"How have you been Babloo?" Sikander asked, putting his arm around me pretentiously.

The other guys smiled at each other. Sikander produced a can of Coke and held it in front of me.

"Here, take a sip of Coke," he said, with mocking encouragement. "Hang out with us."

I didn't like drinking from a can that someone else had put his or her lips to. I didn't even like eating food that someone else had touched with his or her bare hands. The only exception was when my mother made *chapatis* or *puris*. But otherwise, when I was served *chai*, I would refuse to touch it if the person serving it had held the glass by the rim where I would need to drink from. In the past, when the family had been invited for dinners, I wouldn't even touch the food if someone's hand accidentally brushed it while serving. Since this happened a lot in India, I hardly ever ate when I went out. My mother would glare at me and my father sometimes even verbalized his anger, but I just could not get myself to ever eat the "contaminated" food.

"Go on. Take a sip."

I took the can from Sikander. I reasoned with myself that technically speaking, even though they must have all been drinking from the same can, I hadn't seen it for myself.

I took a long sip and made a wry face. The guys laughed. It didn't taste like coke at all. Even though I usually drank only the popular Indian soft drink Thumbs Up, I had tried Coke a long time ago and never forgot tastes. This tasted bitter and created an unpleasant aftertaste. I extended the can towards Sikander but he refused to take it.

"What's the problem? Are we not good enough for you to hang out with?" he asked sarcastically.

I reluctantly took another sip. When I withdrew the can, I felt sick. I wanted to throw up but then I hadn't eaten all day.

Sikander grabbed the can from me and gulped its contents down noisily. He squashed the can with one hand and looked at the others proudly.

"It's a man's drink. You're just a boy. It's not for you," Sikander pronounced arrogantly.

"Maybe he likes it with juice. We could give him some with juice," Mahesh sneered from the car.

"Shut up. We're not wasting anymore of our stuff on this moron. We have a night ahead of us."

Sikander fingered his mobile phone in silence while his cronies looked at him expectantly. Pravin directed Sikander's attention to the second floor balcony of Block B. Sonal Tripathi smiled down at Sikander. He smiled back and blew her a flying kiss. She hid her face in her hands coyly, like a new bride on her wedding night.

"One day I'm going to screw her. Her virginity has my name on it," said Sikander to no one in particular.

He paused for a second thoughtfully and turned towards me.

"How well do you know her?" he demanded.

"She is Mr. Tripathi's daughter," I mumbled.

"Even I know that, you retard. Do you know her well enough to get her down for a walk?" asked Sikander, brusquely.

Sonal was now pretending to do something in the balcony, stealing glances at Sikander. Soon her mother would call her back in.

"Mr. Tripathi is a decent man," I said, slowly.

At this all of them started laughing.

"That Tripathi is a sex-starved pervert," said Pravin.

"He calls me with weird kinds of porn film requests," said Sikander. "I could learn a lot from him about what to do with women!"

At this they all started laughing again. I didn't get the joke but smiled. I would have to think about this whole conversation later and try and figure it out.

"So tell me Babloo," said Sikander, with fake seriousness. "Have you ever screwed a chick?"

I looked at him blankly.

"What I meant is," he explained calmly, "have you had sex with a woman?"

He nudged Pravin to catch my reaction, as I looked directly at them muddle-headed. Sometimes I stared and never realized that it made my face look frightfully strange.

The TV show was over and silence began descending on the

colony as TV sets were abruptly switched off. The quiet was broken every few minutes by the whizzing of the trains in the background at regular intervals. Sikander signaled to Mahesh to turn the music down. Pravin handed Sikander another can of Coke, which he choked down.

The empty silence between us was broken by the sound of hurried heels on concrete. We all looked up and when the source of distraction passed under one of the overhead lamps, the brief light revealed Vandana.

Sikander immediately stood to full attention, as did his backscratchers almost immediately. I kept gazing at her as she walked in our direction. We were standing close to the entrance to her building and she had to walk past us to get home.

As she walked past, she smiled at me and said, "Hi Babloo."

Sikander slicked back his hair with the hope that he would catch her attention. She didn't so much as glance in his direction and walked into her block. Sikander hummed a Hindi film song and watched Vandana strut to his rhythm. He licked his cigarette-toned lips as she disappeared from their view.

Mahesh, Madan and Pravin nodded in approval. I lightly smiled to myself. These guys didn't know that she had spoken to me about her dreams. A woman did that only with a man she trusted.

Sikander and the guys started conversing amongst themselves. They were speaking so fast that I couldn't follow their conversation. They each took out a 500-rupee-note.

I caught Sikander saying, "Give me two months. Man, you guys better kiss your money goodbye."

I wasn't paying attention to them anymore because Vandana had taken over my thoughts. I imagined the both of us holding hands and walking in a park.

"Hey Babloo," Sikander was saying.

I started drifting back into reality. Sikander came over and stood next to me.

"So... tell me Babloo. How's life going?"

I looked at him pensively, still trying to complete the last scene in my head. But Sikander didn't let me.

"Babloo, you hardly ever speak. What's going on in that mind of yours?" Sikander enquired in a softer tone.

I was smarter than that. I wasn't going to tell Sikander what I was thinking about. This was Vandana's and my world and no one else was allowed to enter.

"You're thinking about Vandana, aren't you?" Sikander asked knowingly.

"How did you know?" I asked immediately, I could feel my face lighting up.

"I could make out," he said, smiling. "The way you were looking at her; your reaction when she said hi to you. I'm a guy with a lot of experience. I know these things."

I didn't know what to say, so I kept quiet. I knew that when in doubt it was best not to say anything. The problem was that I was often in doubt.

"You really like her, don't you," Sikander said.

"And I know that she likes you too," Pravin added.

"Really?" I was all smiles.

Sikander glared at Pravin. His smile immediately disappeared. Sikander turned back towards me, flashing that fake smile again.

"Why don't you ask her out?" asked Sikander.

I looked at him blankly.

Sikander shook his head. He squeezed my shoulder and then loosened his grip. This was probably what male bonding was, I thought.

"What I mean," said Sikander, explaining himself, "is that why don't you tell her that you like her? I mean, you like her and it's obvious that she likes you. You both should be a couple!"

I thought about this. I had always wanted to tell Vandana that I liked her but didn't know the best way to broach the subject with her.

"How?"

"You're asking the right person. I am a guy who knows everything about women. I know how women think, what they feel. I've been in love with a lot of women."

At this, the guys snickered. Sikander turned towards them with a scowl. They immediately fell silent.

"Then why don't you have a girlfriend?" I asked, puzzled.

Pravin, who was drinking from the Coke can, choked and burst out laughing. Sikander immediately kicked him hard between his legs. Pravin dropped the can and clutched his groin in pain. He started hopping away when Sikander turned back to face me.

"Tell me honestly, man to man. You really like her, don't you?"

"Yes."

"And you would like for you both to, you know, be a couple?"

I wanted to marry her but decided not to reveal this to Sikander.

I simply replied, "Yes."

"See, I know these things. I know how to win a woman's heart."

As he finished saying this Sikander immediately turned towards the other guys with a challenging expression on his face. They were silent. In the distance, Pravin was squatting down with his hands between his legs.

"So let me help you, Babloo. I can help you win Vandana's heart. I can get you both together."

I looked at Sikander with a blank expression.

Sikander explained, "See, you need to let her know how you feel about her. And it would be risky if you told her yourself. It could be too embarrassing. I mean she's a decent girl and she may take it the wrong way."

"But you said that she likes me," I reminded him.

"Yes she does like you. It's obvious. But she hasn't said that yet. And we have to know for sure before you tell her how you feel about her. We have to find out first."

"How?" I asked.

"You have to get a friend of hers to find out how she feels about you. That way you'll know."

I was getting fed up with the conversation and my restless expression revealed it. I hated lectures and explanations. In short, I preferred telegrams to letters. Even in a newspaper, I felt that the headlines should be effective enough to say it all.

"That way I'll know what?" I asked.

Sikander let his frustration show and his face took on a sour expression. Madan nudged Mahesh to draw his attention. But neither of them dared to smile.

Sikander maintained the calm in his voice. "That way you'll know that she likes you. Someone has to find out for you."

"Who?" I asked.

"You don't know anyone who is close to her?"

I thought about this. I had seen Vandana chat with some elders in the building but she didn't mix much with the building crowd.

"No, I don't," I replied, disappointed.

"God, that's a problem," said Sikander with a thoughtful expression on his face.

This got my attention immediately. I hated problems. A worried look immediately formed on my face. Sikander got his cue.

"Listen Babloo, I understand how difficult this is for you. You like Vandana and it must be so frustrating not knowing exactly how she feels about you. Someone has to help you out here, before it gets too late."

My face took on an expression of alarm. Too late for what?! I didn't understand.

"I'm going to help you," Sikander said.

"How?" I asked.

"Someone has to talk to her. To ask her indirectly, how she feels about you. Since you're a childhood friend of mine, I'm going to do it for you."

After all, Sikander did have a nice side to him. At the end of the day we were childhood friends, I thought. And childhood friends helped each other out. Sikander was a nice guy. It was true that bad boys did have a nice heart. The perfect example was Riyaz Khan who kept reaching out to people, from what the papers said. He helped out friends, accident victims, patients and many other people he didn't know.

"Would you really do that?" I asked eagerly.

"Yes I will. Just for you. I mean, I'm a very busy guy. But I'm going to take time off and help you. But I'll need your help for that."

Now I was getting confused. Sikander needs my help to help him?

I simply asked, "How?"

"First, I would have to become a friend of hers. Then when she and I become friends, I can ask her. Simple."

It seemed simple enough to me. Problem solved. Such a long conversation for such a simple solution.

"Babloo, I don't know her personally. You'll have to help me become friends with her. So you'll have to introduce us next time."

I was confused again. I couldn't remember what 'introduce' meant. Sikander sensed that.

"What I mean is that the next time we see her, you'll have to take me up to her and tell her – 'Vandana this is Sikander. He is a very good friend of mine.' That's all."

That seemed simple enough. I felt I could do that.

"Do you understand?" asked Sikander.

"Yes," I replied.

Now Pravin had rejoined the group. But he kept a safe distance from Sikander.

"What did you understand?" asked Sikander, in an authoritative tone similar to that of a teacher questioning a pupil.

I was silent. I was already imagining my wedding. I would make Sikander my best man. In Indian weddings, there was no such concept but I decided I would change that.

Sikander brought me back to reality.

"So the next time that Vandana comes back home, make sure you're with us. Then you stop her and introduce us, OK?"

Now I knew what 'introduce' meant. I could understand things when they were explained slowly to me. Sikander had explained slowly.

"Ok," I replied.

"Good," replied Sikander with a tone of finality. He gave a 'thumbs up' to the other guys and turned towards me as he opened the door of his car.

"See you later Babloo. We have to go now. Have a good night."

Sikander and the guys got into the Maruti Esteem and drove away. The screeching of his tires echoed throughout the colony. A few figures came out onto their balconies.

The sound of the crickets intermingled with the jingle of the 10 o'clock news and the sounds of the Mumbai local trains. It was late and I knew I should be heading home. But instead, I decided to take a walk along the tracks and skip dinner. I had a lot of thinking to do that night.

# 5

THE MUMBAI SUBURBAN RAILWAYS RAN ON TWO separate routes. The Central line headquartered at Victoria Terminus station was a magnificent edifice viewed by Mumbai citizens with deep pride. The Western line, one of the busiest circuits in the Indian railways, commenced from Churchgate and linked the prime suburban and commercial areas of the city. Both these train systems intersected at various stations. Bandra was one of them.

Amar Srivastav, my father, was a well-respected clerk with the Bandra Railway Office. It was his first job and he had diplomatically survived office politics, threatening innovations and varied temperaments over the years. At the time of being recruited straight out of school decades ago, multinational companies had not yet realized the booming potential of India and it was the government services that were considered the most respectable form of employment.

Papa saw Ma for the first time through an arranged marriage, set up in true North Indian fashion through their parents, in their hometown of Panipat. Shortly after, the eager, newly-wed couple consulted a renowned astrologer in the holy town of Rishikesh, to see what the stars had in store for their new life together. They were told, among other things, that they would bear two boys, the elder of whom, would do something really big in his life. One part of the astrologer's prediction had come true when Ma gave birth to Raghu and me within a year of each other. But within a few years, my parents were convinced that the second part of the prediction held no truth in it, when I started displaying abnormal behaviour early on.

I turned out to be slow and very obviously strange, eccentric and aloof. Communication between my parents and me was virtually non-existent. If they probed too much, I clammed up and simply stared at them vacantly.

A visiting psychologist at my school, St. Andrews in Bandra, had diagnosed me with autism but offered no real solution to the problem. My parents were merely told to be calm, patient and understanding with me. Over the years, they had tried to adhere to this advice, but Papa soon lost his patience with my perceived lack of responsibility or concern. He began to be harsh with me, hoping that it would propel me to do something worthwhile with my life. All their efforts proved futile and I became more and more difficult to handle.

Though Ma secretly harboured some hope in the form of a miracle, Papa had washed his hands of me. He said that I brought the family nothing but shame and gave the Colony a reason to talk about the family that he had protected so carefully all these years.

It was a Wednesday morning and the Bandra station road was devoid of any activity. There were neither any hawkers, nor the usual hustle-bustle that was characteristic of the ever busy road. It was Mumbai *Bandh*.

*Bandhs* were usually spearheaded by a prominent political party to either direct the Government's attention to an issue or event that needed reviewing, or to reassert their importance to the helpless masses. As a result, all the city's services and businesses were shut down. This not only affected the financial health of the economy but also inconvenienced the common man who survived on daily wages.

The railways were brought to a halt as well so Amar was on a forced holiday. A break in his six-day work week made him very restless. His only source of entertainment at home was the news on TV. But the same stories kept repeating themselves and in no time Amar was bored, surfing channels aimlessly.

Seated in his small 10 by 15 foot living room, he was wearing a crumpled kurta pajama, which had become loose over the years as his frame shrank with age. The few strands of hair on his crown had been dyed and oiled back. This, his thick, black-framed glasses and his slightly crooked teeth, all these gave him the typical look of a

Government employee.

Mumbai was not the same as it had been many years ago when Amar first came to the city from his hometown of Panipat. It had now become the hub of the underworld and there were daily reports of gangster shootouts. Terrorists realized the potential of the city to further their causes which they had already proved with the Mumbai bomb blasts of 1993, among others.

The landscape of Bandra had changed drastically. The greenery and virginity of the then far off suburb had been replaced by buildings, traffic, people and more people. The roads bore the added weight of hundreds of new cars everyday and weren't wide enough to accommodate them all, resulting in major traffic jams at all times of the day. Reports indicated that more alarmingly increasing numbers migrated to 'the city of dreams' each year in search of better livelihoods. The city seemed so promising to rural folk, that once a person was sucked in, he or she stayed back. Amar was one of them.

But Amar was unaffected by the rapid, haphazard changes that the city underwent, termed as 'progress' by politicians. He never had to commute to work, just a five-minute walk took him straight to his solitary desk in the cramped Bandra railway station office. His government job was secure, and his life started and ended in Bandra.

On the marriage front, he couldn't have been more content. Despite Sudha's mood swings and melodramatic personality, she had converted their bare quarters into a comfortable home. He valued her companionship and considered her the ideal Indian wife. Lately he had grown concerned about finding as perfect a life partner for Raghu.

He didn't have to look really far because the right proposal had recently, literally, come to their doorstep. It was the alliance he had always hoped for. The union of both families would escalate him to higher society, both in the colony and within his community.

He let his sight wander around the circumscribed room and marvelled at the way his traditional wife had modestly furnished the house, giving it a sense of comfort. The furniture had withstood the tests of time and remained intact and dependable even after all these years. There was not much space to fit in a living room set and dining table. But Sudha had expertly managed the small space as well the limited budget she was provided with. The result was a wooden three-seater with comfortable cushions, flanked by matching one-seaters on either side. In the centre was a wooden coffee table which held a vase that saw fresh flowers every day. Facing the three-seater was a shelved cabinet that housed family pictures, memorabilia collected over the years and their 21-inch color TV. Behind the couch was a wooden board fastened against the wall with a small latch. When unlatched, four legs pulled out transforming it to a dining table. Four matching wooden chairs meant to complete the dining table, were set against the wall and served as extra seating when they had to entertain guests, or were lent to neighbours for the same purpose. Two of these chairs were moved into the balcony where Amar and Sudha sometimes spent their evenings, when they weren't taking walks in the colony compound.

Amar abandoned his musings about the furniture when Raghu entered the room. Raghu was clean-shaven, lanky, and carried around what seemed to be the beginning of a paunch. He had joined eyebrows giving him a sinister look. When he smiled he looked awkward, sometimes scary.

Raghu's hair was damp from a shower. He sat down on one of the single sofa chairs. His sleeveless T-shirt and long flimsy shorts were far from flattering to his bony structure.

"Good morning Papa."

"Good morning, beta," said Amar happily, glad that his son had rescued him from the monotony of the news. The morning news had been repeatedly airing a news feature about a girl on a moving train who lost an eye to a stone, thrown by some hooligans at the passing locomotive. Amar picked up the remote control and lowered the volume to a bare minimum, keeping it audible enough in case something interesting caught his attention.

"So is the *bandh* going to be bad for the stock market?" asked Amar curiously.

Raghu enjoyed talking about his work. It was the only thing that gave him a sense of importance in his otherwise uninteresting life.

"Yes, it will be," replied Raghu smiling, straining his ears to listen to the news story of the *bandh*. He knew that the fall in share prices that the *bandh* would instigate would make no difference to his life. His job was only to analyze stock prices and present reports to Mr. Trivedi, his boss and a leading Mumbai stockbroker.

"Oh," acknowledged Amar.

Amar hardly got to spend any time with his younger son. Raghu returned from work very late in the evenings and usually by that time, Amar would be getting ready to retire for the night. But he never questioned his son's whereabouts because he knew that Raghu had to slog it out, as his chosen field was very demanding.

"So how's work going? Are you enjoying it?" asked Amar.

"It's going great," replied Raghu. His eyebrows settled into a straight line as he turned his full attention to his father. "I am learning a lot from Mr. Trivedi. He told me that he's very happy with my work and is going to offer me a full time position soon."

"That's great, Beta. How much will he be offering you?"

"That's what I wanted to ask you Papa," replied Raghu respectfully. "He's offering me 20,000 rupees a month. Should I accept it?"

Amar's eyes glowed in amazement. That was more than he was making now, including benefits. His face took on a more cheerful expression.

"That's a great salary. You should accept it gratefully!"

"But I can get more if I apply for a job with a good investment firm," reasoned Raghu.

"Yes, but you must not forget that Mr. Trivedi gave you a break in this industry. He values your work which is why he is offering you a permanent position. Besides, 20,000 is a lot of money. You are still in your learning phase in life. There will be a lot of opportunities later to make more money."

"Yes Papa."

Amar truly believed what he said. He knew that Sudha and he had produced a bright son in Raghu.

Sudha was in the kitchen preparing breakfast in a gaudy nightgown, humming a *bhajan* to herself. Short by Indian standards, her small frame made her appear even shorter. Her waist-length hair, which she usually left untied, made her feel taller. She had big expressive eyes, which changed sizes innumerable times during each episode of her favourite soap opera.

She finished pouring out the tea and carefully carried the two steaming cups, nestled between her index finger and thumb in either hand, into the living room and placed it in front of Amar and Raghu. This was Amar's third cup since morning. He had been addicted to tea for years. The reason – working with the railways, the canteens of which were home to good, authentic tea.

Sudha retreated into the kitchen, not missing a beat of her indecipherable *bhajan*.

"Beta, now that you will have your job in place, have you thought about getting settled?" asked Amar.

Sudha caught a whiff of the conversation and immediately reappeared in the living room. Amar and Sudha had decided that they would have this conversation together with Raghu. They had planned on waiting till Sunday, Amar and Raghu's day off, but the *bandh* had presented them with the right opportunity.

"You know Raghu, it is good to get married at a young age," Sudha blurted out quickly. "I don't agree with today's youngsters who wait to get settled in their careers and then get married. By the time they're ready to have children it's too late. Think about your father and me. We did everything at the right age. Your father was able to educate you well while he was still in service. If we had had you late, then he would have been retired by the time you went to college and..."

"We have seen a good girl for you," interrupted Amar, cutting to the chase. "What do you think of Vandana?"

Raghu's eyes almost popped out on hearing Vandana's name. He had always considered her gorgeous, with an amazing figure, and a certain kind of grace that made her any man's dream. Life couldn't get any better for this below-average-looking guy who had never even kissed a girl.

"Whatever you both think is right," he answered casually, trying to conceal his excitement.

Both the parents looked approvingly at each other. Sudha was enthusiastic about the alliance. Vandana was a cultured girl from a good family whose untarnished reputation had never dragged her into any colony controversy despite her modern way of dressing. She considered Vandana the kind of girl she wished she herself could have been when she was a young woman.

Amar was keen on this matrimony for different reasons. Amar had tremendous respect for Vandana's father Shekhar Gupta, (the Chief Manager, Commercial/Operations, and senior-most official in the Bandra Railway office), who had climbed the ranks on his own merit, unlike most Government employees who scored jobs either through reservation quotas or recommendations. Gupta was always respectful towards him yet maintained that distance created between the ranks of senior and subordinate. But that would all change now, thought Amar. Through the alliance of their children, they would be equals.

"Good, Beta. She would be a perfect match for you. We shall take it forward then."


I awoke with a start. It was broad daylight. I lay in bed and waited for the familiar, light vibration in the room brought on by the intrusive local trains. A few minutes passed. It was quiet, except for the sound of pigeons fluttering on the window sill and the distant sound of a Hindi film song playing from the other side of the tracks.

I got up and peered outside the window. The empty tracks stared back at me. I waited for five more minutes, but there was no indication of any train approaching. The sounds of blaring horns, characteristic of the busy Bandra station road, was also replaced by silence. I glanced upwards at the ceiling fan. It was still rotating with a mind of its own so there was no power cut.

I hastily got out of bed and proceeded to do my daily pushups. Upon reaching the 100th mark, and still not out of breath, I positioned myself in front of the mirror and flexed my muscles.

My conversation with Sikander had given me a peaceful sleep at night and a pleasant dream of Vandana. Usually my dreams were left incomplete when the first train rumbled across the track outside my window. But last night I was able to dream completely because for once, the Mumbai local trains seemed to have some consideration for me.

I changed into my favourite shirt, jeans and sneakers, and entered the living room to find the other members of the family chatting animatedly at the dinner table, now converted into the breakfast table. I caught the word 'celebration' in their conversation before they all fell silent upon seeing me.

Papa frowned on seeing me in the same clothes that I wore almost every day. Because of this, Papa could never quite remember when he saw me last.

I acknowledged them with a quick glance and sat on the couch facing the TV. My back was towards them. I sensed they had stopped eating since there were no sounds of movement or of spoons scraping against steel utensils behind me. My senses had always been sharp.

I felt for the remote by my side and switched on the TV. My father's angry voice didn't startle me.

"Where are your manners?"

I turned around suddenly, which in turn startled the three occupants of the table. In school, I remembered it being termed 'response to stimuli.'

Raghu's steel glass fell from his hand creating a loud noise that broke the silence. My eccentric behaviour scared him sometimes. When Raghu was younger, he told our parents that he would get nightmares about me killing him in his sleep.

"Where are your manners?" asked Papa once again, the anger rising in his voice.

I couldn't figure out what the fuss was all about. Papa had made a golden rule that the TV should always be turned off when the family was having a meal. But technically speaking, I wasn't eating. And even more technically speaking, I was never made to feel a part of the family.

I pondered the other possible reasons behind Papa's ire. It could also be because I hadn't wished them a good morning. But in the past, I had tried explaining to Papa that I never found anything good about the morning. If Papa did, then he should wish me first, shouldn't he?

I heard my mother's adamant voice, "Please, ji. Eat your breakfast. Let him be."

Her voice took on a softer tone.

"Babloo, come have breakfast with us."

I knew that she was secretly hoping I would stay on the couch and not sit face to face with Papa. I was concentrating on the News now and Ma's repetition of the same sentence stood no chance against the TV volume. The news reporter was talking about an incident where a college-going girl travelling by a local train to Churchgate lost an eye when a stone hit her. Even though this wasn't the first incident of stone throwing on the tracks, the railway authorities hadn't taken any action. I knew that this story had made headlines only because there was nothing more glamorous to broadcast, such as a film party or a politician's speech full of empty promises. If there were, something as important as this would get a mere 30 seconds of news coverage.

The feature proceeded to show a photograph of the bloody-eyed girl in the hospital; a visual shown to increase the channel's TRP ratings, and not to propel the authorities into taking any action. This made me angry.

I banged my fist hard on the coffee table and screamed out, "Shit!"

This time Raghu's spoon escaped his hand and hit the old flooring.

"This behaviour will not be tolerated in my house!" shouted Papa from behind me. "You will learn to behave yourself, do you understand..."

"Please, ji. Forget it. Let him be," Ma's voice intervened.

"Who does he think he is? He doesn't talk to any of us. He comes and goes whenever he feels like. This is a home, not a hotel. When will he learn to show some respect?" continued Papa, his tone full of rage.

"Please," said Ma sedately. "Now's not a good time."

"Then when is a good time?" I could sense Papa turning towards her. "When? If you will not let me handle him my way, then make him listen to you. He acts as if we are not even in the room."

Ma fell silent. I hated my mornings when they began in such a tense manner. All I had done was watch television in peace. Now I wished that the trains were running so that I could have woken up early and escaped in time, but better now than never.

I got up and walked to the breakfast table. With a sudden motion I picked up two *puris* and headed for the main door. Papa didn't know how to react to this. He seemed to have forgotten that I was either very slow or when provoked, very sudden. But Ma understood my behaviour and felt helpless in such situations. I in turn knew that she was secretly relieved that I had disappeared for the day. Now she would have to calm Papa down so that the rest of his day passed in peace.

# 6

THERE WAS NOT A SOUL IN SIGHT FOR MILES IN either direction of the tracks outside the railway colony. I understood that it was the sign of a total *bandh* and the city was completely paralyzed. Otherwise at least a few people would have ventured out of their homes.

I didn't know what the issue was and didn't really care. There had been several *bandhs* that year – sometimes to oppose fuel hike prices and at other times to protest against a change in policy that would affect the common man – but they were always politically motivated. The working classes never had a say in the matter even though they suffered the most. A day's loss of earnings was a huge setback for these people who survived on daily wages.

I valued my freedom and no politician could take that away from me. So just as I had done on previous occasions, I got out of the house. During the last *bandh*, I had ventured out on the street and witnessed a rioting mob burning a row of taxis parked on Linking Road. I was a fast runner so managed to get away before they could catch up with me. Being out on the streets was considered a sign of disrespect towards the 'noble cause' behind a *bandh*. Considering my narrow escape, this time I deemed the railway tracks a safer place to wander around.

I stood in the centre of the first railway track and looked in both directions. Being alone on the tracks gave me a complete sense of freedom. I never thought that the merciless Mumbai railways could in any part make me feel that way. These were the same tracks that had disturbed my sleep over the years. And now they brought me such calmness.

The sun hovered directly overhead, indicating that it was sometime around mid-day. I re-confirmed my estimate, looking at my watch, and beamed with pride when I saw that I was just a few minutes off. I felt the heat of the metal bracelet burning into my wrist, but made no effort to take the watch off. I took another look in both directions. On one side, a 100 meters away, was the familiar outline of Bandra Station, majestic and lifeless. On the other side, the tracks stretched away endlessly, disappearing around a curve.

I turned in the direction away from Bandra Station and started walking briskly. I never strolled. I felt that a person who strolled had no purpose in life and I liked to believe that my life had some specific purpose.

As I approached the next station, Khar Road, I came across a train parked in the middle of the tracks. Some of the windows were shattered. The train must have tried to follow its schedule but was stoned to a halt by some *bandh* activists.

I gathered some stones from the rugged surface between the tracks and started tossing them around in my hand. I glanced around. There was no one in sight. Keeping a safe distance from the train, around 30 feet, I took aim at one of the unbroken windows and flung the stone with full force. The glass shattered instantly. I rarely missed my target.

I threw more stones in quick succession, hitting my intended target each time. The consecutive shattering of glass windows echoed through the pin drop silence. Even the usually noisy crows seemed to be observing the *bandh*.

I pondered over the scene that had transpired earlier at home. All I had done was sit down in the living room and try to be a part of the morning household activity. After all, families sat in the same room as each other and shared conversations. I couldn't understand why it had bothered Papa so much. Maybe Papa hated me. In fact, maybe my whole family resented my presence.

I recalled various previous instances when I was ostracized from their inner circle. Whenever I would enter the room, they would all fall silent. Whenever there were guests at home, I was not included in the gathering. In other incidents, my family would disregard my presence completely, like the time they decided to buy a colour television. Papa, Ma and Raghu would discuss and compare brands and prices without even asking me for my opinion, even though I was in the same room. Or the time they were debating whether to take a car loan and upgrade our family mode of transport from the old rickety scooter we had for years. Weren't these decisions that were supposed to involve the entire family?

Whenever I thought about my family, clouds of resentment shrouded me. It took me into a negative zone in which I started despising everything. My parents had always been very supportive and encouraging of Raghu but had left me completely on my own. The only bright spot in my life was Vandana but I hardly ever got to see her. I realized I would have to make more of an effort to get close to her, even if I had to take Sikander's help.

I focused once more on the train and hurled another stone, shattering a window of the ladies' compartment. It provided solace to my desolate frame of mind.

I dropped the last stone left in my hand and started walking energetically even though I had no particular destination in mind. The cinema halls would be closed that day. And the empty streets would make me too conspicuous and could possibly invite danger.

"Hey!"

I heard a dauntless, deep voice behind me. For a few seconds, I thought I had imagined it. There were times I would hear voices but when I looked around, there was no one there. I figured that maybe this was one of those times.

"Hey!" "Hellow!" "You!"

Now it was a succession of different voices. Usually, I didn't hear so many voices at the same time. Mostly it would be the same voice talking in different tones.

I mentally traced the source from diagonally across the tracks behind me. The voices were approaching me but I kept moving at a steady pace, still engrossed in my thoughts.

The voices came closer. "Hey, you! Stop!"

I didn't stop.

"Stop!" The voices ordered. They were right behind me now.

I stopped suddenly and turned around. Facing me was a group of seven angry looking men wearing bands around their heads. The bands were the colour worn by a prominent political party.

"What the hell are you doing out here?" one of them demanded, a bearded man in a loose kurta and black trousers, more menancing than the others. He wore beads around his neck, camouflaged against his dark skin, and duplicate designer glasses. Probably the leader of the pack.

"I don't have any money," I said frankly.

The leader's eyes took a terribly frightening tone as he pondered over this for a few seconds.

"Who is asking you for money? What are you doing out here?"

I stared silently at the leader whose brow furrowed in irritation. He glared threateningly at me.

"Who are you? What are you doing here?" he shouted again, this time at the top of his voice.

I continued looking at him blankly. I didn't like people demanding answers from me.

"Were you breaking the windows on that train?" enquired another in a similar tone.

I turned to face the other man. The leader advanced towards me.

"Don't just look at me. Say something. We'll break your bones, your family will not even recognize you, you *chutiya*."

*"How can you let him abuse you like that, Babloo?"*

*"What should I do?"*

*"Do what a man would do. Do what a hero would do!"*

I listened to my best friend carefully and quickly referenced a concept I found consistent in the many Hindi films I had watched – the element of surprise. I had keenly observed the hero in a hopeless situation, using surprise as his weapon to overpower his adversary. And when the villain least expected it, he rarely stood a chance against the quick, unexpected attack by the hero. It always worked, regardless of inequality of strength or power. Translated to real life, I understood that it took one a few minutes to adjust one's frame of mind to a fight. And a few minutes was all that was needed to overpower the enemy.

I let out a shout of anger. I acted possessed and in a swift action, bent my head and charged at the leader in a raging bull-like fashion. The leader didn't have enough time to defend himself and spiralled backwards as I butted into him. He spiralled, lost his balance and fell, banging his head on the tracks. He screamed in pain, his agonized voice echoing all around. Before he passed out, the last thing he looked at was the glistening metal on the dial of my watch.

I snapped out of my pretended rage almost immediately and realized that I had done something dangerous. I immediately started running in the direction of Bandra Station, towards home. Earlier I had wanted to get away from home. Now, I just wanted to get to the safe confines of my cramped room.

A few of the others took chase but they couldn't match up to my speed. I was very fast and had the added advantage of my sneakers, against the flimsy chappals of the others. Within minutes, I lost my pursuers.

As I approached Bandra, I headed for the fence that divided the railway lines from the Gaiety Galaxy Multiplex. I heaved myself over the barricade and ran alongside it on the straight, pothole-infested road that led to the colony. Once I entered the gates, I felt a sense of relief.

I suddenly realized the danger that I almost got myself into. I had encountered a group of people driven more by fanaticism towards their party rather than a real purpose. They could have killed me and no one would ever have known. That was not how I intended to die.

As I walked through the colony, my worried expression relaxed as a new realization dawned on me. This was the first fight I had gotten into in which I had outsmarted more than one opponent. I felt powerful. I recalled Vandana's words – *Sometimes you have to talk back to people in the same language and only then do they understand.*

The element of surprise had proved to be a reliable weapon.

## 7

VANDANA GUPTA WAS BOTH BEAUTIFUL AND INTELLIGENT, and never ceased to attract male attention. Among her list of admirers was Firoze Mehta, owner of the advertising agency where she worked as a receptionist.

Firoze made passes at her whenever they were alone. They were always verbal in nature – dinner after work or a ride home. But Vandana always maintained her distance and politely refused. He was a married man with a roving eye, and she found him very repulsive. She was a romantic at heart and was still hopeful of being swept off her feet by that special someone.

It was 7 p.m., an hour later than the time Vandana usually left for the day. She had lost track of time till she heard the familiar gong from the small Shirdi Sai Baba temple nearby which indicated the commencement of its daily *aarti*.

Vandana activated the answering machine, and put her computer in sleep mode. A Garfield icon waved at her before merging into the black of the screen. She rose from the chair, straightening her tight skirt. As she was about to pick up her purse, her extension buzzed. It was Firoze.

"Yes sir?" she quickly answered.

"How many times have I told you Vandana? Call me Firoze."

"I was just leaving sir."

"Come into my cabin."

She replaced the receiver and quietly cursed herself. She adjusted her low-cut blouse to make sure she wasn't revealing too much before knocking on her boss' door.

"Come in."

The office was a small cabin adorned with *fabindia* lamps, with huge windows overlooking the semi-circle of the dazzling streetlights on Marine Drive popularly called The Queen's Necklace. Vandana admired the splendour of the brilliant array before turning to look questioningly at her boss seated behind his desk.

Firoze, with his pot belly hanging heavily over his belt, got up and walked around his desk towards her. He was slightly shorter than her, around 5'3" in height, and had a receding hairline. His collared Polo T-shirt and creased khaki pants emphasized his roly-poly shape. Aside from his lascivious ways, he had a subtle approach when dealing with his staff. He was always friendly yet business-like with all his employees down to the peons. He wasn't a freak when it came to punctuality as long as client deadlines were met.

He silently directed her to the two-seater couch by the door. Facing the couch was a 32-inch, flat screen Samsung television mounted on the wall, playing TV commercials. She seated herself and positioned her writing pad on her bare knee.

"What do you think of this commercial?" Firoze asked earnestly pointing towards the screen.

She put her pad by the side and looked up at the screen.

A man was riding a motorcycle. There was spilled oil ahead on the road. The motorcycle skidded for a distance of a 100 meters on the oil patch after which it regained balance and sped off normally.

Vandana watched intently. After the commercial faded into black, she found Firoze sitting right next to her.

"So what do you think?" he asked, breaking into a zealous smile.

Vandana had joined the agency as a receptionist merely to get her foot in the door of the advertising world. She was just a Bachelor of Arts graduate and didn't have the connections required for an entry-level position in the creative department of a multinational advertising agency, her dream job. Maybe I can impress Firoze with some impressive ideas and ask for a change, she thought.

"I like the concept, but it's not really convincing. I feel that..."

He inched towards her as she continued eagerly.

"...there should be a message at the end, before we show the product. Or a caption... gripping the roads."

"Tell me Vandana," he said softly. "Where do you see yourself a year from now?"

"Well," she replied carefully, "I guess I would be married and living abroad."

"No Vandana. What I mean is where do you see yourself in this company a year from now?"

"Well, I would like to be a part of the creative department. I know I have the necessary skills to..."

"Vandana," he interrupted her and rested his palm on her shoulder. She immediately brushed it away. He stole a glance at her bosom before continuing.

"Swati was a receptionist, just like you. In just six months she became the head of the films department and reports directly to me now. Do you know how?"

Vandana did know how. The news had travelled through the office grapevine in no time. The afternoon-long meetings even when they had no projects in hand, the after-work dinners they were seen at – who were they kidding?

Vandana looked sullenly at Firoze and stood up. Firoze held her gaze, eyeing her expectantly.

She remembered to bang the door behind her.

It was 7:15 by the time Vandana had collected her things, composed herself, and stepped into the bustling street. Horns blared, while abuses travelled through the cool evening air. Pedestrians found their way around human obstacles on footpaths already obstructed with illegal mini constructions of *paan* stalls, juice vendors, and magazine stalls.

Vandana skillfully maneuvered her small frame through the crowd as she brooded over the episode that had just transpired with Firoze. He had flirted with her many times in the past. But after the second time, she had learned to handle the matter diplomatically by pretending that nothing had happened when she saw him next. But today, Firoze had crossed all boundaries. She knew that even if she tried to change jobs, it would be the same story there as India was a chauvinistic, male-dominated society, no matter how progressive the world perceived it to be.

She had encountered men coming onto her in the past. But that evening, Firoze had crossed the line, by directly insinuating that she sleep with him. Vandana was seething with anger and frustration, especially since she knew she would have to go back to work tomorrow. Even if she decided to randomly quit, it would take her a good few months to find another job. And the thought of sitting at home with her pushy mother, who would try to domesticate her and forcibly train her to be a successful future housewife, was daunting.

Vandana didn't have a sister whom she could share her problems with. And she found it difficult to find a confidante in another woman. All her female friends in the past had proven to be either insecure of her or too self-absorbed. She had made a few close male friends but in no time, they started asking her out.

In college, she had come close to having a relationship with a classmate who wooed her and seemed to stimulate her senses. He was not anything great to look at but was very intelligent, warm and made her feel special. They would have long conversations, go for drives and even long dinners. One day, when she thought he was going to hint at a relationship with her, he suggested that they spend some time alone at a friend's empty flat.

Since then she had grown wary of men. But she still harboured the cureless hope of meeting that special someone, a man who would love her for the person she was. Otherwise she would have to settle for an arranged marriage with a boy chosen by her shortsighted, traditional parents. And she couldn't come to terms with such a bleak eventuality. She was a romantic at heart.

Her life was lonesome, and like other girls she couldn't find a best friend in her mother. Her mother vehemently imposed her small town mentality, sparking off a benign resentment in her. In that respect, Vandana considered this job a godsend. It had given her a way to make her own money and assert her independence. Her next step was America and she prayed to God every night to take her there somehow.

Vandana had read a lot about America in books and was totally enamoured by the country. She was fascinated by the fact that freedom of thought and action was a way of life there. In India it was almost considered a sin, especially for women.

Her uncle in Chicago had offered to support her further education. But her parents flatly refused. Their old-fashioned mindset considered it unsafe for a decent girl like Vandana to leave home before getting married.

She dodged through the crowded streets till she found her way into the pandemonium that was Churchgate Station. The massive interiors of the station echoed with the voices of thousands of people speaking in various languages, making it sound like white noise. This was arrested by the periodic announcement of the various trains leaving at various times, over the loudspeaker.

The ticket counter was a picture of utter chaos. Bodies were moving in and out of lines combatively, resulting in a lot of shoving and arguments between people, each trying to get access to the window before the other. Vandana had a monthly pass, which spared her this misery.

People have no consideration or sense of personal space when it comes to rushing back home, she thought. She walked towards the platforms with her head up which helped her find her way through the crowds. But as it happened every other day, she occasionally felt purposeful hands brushing up against her. When she first began taking the trains to commute to work, she would create a scene and embarrass the culprit in such situations. But after a while, she got fed up and just looked upon it as a temporary way of life.

As the four parallel platforms came into view, she scanned the four illuminated electronic boards to find that the Virar Fast would be on Platform 4 in three minutes. She heaved a sigh of relief as she fanned herself against the muggy air, with a few successive waves of her hand. The fast train stopped only at the busier stations, and would save her a few minutes of torment that plagued peak time commuters like her.

Vandana found her way to Platform 4 just as the train pulled in. The anxious crowd of commuters jumped on the train in a frenzied manner to secure a seat for the long journey. The ladies' first class compartment was less crowded than its male counterpart. Vandana managed to find standing space by the door and held on to an overhead steel railing to maintain her balance once the train lurched forward again. After the passengers boarded, hawkers pushed their way through the compartment announcing their cheap wares such as combs, clips, *chikkis*.

Just as the train pulled away, a beggar woman accompanied by a small child and a harmonium jumped on. They would sing for their alms. Vandana was glad there was some form of entertainment, jarring and tuneless though it was, that would break the monotony of her typical day.

The waiter and the customer regarded each other suspiciously in Bandra Station's reputed, low-budget, quality restaurant – National Dhaba – the waiter because this was the third plate of *rajma* curry he had brought for the customer, while the first two still remained untouched; I, because this was the third time the silly waiter had served me my favourite dish of kidney beans with his fingers dipping slightly over the edge of the bowl. Why didn't he just get it?

I created a mental character sketch of my adversary. The waiter probably didn't have sufficient experience at waiting tables. His shabby appearance indicated that he must have come from a small town or village in search of employment. The owner must have given him a job at a meager daily wage. The waiter must have considered it a favour and in his gratefulness worked extra long hours. I deemed it exploitation.

The waiter hesitantly placed the third plate of *rajma* curry carefully on the table. To him, I probably seemed strange and if I turned out to be the non-paying type, the owner would have to take care of me. However, if extra man power was needed, he would have to join in.

I eyed the third plate of *rajma* curry on the table. Even though I was famished, I couldn't get myself to touch it. I wished I could have sat the waiter down and explained my problem to him. But words did not come easy to me. I usually spoke slowly and out of fear of jumbling up my words, spoke only a few at a time. By the time I collected my thoughts to put into words, the waiter was gone.

I usually didn't eat out. But today I felt the urge to treat myself to my favourite dish after watching a sloppily made adult film at Nandi theatre. Besides, Raghu wasn't really fond of *rajma* curry so it was hardly made at home.

The film was a C grade film called *College Ladki*. It was based on a true incident in which a girl was raped at a Mumbai college. The film caught my interest because its publicity posters depicted a shoddy image of a court battle. And I loved court scenes in films.

Usually such a controversial incident would have been grabbed by a top A grade filmmaker. Unfortunately a topic like this, that needed the right exposure, caught the attention of a sleazy filmmaker first.

The filmmaker had disregarded the actual truth behind the story and instead, had glamourized the sex scenes. The victim had been dressed up provocatively, almost as if to insinuate that she called this barbaric episode upon herself.

The theatre had been filled to capacity. Men had filthy minds and basically loved watching women being exploited sexually. Some men even brought their wives along. I felt sorry for them because I understood that their limited budget was too low for Gaiety Galaxy's air-conditioned halls, and this was their only way to give their spouses a cinematic experience.

I did not sit through the entire film because a fight broke out a few seats away from me and I couldn't hear any part of the court scene. Besides, I was thinking about *rajma* curry throughout the film. Now I had three plates of the dish to choose from but couldn't get myself to eat any of them.

A taxi driver in his khaki uniform sat down at my table, facing me.

He was a pleasant looking Sikh guy with a well-fitted turban and appeared to be in his mid-30s. The *dhaba* had a 'sit where there's space' policy and patrons often found themselves sharing a table with strangers. The taxi driver looked at the plates of *rajma*, and then at me.

"Do you want it?" I asked him.

The taxi driver seemed to have a smile pasted on his face.

"Why are you not eating, brother?" he asked pleasantly. "You don't like it?"

"No," I replied slowly, "I like *rajma* curry but don't want to eat this."

"Why?" asked the taxi driver, more concerned than suspicious.

"Because he put his fingers in it," I replied, trying to follow the passing waiter with my pointed finger.

The taxi driver thought for a few seconds and then let out a hearty laugh. I responded with a confused expression. I couldn't figure out what could possibly be funny about this.

"Such a small matter," said the taxi driver, "I will fix it."

The taxi driver shouted something in *Punjabi* at the owner, seated behind the counter by the main entrance. From the brief exchange, I recognized only the word '*rajma*'.

The service was very quick there and in a few minutes, the same waiter presented a plate of *rajma* curry, this time holding the hot dish on his palm. The taxi driver praised him with a '*Shabash*, good job!' and looked at me, this time with more of a smile on his face. The waiter walked away with an irritated expression as he tried to soothe his scalded palm by blowing on it repeatedly.

"Here... problem solved. You have that plate and I shall have this," he said, reaching out for one of the three plates I had discarded.

"How can you eat that?" I asked.

"In my house, sometimes we all eat from the same plate. I am very used to people dipping their fingers in my food."

I conjured up this picture in my mind and almost immediately I could feel the nausea welling up at the back of my throat. I quickly chased away those disturbing images and looked at the man seated across from me, eating happily.

"I am Babloo." I had made an introduction.

The taxi driver took a break from his food.

"I am Manjit Singh. I am a taxi driver. What do you do?"

I pondered for a minute. The last time someone had asked me that, it was a little less than a year ago. That time my answer was that I was looking for a job. Now I didn't have an answer so I replied with a blank expression.

"Are you looking for a job?" asked Manjit, as if reading my thoughts.

Manjit took a green chili from his plate and devoured it in one whole bite without a change of expression. On seeing that, I immediately took a long sip of water.

Manjit Singh looked at me expectantly. I wanted to continue the conversation. It was the first conversation of the day for me.

"I was looking. Now I stopped."

The taxi driver went back to his food slowly.

"I understand," he said, shaking his head sympathetically. "Don't give up. I am a B.A. pass from Punjab University. I came to Mumbai because my Uncle promised me a job in his toothbrush factory. But when I came, forget about picking me up from the station, he didn't even take my calls. I had to survive somehow. So I took the first job I got."

I stared at Manjit Singh blankly.

"What I mean to say," continued Manjit Singh, "is that no job is small. Take whatever you get. You can cut down on everything but *this* doesn't stop growling."

He patted his stomach and let out the same hearty laugh.

I decided I liked this guy. He was one of the few people making an effort to talk to me normally. Vandana was another.

Manjit Singh let out a huge burp. For a second the loud chatter of the *dhaba* dropped in volume as people from nearby tables turned to look in our direction. This time it was my turn to laugh.

"See," said Manjit Singh. "That's the way. Be happy. They say that life may not be the party we hoped for but we may as well dance!"

The line was too complicated for me to decipher. I decided to retain the 'Be Happy' part.

Manjit Singh finished the last of his food and quickly got to his feet.

"Ok, Babloo. Thank you. It was nice eating with you. I have to get back to work."

I hadn't started eating yet so technically speaking we hadn't eaten together, I thought. But I hoped that one day we would.

"You offered Manjit your food," Manjit Singh was saying as he wiped his hands with his crumpled handkerchief, "Manjit will never forget."

He waved at me and stopped at the cash counter to have a brief chat with the owner before leaving.

After finishing dinner, when I went to pay, I was told that the taxi driver had paid for all four plates. There were some good people in the world after all.

The pace of movement on the Bandra station road had reduced to a crawl. Weary commuters were using their last ounce of energy to drag themselves home. I looked at my watch. It was 8 p.m. – too early to go home. I didn't fancy being confined to my bedroom and counting the rotations of the fan while my family enjoyed a film on cable TV in the next room. In the past, I used to sit with them and watch movies. But soon I started sensing them looking at me while the film was going on, which made me uncomfortable.

There were long lines at the BEST bus stops for the 211, 214, 220 and 221 buses, on the other side of the road, opposite the grand entrance to the station. These bus routes would take commuters into the posh interiors of Bandra. The travellers were civilized, unlike on most other city bus routes, and always stuck to their place. If anyone tried to break the order, they were pushed to the end of the queue.

I walked past the bus stops and came to the huge mosque standing to one side of the station. Every Friday afternoon, the mosque would see many devotees who religiously came to offer *jum'ah*. Since the mosque was not big enough to accommodate all the devotees, they would lay their mats on the road in front of the station and kneel in prayer in unison as guided by the *azan* over the loudspeaker. It was a wondrous sight to watch so many people come together for the same purpose.

Opposite the mosque, on the other side of the street, were small eating joints operating out of open stalls, serving meat curries and *parathas*, giving out heavenly aromas. I stood there for some time taking in the aromas and thought about Manjit Singh.

Despite such a hard life, Manjit Singh seemed to be happy. I wished I could be as content. I knew that my happiness lay in having a sense of purpose. In the colony I kept overhearing people complaining about their jobs and lives. I often wondered how these people led such a purposeless existence.

I instinctively walked to the main entrance of Bandra Station. I stood by the newspaper vendor who never seemed to mind people glancing through his papers and magazines without buying any. I would usually go through the film gossip magazines and look at the glamorous pictures. The actresses were beautiful and every man's dream. But to me, none of them came even close to my Vandana. She was smart, beautiful and above all a very nice person. Absorbed in my thoughts, I had been unconsciously staring at the same scantily clad picture of actress Mamta Kulkarni for five minutes without really looking at it, when a familiar voice distracted me.

"Hi Babloo," Vandana greeted me with a full smile on her face.

I looked up at her. She was wearing a long, white skirt and matching blouse, giving her a pure appearance. Even the slight revealing dip of her cleavage didn't spoil it. I decided that I would tell her to wear it on our honeymoon.

I gave her a fleeting smile, which almost immediately changed back to my blank expression. I could never hold smiles for long.

Vandana kept smiling. "What are you doing here?"

She looked at the page that I had open.

"You like her, huh?" she asked.

"No."

I didn't want her to get the impression that I liked any woman except her and closed the page, slamming the magazine down on top of all the others. The newspaper vendor looked at me angrily and straightened the magazine, rearranging it neatly on a stack.

"Are you going home?" asked Vandana.

Her eyes sparkled, reflecting the bright lights of the electronic schedule board in the distance.

"Ok," I replied.

Her puzzled expression indicated her confusion at whether that was a yes or no. Nevertheless, she started walking. She stopped after a few steps and saw me still standing at the same place, looking at her as if I had just seen a ghost.

"Well," said Vandana curtly, "are you going to walk me home or not?"

"Ok," I replied.

"I didn't mean to force you." She laughed. "You can go back and look at Mamta Kulkarni if you want."

I wished I hadn't been looking at that magazine. Now Vandana might remember it and wouldn't believe Sikander when he conveyed my message.

"So, tell me, Babloo," said Vandana animatedly, "do you like any girl?"

A flurry of thoughts started flowing through my head but I kept them to myself. Sikander had promised to do the needful.

"You're a nice guy, Babloo. And trust me, only nice things happen to nice people. The right girl will find you."

Vandana got no response from me. She turned towards me. I was staring at a police constable slapping an *auto rickshaw* driver. Apparently, the *rickshaw* driver hadn't seen the constable in time and had rammed into him. I could sense Vandana closely observing the blank expression on my face.

"So how was your day? What did you do today?" she enquired.

"Nothing."

"Well, you're out here. That is doing something. So don't say you didn't do anything."

I always found her to be sweet and encouraging. She would make a good wife, I thought.

"How was your day?" I asked her.

"It was horrible," replied Vandana eagerly, "My boss is so creepy. You know, sometimes I wish that something really bad happens to him. You think that's bad?"

"What?" I asked blankly.

"That I wish bad for him?"

I was wondering how anyone could be bad to someone as nice as Vandana. Before I let my thoughts take me back to that park and house by the sea, I quickly spoke.

"No."

"Thank you," she said.

Vandana could be strange sometimes. Why was she thanking me? I thought.

"So did you do anything interesting today?" asked Vandana.

"I saw a film."

"Really? Which one?"

"*College Ladki.*"

Vandana seemed puzzled. She hadn't heard of the film. There's no way that she could have because those kind of films were never advertised.

"Was it an educational film?" she asked curiously.

"Yes. I learned a lot."

As we approached the colony gates, a Maruti Esteem came to an abrupt halt in front of us. I recognized the vehicle.

"Hi Babloo," said Sikander, as he got out of the car.

"Hi."

"So, what are you doing?"

"Nothing," I replied, looking at him with the usual blank look on my face. I had no control over that expression.

Sikander tried to stay focused on me but let his eyes slip quickly to look at Vandana's low cut blouse.

"So," said Sikander, turning towards Vandana, "are you going to introduce me to your friend?"

Vandana looked at me and then back at Sikander. I was confused. I knew I had to introduce them but forgot what Sikander had told me to say. Sikander came to my rescue.

"Hi. I'm Babloo's friend Sikander," he said politely, popping a piece of chewing gum into his mouth.

"Hi, I'm Vandana. I have seen you around. You're the cable operator, right?"

Sikander stood up straight.

"No. Actually, I own the business," he said, trying not to act arrogant. "Any complaints?"

"Well... actually yes. We could do away with the late night porn. Not a good influence on the kids, don't you think?"

Sikander almost choked on his gum, but immediately tried to cover up with an expression of surprise.

"Really? I didn't know that. You know these guys who work for me must be doing it. Thanks for bringing it to my notice."

"My pleasure," she said.

"So where are you guys coming from?" asked Sikander, trying to change the topic.

"We were just walking back from the station," she replied.

"Oh," said Sikander, feigning concern, "It's not safe for a girl to be walking alone so late at night."

"Don't worry," she said, "I have Babloo here to protect me."

I beamed with pride.

"Ok, I have to go now. Nice meeting you." She turned towards me. "I will see you later Babloo. You can stay here with your friend."

"Ok," I said.

Sikander looked at her shapely behind as she walked through the gates and disappeared into the shadows that enveloped the complex. By the time she disappeared from his view, I was standing close to him staring into his face intently.

"Get away from me, you *gaandu*," shouted Sikander, stepping back.

I was focusing on my thoughts. I tried to verbalize them.

"Why didn't you tell her?"

"Tell her what?" he asked annoyed.

I fell silent and looked at Sikander with my typical strange expression. Immediately Sikander's expression changed to a calm one.

"Oh that," he said putting his arm around my shoulder. "This is the first time I met her, Babloo. I have to get to know her. Give me some time."

He opened the door of his car. I took another step towards him.

"What?" asked Sikander, irritated.

"Vandana said to stay with you."

Sikander shook his head. "Ok, get in."

The bright lights of the line of restaurants on Linking Road brought out the true glamour of the city, hidden during the day under layers of concrete and grime. There were cars parked along the entire stretch, haphazardly filling every foot of empty space available. Young families were entering restaurants, while the early eaters were leaning against their parked cars chatting with each other over *paan* or ice cream. The person who had designed the huge Citibank billboard that read "The Citi never sleeps" had sensed the true pulse of Mumbai.

"So, tell me Babloo. What's Vandana like?" asked Sikander, as he skillfully dodged cars on the busy road.

"What?"

"What kind of stuff does she like?"

"Stuff?" I asked confused.

"Does she like perfumes, flowers, chocolates," explained Sikander, "what makes her happy?"

I suddenly became pensive. I realized I didn't know her as well as I thought I did.

"I bet she likes fancy stuff. She seems like a woman who's fond of classy things, like designer stuff. What do you think?" asked Sikander.

I was staring into space, still lost in my thoughts.

"You know, Babloo," said Sikander impatiently, "you have to help me out here. How am I going to help you if you don't give me any information on the girl?"

"She likes America. She wants to go there."

"Oh," he said, as if thinking aloud, "she's one of those types? I understand."

I smiled. I was glad that I had helped Sikander understand her better.

"I'm getting bored. Let's have some fun."

"Ok," I said mechanically.

Sikander slowed down and came to a full halt by a rundown

building opposite McDonalds. A shady looking man in a white kurta pajama, smoking a *beedi*, came to Sikander's side of the car.

They proceeded to talk in low tones. I couldn't figure out what they were saying but I wasn't even interested. My future with Vandana was on my mind.

The man disappeared into the building and in a few minutes returned with a young girl, completely dolled up. She was wearing a short black dress and reminded me of one of the actresses from the film *College Ladki*. Sikander nodded at the man and the man gestured towards the girl. She quietly sat in the backseat. Sikander pulled the car away from the building going towards the interiors of Bandra.

We drove for a few minutes till the girl spoke. Her husky voice startled me.

"I will charge double for the two of you."

"Relax sweetheart. It's just me. Trust me, I'm enough."

"What about him?"

"He will mind his own business."

Sikander snickered to himself as we continued the rest of the drive in silence. At periodic intervals I saw his hand going towards the backseat till it merged with the darkness.

Sikander parked the car in the shadows outside the *Le Pappilon* building in the quiet suburbs of Mt. Mary. He opened the door and got out. Within seconds, the backdoor opened and Sikander slid in next to the girl.

I turned around and saw him whispering something into her ear. She giggled as Sikander's hand found its way steadily up her skirt. He unzipped his pants with the other hand to reveal his nakedness and adjusted himself over the girl with his back towards me. Her eyes squinted as he maneuvered himself inside her but opened them wide when she noticed me staring at her.

"What's with your friend?" she exclaimed angrily.

Sikander turned around to look at me. I was less than a foot away observing them like an anxious spectator.

"Hey, turn around," ordered Sikander.

I didn't move and kept staring.

Sikander turned back to her. "Don't worry about him. He's a psycho. Come on. Let's do it."

She guided his hairy buttocks into her when her eyes opened again suddenly, this time with the impact of my head against hers. I had moved in closer to get a better look. Now my head was almost alongside Sikander's head.

"Hey, you guys are sick," she said, pushing Sikander off her, "I am not doing a bunch of gays together. Fuck you!"

She got out of the car, pulling up her panties.

"Fuck you too," shouted Sikander, as she hailed a passing *auto rickshaw* and climbed inside it.

Then he turned towards me. "What the hell is wrong with you?"

I was smiling to myself. I had seen these kinds of scenes in C grade movies at Nandi Theatre. But this was even more enjoyable and as Vandana said, "educational."

## 8

SUNDAY WAS VANDANA'S DAY OF GRATIFYING RELAXATION after her hectic work week. But today was going to be different. Her parents had sprung the most heartless surprise on her. Her stubborn father was sitting across her at the dining table, and her mother sat next to him, with her strict eyes open wide, staring at her.

Vandana's father, Shekhar Gupta, was a tall, authorative looking figure. Fair complexioned and presentable, he always wore safari suits, a fad that went out of fashion years ago. With a full head of hair dyed black and a peaceful expression on his clean-shaven, soft face (courtesy early morning yoga), he looked much younger than his middle-aged years.

Madhu Gupta was a loud woman, well groomed, but without much to offer in the looks department. She always wore striking, expensive sarees, gold jewellery, tying her hair in a bun, with a concerned expression on her round face, giving her a somewhat regal look. Though Vandana looked nothing like her, they could be mistaken for sisters, solely based on their petite frames and jet-black, gorgeous eyes.

"Raghu is a good boy," her father was saying casually, in between bites of *parathas* and *dahi*. "He has a promising future. That boy is going to go places and keep you very happy."

"Yes. And he will make lots of money," her mother added in approval, shaking her head from side to side.

"But you could have asked me, Papa," said Vandana, in a pleading tone. Her earlier reasoning hadn't proved successful.

"See Beta. You have to get married someday. And Raghu is a good boy. I know his father very well. He is an honest and principled person. That boy belongs to a good family," he said.

"And you have to look at the family when getting married," her mother added.

Vandana didn't look at her but sensed her mother shaking her head from side to side in approval.

"But Papa, I want to work for a few more years. I want to see the world. I thought you understood that."

"You can do that after you get married," he said, giving more attention to her than to the food now. "That's what we're trying to tell you Beta. This boy will give all that to you. I have seen many people in my career and I know who is capable and who is not. This boy is."

What about personality? He has none, Vandana wanted to say. But her traditional parents wouldn't understand that. After all, they had married each other.

"But Papa, I don't want to get married so early. I need a few more years," she said.

"*Haay Raam!*" her mother exclaimed, in a melodramatic tone. "So you want to sit at home unmarried for so long? What will the colony say? That we are unable to get our daughter married?"

That's exactly what she expected her mother to say. Her mother had married her father, who was 10 years senior to her, when she was just 16. Now, by law, that was illegal. The legal, marriageable age for a woman was 18. And Vandana was three years past that.

"Your mother's right," said her hen-pecked father. "What will the colony say? Beta, it is not good to keep an unmarried girl in the house for too long. People will start talking."

Vandana detested the narrow-minded mentality of the colony. People loved to gossip and had nothing better to do than to poke their noses in other people's affairs. Jealousy and frustration was in the air all around, and getting in the line of fire was the last thing her father, the Chairman of the Railway Colony Society Committee, wanted.

Vandana had dreams and thought that the right opportunity would come and take her away. But this opportunity was keeping her confined to the colony, a place she badly wanted to get out of.

She had overheard her mother talk to her father many times, of the marriage proposals that were coming their way. But she thought her father would use his good sense of judgement and keep his promise of letting her get married only when she was ready.

Her mother's face took on a rigid expression. "If you had studied further, we would have understood. But now you are working in a job in townside and coming home so late every day. How long will this go on? You have to start thinking ahead."

There are many men, not only in the colony but in all of Mumbai, thought Vandana. She believed that the right guy was somewhere out there and would find her, genuinely love her and make her feel special. But, Raghu? She had never given him a second glance and considered him dull, boring and devoid of any personality. She could never see herself having an intelligent conversation with him. And the thought of him ever touching her disgusted her. Is this the kind of guy she had saved her virginity for? She shuddered at the thought and turned towards her father.

"But Papa, you could have at least asked me. I mean, it's such an important decision of my life. How could you not speak with me? How could you make this decision for me?"

Shekhar was about to say something, but Madhu beat him to it. Her voice was firm.

"Vandana, we have let you do whatever you wanted to all your life. You wanted to go to a co-ed college, we didn't say anything. You wanted to take a job so far from home, we let you do it. We even let you dress the way you want. But we will now decide whom you will marry."

The finality in her mother's last sentence indicated that the topic was closed. Her father got up from the table and left in silence while she wordlessly fought back her tears.

"Now come and get dressed. The Srivastavs will be here in an hour. You have to make a good impression. Now listen carefully."

Amar, Sudha and Raghu walked in silence from Block A to Block B, each consumed by their own thoughts.

Amar was wearing his favourite white, embroidered kurta *churidar*, an outfit that he reserved for festive occasions. He was elated that he was going to fulfill his final responsibility as a father. In his mind, where Babloo had failed him, Raghu had more than made up. An alliance from a well-respected family had been his cherished dream.

Sudha's green and red silk sari caught many glances and whispers from residents passing by. She had adorned herself with gold jewellery and her heavy *kajal* and shining *bindi* indicated that she was dressed up for something auspicious. Sudha was aware that Madhu Gupta was extremely fashion-conscious and she was determined to match up to her standards. She too was jubilant, but more so because of the dowry that the groom's family reaped in their community. Shekhar Gupta was known to be a very well-invested man. The colony grapevine had it that he had invested in a flat in the far-flung suburb of Mira Road. One day that property would be Raghu's, thought Sudha.

Raghu was the most excited of the three. Vandana was the bombshell of the colony. To be sleeping next to her every night was something that he could only dream of. And being married to her would make him popular both in the colony and in his workplace.

As they entered block B, a passing family stopped in their tracks and took notice of them. Sudha knew that they would soon start wondering as to why the Srivastavs were going all decked up to the Guptas' residence. And when they would find out, the Srivastavs would be the talk of the colony.

They walked up the creaky staircase, their differing footwear making further inharmonious noises that echoed in the Sunday silence. It took them a good 10 minutes to cover the long set of stairs to the sixth floor. None of the buildings had elevators. In that sense, the lower ranking personnel, delegated to the lower floors, were better off.

On reaching the Guptas' main door ornamented with Feng Shui paraphernalia, Sudha adjusted her sari before pressing the electric doorbell. She was almost instantly greeted by an equally decked up Madhu Gupta, wearing an even more expensive silk saree.

"*Namaste* ji. So nice to see you," Madhu said with her hands folded in the traditional Indian gesture of a respectful greeting.

The Srivastavs reciprocated the gesture and were invited inside the well-furnished house. Shekhar Gupta appeared from the bedroom now dressed in formal trousers and shirt.

"*Namaste*," he folded his hands in respect.

Amar was pleased. This was just the beginning. In the office, Shekhar addressed him as Srivastav.

"Come, please sit," said Shekhar.

They all took a seat, being careful enough to leave the seat on the couch next to Raghu empty.

"You have a very nice house," said Sudha. This was her first time in an apartment in Block B. She had always been confined to interacting with the women of Block A, the junior officers' wives.

"Thank you," replied Madhu. "So what will you have? Is tea ok?"

Everyone nodded in agreement. Madhu had purposely told her husband to invite them in the late afternoon, way after lunch so she would not have to undertake the cumbersome task of cooking exclusively for so many people. She disappeared into the kitchen.

"Where's Babloo?" asked Shekhar.

Amar looked at Sudha for a reply.

"He went out for some work. He might come a little later," said Sudha smiling.

They all fell into an awkward silence, which made Shekhar fidget in his seat. He quickly spoke.

"So Raghu, how's work going?"

"It's going well Uncle, very busy."

"Your father told me that you have been offered a lucrative position by Tanmay Trivedi. Tanmay Trivedi is a really well-respected stockbroker."

"Yes he is. I guess I'm very lucky to have been offered such a position," said Raghu.

"There's no such thing as luck, Beta. It's your hard work that got you here."

Raghu smiled.

"Mr. Gupta, we are so happy that you considered our Raghu to be your son-in-law," said Sudha.

Amar gave her a stern look. He had drilled it into her that this was the girl's father and he should be thanking them.

"You are so humble Mrs. Srivastav. We are the lucky ones to have such a fine boy as Raghu for our daughter."

The pleasantries were broken by the arrival of Madhu, followed by Vandana. Madhu was carrying a tray of *samosas*, *pakoras* and *mithai*. Vandana followed her with a tray of tea in her hands.

Vandana's simplicity overshadowed the decked-up ladies. She wore a lovely pink sari with a sleeveless blouse and basic make-up which accentuated her gorgeous looks. Raghu couldn't take his eyes off her as she placed the tray on the table and sat next to him.

Vandana's mother had rehearsed this scene with her for the past hour and told her to seat herself only when the boy's mother told her to sit. But Vandana sat down anyway. She was determined to get this over with as soon as possible. She proceeded to make tea for everyone. Sudha smiled at her when their eyes met but Vandana averted her gaze.

After everyone had sipped their tea, the typical Indian scene ensued, where a boy and his parents came to see a girl and her parents, to ask for her hand in marriage. Sudha asked Vandana if she could cook and what her favourite dishes were; Amar asked her what her educational background was and her future plans for her career. Vandana gave all the right answers as she had been programmed to, by her mother.

The conversation reached the point where someone suggested that the boy and girl should talk to each other alone. Vandana immediately held her head.

"Excuse me. I have a headache. Papa, can I go and lie down?"

He remained silent. She said bye to everyone and retreated to her room, hoping that they wouldn't send the idiot inside to have a conversation. They didn't.

"She works very hard all week and wasn't feeling well today," justified Shekhar.

Amar replied, "Then you should have told us, Mr Gupta, we…"

Shekhar cut him off politely, "Call me Shekhar."

Amar smiled, "We would have cancelled, Shekhar. We could have done this some other time."

"No," said Shekhar, holding up his hand, "I had given my word."

"That's what we respect about you Shekharji," said Sudha, "everyone in the colony has high respect for you."

Shekhar smiled proudly.

"Well, we didn't ask the boy and girl what they think of each other," said Amar, "Raghu respects whatever we say. That's why we are here."

"Vandana is as happy with this as we are," said Shekhar. "Besides this is not the first time they are seeing each other."

"But don't you think that Raghu and Vandana should talk and get to know each other? After all, they are going to be spending the rest of their life with each other," said Sudha concerned.

"We should let them spend some time alone," said Amar carefully, "Raghu, maybe you could take Vandana out for coffee. That's only if you don't mind Shekhar."

"No, of course not," said Shekhar, ignoring a glare from his wife. He turned towards Raghu. "Yes, whenever you are free Raghu, you are more than welcome to come and take Vandana out."

"Yes Uncle," replied Raghu cheerfully.

"See, we are doing this for the first time. So what happens after this?" asked Madhu eagerly.

"See Madhuji," replied Sudha. "We should set a wedding date. Sometime six months from now. That will give Raghu some time to settle down." She decided that she would mention the dowry at a later date.

"And that will give Raghu and Vandana time to get to know each other," added Shekhar.

"Great," said Amar confidently. "As future *samdhis*, we too shall be meeting more often."

"Don't be so formal Amar. We are family now," said Shekhar.

Raghu beamed with happiness. He couldn't believe his luck.

Inside the bedroom, Vandana had been overhearing the conversation and was cursing her luck. She couldn't believe this was happening to her.

## 9

THE NEWS OF THE PROPOSED ALLIANCE BETWEEN THE Guptas and the Srivastavs spread across the colony within days. And Madhu Gupta was the one instrumental in ensuring that that happened. She knew that now Raghu and Vandana would be seen together and it was better for the colony residents to know that it was heading towards marriage rather than to let them make their own interpretations of the couple's sudden togetherness.

I didn't even get a whiff of the new turn of events that was on everyone's tongue. I didn't read into my family's new excitement and besides, my parents had never included me in any of the family affairs – they had decided to tell me only after a wedding date was fixed. I never communicated with any of the residents, who only cast scoffing glares in my direction, and they never made any effort to chat with me.

These days, I was living in my own bubble. Sikander had promised to convey my feelings to Vandana and I was positive about getting a favourable response from him. Then I planned to take the matter ahead with my parents. This was one responsibility of theirs towards me that I knew they could not shake off.

I returned home at night to find Papa still awake, seated in the living room, staring into space. Ma was sitting next to him with a worried look on her face. When they saw me come in, they snapped out of their spaced-out zones.

"Babloo, come here. Sit down," said Papa calmly.

I sat down. I felt around for the TV remote but didn't find it. Instead I caught sight of the day's newspaper, *The Times of India*, on the coffee table. I picked it up and started slowly mouthing the headlines.

THE RAILWAY MINISTRY PROPOSES A FARE HIKE.

So what else was new? I turned to the next page and scanned the headlines for the city news. In the lower left hand side was an article – WOMAN TRAIN COMMUTER GETS RAPED IN THE LADIES' COMPARTMENT.

I stared at the article's headline in disbelief. Where was there hope? I wished I could do something and get rid of all these people and make the city safe. But what could I do? I banged my fist on the coffee table in frustration.

"Babloo!" shouted Papa.

I looked up and stared straight into my father's eyes. Whenever I did that, it unnerved Papa and he didn't know what to do. Even if he said something, the stare continued. He said something anyway.

"Babloo," said Papa, in a soft tone, "I have found a job for you."

I snapped out of my stare and looked at him suspiciously.

"I have spoken to my department and they agreed to offer you a job in our office."

For the first time in years, I felt my face lighting up.

Ma smiled. She said to Papa approvingly, "I told you."

I knew that as a Railway Officer I could bring about immense change in the system. I had it all planned out. First, I would delegate a screened police authority in the ladies' compartment, where most crimes took place. Then I would initiate a proposal to introduce a metro rail system similar to that in the West, which would run either underground or over the city on specially constructed ramps. I was bursting with ideas and now that I was going to be a Railway Officer, I would ensure that they saw the light of day. I knew that this new appointment would make Vandana very proud of me.

"It's an office boy job. It's something small to start with. But at least you will be earning some money and doing something productive with your day. And I will be there in the office to correct your mistakes," said Papa.

I knew that an office boy was another word for peon. A peon wore a uniform and was at the beck and call of everyone in the office, to serve tea, to transfer papers from table to table, to be the victim of everyone's frustration. I looked at both my parents disbelievingly.

"The job provides good benefits with a Provident Fund, a first class railway pass, and a daily commuting allowance which you could save as your pocket money. Start coming to the office from tomorrow," Papa stated.

"No," I said.

"What?" asked Papa, not sure that he had heard me correctly.

"No!"

"What do you mean by no?"

"NO! NO! NO!" I shouted at the top of my voice. At this time of the night, the whole colony would be able to hear it.

"Shhh…Beta. Just think about it. It's ok," Ma said.

"What do you mean he should think about it?" asked Papa belligerently.

"Just let it go. Let him think about it. If he doesn't want to do it, don't force him," said Ma placatingly.

"It's your lenient attitude that has made him so irresponsible," Papa snapped, in the same angry tone. "Otherwise he would have been motivated to do something with his life."

Ma burst into tears. "So it's all my fault? Our son has turned out this way and it's my fault?!"

With that, she covered her mouth and rushed into the kitchen.

Papa looked at me crossly and disappeared into the kitchen after Ma. I picked up the newspaper again to read the remainder of the article. It mentioned that the woman was raped by a gang of three men. There were other women present in the compartment but they just stood there and witnessed the entire incident in silent fear. When the act was completed, the gang got off at the next station. A police report was only filed the next day when the victim went to an NGO after her parents threw her out of the house for 'the shame she had brought to her family'. However, the case was soon dismissed as no witnesses came forward to testify on the poor girl's behalf and her petition was deemed too weak without corroborating statements. But with the help of a reporter and the NGO, the woman was able to at least take her story to the press.

I threw the paper down on the table, infuriated. My heart went out to the poor victim. I thought of what she must have gone through and how despite all that, she was forsaken by her parents. I knew what it was like to have inconsiderate parents.

I sometimes took a walk at night to clear my head, usually on the railway tracks, as it allowed me space to wander about unlike the humming and bustling Bandra station road.

It was now close to midnight and the trains were infrequent at this hour. The few trains that passed by were brightly lit up within, silhouetting the commuters travelling at this time.

At times, I would walk on an empty track. When a train approached, I would pretend not to hear it. The driver would panic, frantically sounding his loud horn but I would still feign ignorance. At the last minute, when the driver started applying pressure on the brakes, I would move out of the way just in time and disappear into the darkness. It gave me a great thrill to disrupt the functioning of the railways.

My irritation over my father's job offer was replaced by thoughts of the rape victim. She must have screamed and yelled at the top of her voice but it must have been swallowed by the deafening sounds produced by the moving train. She must have looked at the other commuters and begged for help, and they must have just stood there, more concerned about their own safety. Had I been there, I would have helped her.

I trudged heavily on the bare tracks, looking down at them with contempt. These tracks were supposed to carry commuters to their destinations, not change their lives on the way.

Lost in my thoughts, I didn't hear the train coming up just behind me. The train was about 30 feet away, the driver hurriedly applying its brakes, but I was still unaware of its proximity. It came to a full halt less than a foot away from me. I turned around when the driver alighted, hurling abuses at me.

"You *chutiya*, of all trains, did you have to choose mine, to die in front of?" screamed the driver, his face red with anger.

I looked at the train, then at the driver and realized what had just transpired.

"You bastard," the driver exclaimed. "You would have made me a murderer. You people who commit suicide are nothing but weak."

A thought flashed through my head – the element of surpise. The driver did not finish because a swift punch from me cut him off mid-sentence. Before he could regain his senses, I was already running away into the darkness, holding my bruised knuckles. I had just decided that from now on, I would not tolerate anyone telling me that I was weak.

# 10

CAFÉ SEASIDE HAD BEEN POPULARIZED IN MANY Hindi films as the make-up or break-up spot for the hero and heroine. Located in the posh area of Bandstand, facing the Arabian Sea, it had been around for more than three decades and over the years had become a favourite spot for different types of romantic couples – those who would spend the entire evening gazing into each other's eyes, the ones who would be chatting animatedly with parallel action below the tables, and the couples on the verge of a break-up, arguing endlessly. Seated at a corner table, Raghu and Vandana seemed almost conspicuous as they didn't fit into any of these categories.

Vandana had tried to argue her way out of this so called 'date' that her mother had set up for her. But her mother didn't listen. Vandana figured that it was her fault for coming home early from work. She had just wanted to relax at home. Now she felt trapped at both ends.

She found the place to be very sleazy – it gave her some insight into Raghu's taste. She had expected him to at least take her to a decent place like Barista or Café Coffee Day. When she had asked him where they were going, he told her that it was a surprise. Either this guy had no class or he didn't get out much, Vandana thought.

She was highly irked by him and it was clearly visible on her usually calm face. She had had a tiring day and had to travel back home standing in a crowded train from Churchgate to Bandra. She believed that the least Raghu could have done, was bring her here by taxi or at least an *auto rickshaw*. But he had insisted that they travel by the 211 bus. As a result, her aching legs were forced to wait in line for a good half hour and then another half hour in the packed bus. Her mother would term it "being sensible about money".

When they arrived at the café, Vandana was starving and immediately scanned the menu. Just as she was about to place her order for a pizza, Raghu cancelled it telling her that the food wasn't good there and instead, he ordered two coffees. There was no doubt about it; he was plain stingy, thought Vandana – a quality that she despised in a man.

That conversation had taken place around 10 minutes ago. Since then, they had been sitting in silence. Vandana was looking fixedly out at the sea. Raghu was staring at her with a delighted smile on his face.

How she wished she could walk out of there. But she knew that getting out of this café would not relieve her of the entire situation.

She closed her eyes slowly and leaned back in her chair. Her legs ached, and she just wanted to be able to put them up. But Raghu had sprawled out on most of the third, empty chair at the table so that option was ruled out.

She thought about her life and how things had changed all of a sudden. What did she do wrong? She had always chosen her friends with care and had never given her parents any real stress about boys or bad rumours. And this is how they had rewarded her?

The vexatious sound of glass cups banging on the table forced her eyes open. The waiter was hastily placing the hot coffee before them, spilling some in the process. Before leaving, he took one quick look at her revealing tank top.

When Vandana left the house, she had worn a shirt over it. But later on, she had deliberately removed her shirt to scandalize Raghu, desperately hoping that it would put him off, enough to cancel this torturous outing. But Raghu was far from scandalized. In fact, he seemed to be enjoying the view, alternating his gaze between her face and chest.

The only thing that Vandana thought could save her was a miracle. Ever since that day when both families had met at her home, she prayed every night to all the Gods she could think of. Only they could do something, she thought. It was out of her hands now.

Vandana had thought of the drastic measures she could take. She could run away to some friend's place but then she had no real friends. She could leave town and take a job elsewhere, but she didn't have enough money to do that. Like a good Indian daughter she had always given most of her monthly salary to her parents, keeping only some pocket money for herself. Now she found herself left with no option.

Raghu added sugar to one cup and stirred it. Then he emptied a packet of Sweet n Low in the other and pushed it towards Vandana.

"You could have at least asked me if I take sugar or Sweet n Low," fumed Vandana.

"Sugar is not good for you if you want to maintain your figure. This tastes the same," he said, licking his lips just before he took a sip of his coffee.

*Then why the hell aren't you having it, you out-of-shape, low-mentality idiot?* But she had no energy or inclination to argue with him. They were obviously not on the same wavelength. She welcomed any distraction, even Babloo's presence. Even though Babloo was quiet half the time, she found that he always made her laugh without trying to.

Raghu finished his coffee in two long gulps. No manners, no courtesy, thought Vandana. He looked at her, actually more at her breasts, longingly.

"Aren't you excited?" he asked.

The hell I am, thought Vandana.

"About what?" she asked coldly.

"About us," he emphasized.

"What about us?" she asked, disinterested.

"About us getting married?"

She looked at him with a sigh. She just wanted to go home and sleep. But her mother would let her rest only after she had heard Vandana's full report of the evening.

"You know, Ma and Papa said that we should get married after six months. But I don't want to wait. I want to get married soon."

Sure you do, Vandana thought. Your eyes show how horny you are.

"But I need to wait," she said.

"Why?" he asked.

Now she had to think about what to say. She knew that this entire conversation would be repeated to his parents and they would analyze every comment she made. Then she would hear of it from her mother.

"Well, because we need to get to know each other first. You can't just get married to a stranger," she said, surprised at her own sensible answer.

"But I love you, Vandana!"

Vandana nearly choked on her coffee. It was not only obvious that he hardly got out, but also that he had never been out with a girl.

"You what?" she asked disbelievingly.

"I love you, Vandana," he said. "It's true. I have loved you ever since I saw you. All I ever wanted was to be able to be friends with you. This is like a dream come true for me."

"Listen Raghu," she said, losing her temper. "We don't even know each other. We have hardly ever spoken. It's going to take time before we understand each other, ok?"

Raghu was stunned into silence. Now she regretted having spoken to him in that tone. It wasn't his fault, but her parents'. They had initiated the proposal.

"I'm sorry, Raghu. I'm just very tired. I would really like to go home."

"Ok," he said. "But did you have a good time? Did you enjoy my company?"

She rose to her feet pretending she hadn't hear that. Vandana headed out while Raghu paid the bill.

She was standing outside for a few minutes when she realized that she was done being courteous to him. She was really tired and not looking forward to another crowded bus ride back home and decided that she could find her own way back.

The street was a major hang-out spot in the evenings. It was a replica of Carter Road with its zooming cars, coffee joints and a long promenade that ran the entire length of the road. Vandana tried to hail a rickshaw but all of them had passengers and whizzed past her. Frustrated, she started walking and joined the evening crowd on the promenade. The cool sea breeze calmed her down immediately. She sat down on a bench and watched some children playing with each other. They seemed so happy. Vandana missed her childhood and the carefree life that she had had. Just thinking about those days gave her a serene sense of joy. She smiled to herself and started walking ahead, taking in all that was happening.

She passed a group of young girls sitting and gossiping happily. Then she passed two elderly ladies who seemed content with life, talking about their younger days. Two young, teenaged guys were eyeing the young women all around, including Vandana. She took in all of this and realized that she was missing out on a lot in life.

The world around her was so happy. They must all have problems like her but there was a difference. They chose to be happy. Vandana realized that it was her choice and from now on, she would try to enjoy life and just be happy. She had spent enough time whining and feeling sorry for herself.

She felt a sense of joy – a revelation. It was in this frame of mind that she heard a familiar voice.

"Hi, Vandana."

She looked to her side and saw Sikander standing there with a friendly smile on his face. He was in a white, neatly pressed shirt tucked into somber blue jeans, eyes masked behind designer sunglasses. His hair was combed back, with a few strands threatening to break loose on account of the determined evening sea breeze.

"Hi, Vandana. How are you?"

"Well, I didn't expect to see you. How come you're here?" she asked, genuinely surprised, hoping that it didn't come across as rude.

"I love coming here in the evenings for walks," he said. Little did she know that he had followed her right from the time she had left the colony.

When Vandana first met Sikander that night with Babloo, he had come across as the typical Mumbai loafer. But seeing him dressed presentably for a change, and the fact that he spent his evenings here by the sea, instantly changed her impression of him. That night he was arrogant, but now he seemed genuine and very friendly.

"You come here in the evenings for walks?" she asked disbelievingly. "I thought you were the type that would spend the evenings driving around in that fancy, flashy car of yours."

"Me?" he said innocently. "Vandana, I have a flashy car because I love the good things in life. That doesn't mean I'm the spoiled type. I work really hard all day and I like spending on myself and people I care about. It makes me happy."

"That's really nice. Everyone is so selfish these days. It's so refreshing to find a person who still cares about other people."

"It's not anyone's fault. This city does that to you. It gives you no time to yourself. So whenever you have time, you get greedy and just want to do things for yourself," he preached. "So what are you doing here?"

She was longing for someone to talk to. She impulsively decided to trust him.

"Don't ask," she said. "My parents are trying to set me up with Raghu. He brought me here to Café Seaside."

"Where is he?" asked Sikander, looking over her shoulder.

"Oh, I disappeared while he was paying the bill." She burst into a laugh. He laughed with her.

"Where are you going now, if you don't mind my asking?" he asked.

She respected the fact that he didn't probe further. He was proving to be a gentleman.

"I was just heading home," she said. "I couldn't find an *auto* so decided to walk till I found one."

"I hope this doesn't come across the wrong way, but if you're not in a hurry, would you like to join me for a cup of coffee?"

She looked at her watch. She still had time. Besides, what did she have to lose?

"Sure. That would be nice," she said.

They found an opening in the barrier that divided the promenade from the road. They walked through it and crossed the bustling street to the Barista coffee shop.

The place was crowded with youngsters all competing for conversation. The occupants of a nearby table got up and Sikander immediately went to the table and blocked it by holding onto a chair. He held out the chair for her first before seating himself opposite her.

"You are quite chivalrous, I see," she teased. "The women must be lucky."

"What women?" he asked innocently.

"Your girlfriends! Now don't tell me you don't have a girlfriend."

"Have you ever seen me with any girls?"

Now that she thought about it, she hadn't. She had always passed him off as a guy who would be chasing anything in a skirt. But looks can be deceptive, she thought.

"Well, honestly, I have had my share of relationships," Sikander said. "But nothing worked out. I'm a very passionate person but women don't understand that. All they ever wanted was to be taken out and be shown a good time. No one believes in romance anymore which is really frustrating. Do you understand what I mean, Vandana?"

She did understand. All the men she had met were just like that – shallow and superficial.

"You know, Vandana," he continued, "believe it or not, but I believe in love. I don't want to waste time on the wrong kind of women. I don't mind waiting for the right girl no matter how long it takes."

The waiter arrived and handed Sikander a menu. Sikander passed it on to Vandana and said to the waiter, "We'll let the lady order."

Vandana smiled as she took the menu.

"Would a hot chocolate be ok?" she asked.

"Sure," he said. "It's been a long time since I had one."

"Two hot chocolates and a plate of *samosas*," she said to the waiter. He darted off.

"I usually come here by myself," Sikander said. "This is such a refreshing change."

"What about your friends? Those boys from the colony you're always hanging out with? Mahesh, Pravin?" she enquired curiously.

"I've known them for long. They're just company. I cannot really talk to them the way we're talking now."

She smiled. The waiter brought them their hot chocolates and *samosas*.

Either time passed quickly or the waiter had brought the food really fast. Either way, it didn't matter to Vandana. She felt relaxed now and was having a good time.

"Tell me Sikander. Do you have any dreams?" she asked, hoping that she wasn't crossing the line.

Sikander thought about it. The last dream that he had was of him having sex with her.

"I have a lot of dreams Vandana," he said, "Ok, I haven't told this to anyone. I have this dream... no, forget it... you'll think it's silly."

"No no tell me!" she insisted.

"Ok. I have this dream of selling my business and moving to America. I know it sounds stupid..."

"No Sikander, that's a wonderful dream! Tell me more."

"Well, I love this city but don't like the quality of life here," he said. "Life in America is something else. But America is just a part of it. I want to see the world!"

"Really?"

"Yes. Actually, I've been saving money and working on getting a job there. I have some friends there so they're guiding me on the whole visa process. You know, one day I'll just disappear and the next people will hear of me is that I'm in America!"

Vandana felt a surge of energy rush through her. This was so uncanny. She had never imagined that she would meet a guy who had the same dreams as her.

After that Vandana really started opening up to him. She told him about her work, her home, her parents, how they had fixed her up with Raghu. He lied about his life, his home, his business, and his family.

They kept chatting and the two hot chocolates became four, then six. It was only when they heard the distant gong of the Mt. Mary Church that they realized that the 8 o' clock evening mass had commenced. Vandana looked at her watch.

"I should be going now," she said.

"How are you going home?" he asked.

"I was going to take an auto."

"I'm going that way. And even if I wasn't I would still offer to drop you."

"You don't have to be formal with me," she said. "Ok. Thank you."

"Now who's being formal?" he smiled.

Vandana broke into a laugh.

Sikander looked around. "The waiters here are very busy. We'll get stuck waiting for the bill. I'll just go inside and pay the bill. Don't disappear on me!"

"Oh, come on," she smiled.

Their conversation continued throughout the drive back. Vandana was disappointed when they finally reached the gates of the colony; disappointed because such a lovely evening had come to an end.

"Stop here please," she said.

"Why? I'll drop you inside."

"No," she said. "I can't be seen in your car. You know how this colony is. They just need an excuse to gossip."

Before getting out of the car, she said, "Sikander, thanks a lot for this evening. I really had a great time."

"My pleasure. And thanks a lot for making my evening more interesting."

She blushed.

"Vandana," he said, "maybe we can do this sometime again, if that's ok with you?"

"Sure," she smiled, "I would like that. Good night."

She got out of the car and walked through the gates. Sikander looked at her shapely behind. He was proud of himself. He had her exactly where he wanted her.

When Vandana walked in, her mother didn't ask her for a report. That night, before going to sleep, Vandana thanked all her Gods for answering her prayers in some way. She knew that things were going to change.

Sikander drove around Bandra for an hour and then parked outside the colony. He waited for a full 15 minutes before she appeared.

She got into the tinted car and hugged him. "Oh I love you so much, Sikander!"

He hugged her back and muttered, "I love you too."

He put the car in first gear and drove ahead.

"What took you so long?" he asked indifferently.

"I am so sorry. My family got delayed leaving the house. They have gone to the other side of town, to my aunt's place, so won't be back until midnight. They think I'm at home studying," she beamed.

"So when do you have to get home?" he asked, keeping his eyes on the road.

"In an hour's time," she replied excitedly. "My parents will reach my aunt's place by then and will call to check on me. I'm going to spend a whole hour with my *jaanoo!*"

Yeah, whatever, he thought. He couldn't take his mind off Vandana. They stopped at a traffic light and Sikander turned to look at her.

Sonal had a pure face, soft features and delicate curves. She bore an aura of innocence, excitement and wonder, typical of a 16 year old in her first year of junior college.

It had started with that night at the colony when Sonal had been stealing coy glances at him and responding positively to his smiles. Sikander went a step further and started going to the college she was studying at, National College in Bandra. She was totally enamoured by him and started bunking classes to hang out with him outside the campus gate. The most he was able to do in the confines of his tinted car was kissing and necking, he couldn't go any further for fear of the car windows fogging up and attracting attention. And she refused to go with him anywhere too far away from the college campus.

So he started telling her how much he loved her and how he really wanted to spend time with her alone. Spell-bound by his irresistible charm, the naïve Sonal finally agreed to sneak out to meet him. This was the first time she had done that.

Now she was all excited, like a puppy getting out of the house for the first time. She kept chattering away, asking him where they were going for dinner. He was irritated by now and only wanted to get her off his back; that was is, of course, only after he got her *on her* back.

He brought the car to a stop on Kane Road in Mount Mary. Kane Road was the steep, usually secluded slope that connected Mount Mary to Bandstand.

"Why have we stopped here, *jaanoo*?" Sonal asked, eyes fluttering, running her fingers through her permed hair.

He hated it when she called him *jaanoo*.

"Sweetheart, we can go for dinner anytime. But I wanted to spend some time alone with you – just you and me."

"But you promised me dinner, *jaanoo*."

"Sweetheart," he said, "I love you and am dying to be alone with you. I just want to hold your hand and look at you. Can I do that?"

She nodded with a smile and closed her eyes. She was anticipating his hands on hers but felt one slipping inside her kurta and the other trying to find its way inside her jeans.

"Sikander, what are you doing?" she exclaimed.

"Sweetheart, I love you very much," he said without stopping. "Do you love me too?"

"Yes," she sighed.

"Then trust me."

"I trust you."

He took off her kurta followed by her jeans. He wasted no time in getting the rest off. After arousing her with a little foreplay, he unzipped his pants and went for the kill.

She moaned in pain telling him to be gentle. But he couldn't. The evening with Vandana had aroused him completely. She cried out in pain. Only after she dug her nails in his back did he realize he was hurting her.

After he was done, he got off her. She sat there naked, crying.

By the time they reached the gates of the colony, she had her clothes back on and was fully dressed. She was staring blankly ahead. He caught her face and kissed her passionately on her lips.

"I love you very much Sonal," he said in her ear. "Tonight was very special."

Her expressionless face broke into a smile. She kissed him back and then ran into the colony.

Stupid girls, Sikander thought, as he proceeded to clean the spots of blood off his new leather seats.

## 11

I WAS GETTING FED UP OF FINDING WAYS TO PASS TIME and was beginning to feel very edgy and restless. My anxiety had first surfaced after my brief skirmish with the leader of the political gang on the day of Mumbai Bandh. It accelerated further when I punched the local train driver who called me weak. I realized I was developing a passion for action.

I started utilizing my time to exercise feverishly. I practiced punching hard into the walls at home, but only late in the evenings, when the TV was blaring in the other room. My fists hurt but it made me feel alive, and I kept at it. Later in the night, I ran on the tracks and tried to race with the local trains.

The only similarity to my previous routine was watching films or waiting to talk to Vandana. Now I was sticking to the latter part of my routine as I waited patiently outside Bandra station. It was 6:30 in the evening and I knew that Vandana could come anytime between 6:30 and 9 p.m. I decided to wait however long it took because I really wanted to talk to her.

I hadn't eaten all day. These days I was abstaining from food deliberately, limiting myself to only one meal a day. Even though I was in good shape, I now wanted a really developed physique and a six-pack, flat stomach like my favourite star Riyaz Khan.

The only exception I made to my diet was my favourite cold drink, Thumbs Up. The first sip always gave me a head rush and I loved the feeling of the effervescent gas stinging my nostrils. The craving for a Thumbs Up suddenly filled my mind and I found my way into the station, to the canteen stall near the entrance.

"One Thumbs Up," I ordered.

"No Thumbs Up," replied the man behind the counter, "only Pepsi or Coke."

"One Thumbs Up," I repeated.

"Didn't you hear me?" said the man irritated, busy serving other customers. "I said no Thumbs Up."

"One Thumbs Up," I said again, in the same demanding tone.

The man was angry now. He looked straight into my eyes and was greeted by a very strange look. That didn't deter him.

"Hey *chutiya*," shouted the man. "Go away from here. Don't mess my head during business time."

The stream of abuses began turning into background noise. I felt the adrenaline pumping through my veins. I had decided that no one was ever going to abuse me anymore. I was done being the victim of other people's frustrations. In my mind, all I had asked for was a Thumbs Up and this man had no business cursing me like that.

I clenched my fists and felt my strength collecting in my arms. I was going to give all I had in this one punch. The man kept shouting, oblivious to my rising fist. A crowd was beginning to collect, eager to watch anything to break their purposeless, monotonous lives.

I raised my hand and was about to strike when...

"Babloo! Hey Babloo!"

It was Vandana. I immediately forgot my anger and looked around. A crowd had gathered at a safe distance from me, looking on uncertainly. I looked past them at Vandana and rushed towards her.

"Hey you madman! Where are you running, you bastard?" shouted the man from the shop.

The crowd immediately dissipated, looking for their next source of entertainment. The man's voice faded in the background as I approached Vandana. She stood out from the hustle around her, dressed in a simple orange cotton kurta and white, slim-fit jeans. I wanted to hug her, but knew that the time for that hadn't come yet.

"What happened, Babloo?" asked Vandana concerned. "Why was that man shouting at you?"

"I don't know," I replied honestly. "I just asked for a Thumbs Up."

"That's strange. This city has some crazy people."

"Yes."

"So what are you doing here?"

After asking me that, she seemed to immediately realize that she shouldn't have. She knew, in fact the whole colony knew, that I didn't really do anything all day.

"I came for a Thumbs Up," I answered.

A sympathetic expression overcame her cheerfulness.

"So, do you still want a Thumbs Up?" she asked excitedly.

"Yes."

"Come with me," she said smiling and started walking ahead.

She ignored the remarks of the man at the canteen as we passed him. He was warning her to be wary of the guy she was with.

She stepped outside the station and saw the long line at the *auto rickshaw* stand. She looked by her side for me and found me standing a few steps behind her.

"I told you to come with me, not follow me," she smiled.

I stepped to her side.

"Let's go," she said.

There were cars going in all directions, trying to maneuver their way through the peak hour traffic. It was that time of the day when no one had consideration for traffic rules or right of way. Everyone just wanted to get home. The cops present were more interested in making some under-the-table, quick money from traffic violators rather than bringing the situation under control.

We passed the mosque and the huge bus depot from where many bus lines commenced their journey. The beserk sounds of horns, brakes, and people on the street made it difficult for us to have a conversation.

We dodged the roadside vendors in silence till we reached the S.V. Road traffic signal. Beggars attacked us from all sides, but dispersed when the WALK sign came on. We crossed the traffic-laden street and found ourselves standing in front of one of Mumbai's favorite eating joints, Lucky Biryani.

Vandana walked straight into the air-conditioned section of the restaurant. I followed her slowly, taking in my surroundings. The furniture was contemporary, and the walls were adorned with long mirrors. There was only one family seated in the centre of the room. At the far corner, Sikander was alone at a table, talking on his mobile phone. He finished his conversation abruptly and hung up by the time we reached his table. On seeing me, he gave a displeased look but immediately changed it to a smile.

"Hi Babloo," said Sikander.

"Hi."

"Hi Vandana. How was your day?" asked Sikander.

"Sikander, I'm so sorry I'm late. I really am. I hope I didn't keep you waiting for too long."

"That's ok," he said, "I figured that you must have gotten stuck somewhere. But I'm glad you made it."

"I'm glad you waited," she said, relieved.

I couldn't figure out what was going on. Had they planned to meet here?

"So where did you both meet?" asked Sikander.

"I saw him at Bandra Station," said Vandana. "He wanted a Thumbs Up so I brought him here. I thought you wouldn't mind since you guys are good friends."

"No, it's great that you brought him here," said Sikander. "Vandana, if you don't mind, I need to speak with Babloo in private."

"Ooooh. Guy talk," she teased. "Just kidding. Go ahead."

Sikander got up and pulled me up with him. He put his arm around my shoulder and walked me to the entrance of the restaurant.

"What the hell are you doing here man?" exclaimed Sikander, as he moved out the path of a cyclist going the wrong way.

"I came for a Thumbs Up," I replied, confused.

"My friend, my friend," said Sikander shaking his head, "this is not going to work."

"What?"

"You coming here with Vandana."

"Why?"

"Because I need time with her alone."

"Why?" I asked.

"Why what?"

"Why?"

"WHY WHAT?" shouted Sikander in frustration.

I went silent and stared straight into Sikander's eyes.

"Listen Babloo," said Sikander calmly, "I'm doing this for you. I'm meeting Vandana because you wanted me to tell her how you feel about her, remember?"

"Yes."

"So if I'm to help you and tell her how you feel about her I have to win her trust," he explained slowly.

"Yes."

"And to do that," Sikander continued, "I need to spend time alone with her so that I can get to know her. Do you understand?"

I remained silent.

"So from now on, when Vandana is going to meet me, you have to stay away. Do you understand that?"

"Yes," I replied.

"Good. Now you have to leave us both alone so that I can do your work, ok? The more time you spend around us the longer it's going to take, ok?"

"Ok."

"Good," said Sikander. "Now you go ahead and I will see you later."

"When?" I asked.

"When what?" asked Sikander, now visibly irritated.

"When will you see me?"

"I don't know, Babloo. I will see you, ok? Now go and don't come back inside."

Sikander turned to go inside but stopped after a few steps. He whirled around and saw me standing in the same place looking at him.

"What is it?" asked Sikander.

"I want a Thumbs Up," I said.

Sikander sighed and barked out an order to a passing waiter before going back into the air-conditioned section.

As I happily drank my Thumbs Up, I wondered why Sikander repeated the same thing over and over again.

## 12

ANXIETY GNAWED AT SUDHA'S GUT BUT SHE DECIDED to contain it. She wanted to play her cards well. When Raghu had related how Vandana had abandoned him, Sudha decided not to think much of it. She wanted to believe that maybe Raghu didn't see her when he exited the cafe.

That had been more than a week ago. Since then, she had made three attempts to fix up a time with Madhu for Raghu to take Vandana out again. But all three times Madhu politely told her that Vandana had a lot of work at the office and was returning home late.

Sudha tried to read deeper into it especially because Madhu seemed very casual about it. Ever since both the families met that Sunday afternoon, Sudha's social status in the colony had changed for the better. She would spend every other afternoon at Madhu's house and they had become good friends. Through Madhu, Sudha had become a part of the exclusive group of the Senior Railway Officers' Wives.

Sudha and Madhu spoke about everything that housewives usually spoke about. It had started with them making plans about the kind of wedding they wanted, the guests they would invite, even what the bride and groom would wear. Then it extended to building gossip, recipes, clothes and even film stars. Everything seemed fine and even though Sudha looked for signs constantly, Madhu had given her no indication that there was cause for worry as far as the proposed alliance was concerned.

But on Madhu's side, she too was actually very worried. She expected Vandana to change her lifestyle and start coming home early to spend time with Raghu. Today, on a whim, she had called Vandana's office to learn that she had left three hours early and the travel time from her office to her house was only an hour. And Vandana refused to carry a mobile phone, so there was no other way to trace her whereabouts.

Madhu had wanted to discuss the matter with Shekhar, but then decided against it. She had spent more hands-on time raising her daughter and the last thing she wanted was her husband pointing a finger at her for not being able to handle the situation.

It was 10 o'clock and her husband had retired for the night. Madhu usually watched television till 11 o'clock but now her watchful eye was concentrating more on the door which Vandana would use her own key to open. Madhu was determined to find out what was going on with her daughter and regretted having given her so much freedom. She was secretly hoping that this was just temporary and that Vandana would have no problem in adjusting to her new home after marriage.

She knew that her daughter was so unlike her. Vandana had inherited her paternal grandmother's good looks, quite a cut above her mother's ordinary middle-class looks. Vandana always dressed well and wore clothes that flattered her naturally full figure. Like all mothers, Madhu hoped that Vandana would not get into the wrong kind of company.

But Vandana had spent most of her time reading and being productive in general. She had grown up to be an intelligent, smart woman, choosing her company carefully and never giving them any reason to worry. So why was Madhu worried now?

Her maternal instinct never failed her. Over the past year she had started noticing a rebellious streak developing in her daughter. Vandana stopped discussing her day with her mother and never revealed details about her work. Madhu feared the worst and convinced Shekhar that they should start looking at getting Vandana married before her independence made her completely distant.

The Guptas were North Indian *bhaiyas* from the state of Uttar Pradesh (UP). *Bhaiyas* were essentially from a business community or at least well-placed in the Government Services. Since Vandana had been brought up in a modern environment, they deemed it appropriate to get her married to someone suitable in Mumbai itself. That way, their only child would be in the same city as them.

With the help of other members of her community and her trusted *pandit*, Madhu had browsed through the pictures and resumes of many eligible bachelors. But the saying was true that you can take a *bhaiya* out of UP but you can't take UP out of a *bhaiya*. None of the suitors were up to the mark as far as Madhu was concerned. They seemed complacent in their family businesses or government jobs and most of them lived in joint families. Madhu knew that she would have to find someone dynamic, someone who was ambitious and would be able to match Vandana's zest for life.

When Shekhar had suggested Amar Yadav's son Raghu as a potential suitor for Vandana, Madhu was initially not in favour. The Yadavs lived in Block A and Amar was a Railway Clerk, definitely not at their level by any standards. But then Shekhar explained about the boy's potential career as a stockbroker, which got her thinking. Stockbrokers earned a lot of money and their earning potential was on par with that of industrialists and film stars. It gave her a glimpse into the life that Vandana would have and consequently, the status that Madhu would achieve when her future son-in-law made it big.

Madhu understood that the boy lacked personality, but knew that a few years of living with her daughter would change that. Besides, they lived in uncertain times and she felt more comfortable giving her daughter to a family known to them for many years. It all seemed right.

Madhu heard a key turning in the lock and a second later, the door opening. Vandana walked in, looking as fresh and energized as ever – very unlikely for a girl who had had a long day at the office.

"Hi Mama," she chirped happily.

Vandana was always positive and happy. Maybe Madhu was thinking too much. But it had been on her mind for long and she had to clear it out.

"How was your day, Beta?"

"It was good, Mama. How was yours?"

"So... long day at the office... lots of work?" Madhu asked suspiciously.

"The usual, Mama. I am going to get ready for bed. I'm very tired."

"What about dinner?"

"I've already eaten," she replied and walked into the bathroom, closing the door behind her. Madhu heard the shower come on. She waited patiently as Vandana slept in the living room and would have to come back and face her.

In 10 minutes, Vandana returned, dressed in a clean nightgown. She saw the impatient look on her mother's face and sensed that she was gearing up for some sort of lecture.

"Where were you, Vandana?" Madhu came straight to the point.

"I told you I was at work Mama," said Vandana defiantly, seating herself next to her mother.

"I called your office and they told me you left early."

What business did her mother have calling her office, thought Vandana. She had given her mother her work number, instructing her to call on that number only if there was an emergency. The last time her mother had called was six months ago to tell her to come back early because of an accident on the railway tracks due to which protestors had threatened to shut the trains down. Considering there were limited alternate means of transportation to get back home, that call was still somewhat valid. But to keep tabs on her like this was definitely not acceptable.

"Why did you call up at work, Mama? I told you to call only if it's something important."

"It was, Vandana," replied Madhu evenly, "you lied to me."

"What makes you think that?" asked Vandana angrily. "I mean you're saying you called my work because I lied to you? What sense does that make?"

"But you did lie to me. You just told me that you were at work and when I called, you weren't there."

Vandana gritted her teeth in frustration. Her mother was impossible.

"Don't show me eyes, Vandana," said her mother, trying to keep her voice low.

'Showing eyes' was something that one did to someone younger to keep them in check. The other way round, it was considered disrespectful.

"Mama," said Vandana, now calmer, "when I said that I was at work, I didn't mean that I was literally at work. I was out on office work."

"What do you mean?"

"I had gone to a client's office with Swati to make a presentation."

"But when I called, they said that you had left for the day," said her mother suspiciously.

"Mama, it's a huge office with a 100 employees and many different departments. Not everyone knows where everyone else is."

Her mother fell silent.

"So the person who answered," continued Vandana cautiously, "must have seen me leaving but didn't know where I was going. He or she must have just assumed I left for the day."

Her mother was still silent, now shaking her head from side to side letting the new information filter in.

"Tell me Mama, did you ask the person who picked up the phone, who I left with?" asked Vandana innocently, knowing well enough that her mother would not have gone that far.

"No," replied her mother.

"If you want, you can call the office tomorrow and ask Swati, Ok?"

Her mother nodded silently. Vandana knew that her mother would not go to the extreme of talking to Swati the following day. But just to be safe, she would remember to prep Swati in case her mother did call. Swati owed Vandana many favours because Vandana had covered up for her many times, when Swati's husband called for her after finding her mobile phone switched off.

For a second, Vandana felt as if she belonged in the same category as Swati, who lied to her husband about her whereabouts when she was probably shacked up in Firoze's empty flat on Nepean Sea Road in the late evenings or busy in long meetings in his cabin during the day. But then, when Vandana thought about it, she realized her reason for being untruthful to her mother was different. While Swati's purpose was to satisfy her ambitious cravings, Vandana's was merely to have the freedom to follow her heart.

Madhu wished her good night and went into her bedroom.

As she lay down beside her husband, Madhu knew that she would not get sleep so soon. Her mind was not at rest. Vandana had probably given her the right answers, but something was not right. In the past when Madhu cornered her, Vandana usually dismissed the matter casually and joked about her mother being so paranoid. But today, for the first time, Vandana had been enthusiastically forthcoming with an answer. Madhu instinctively knew that her daughter had lied to her. She was her mother after all.

On Vandana's part, she couldn't believe she had gotten off the hook so easily and felt very guilty lying to her mother. She had a clear conscience and felt that she had broken her mother's trust.

But her mother had given her no choice. If she had been honest and said that she had spent the evening with another guy, her mother would freak out. Her mother's traditional mindset would not allow her to see how her daughter could be in the company of a male friend when she was to be married to another man. Then Vandana would be grilled and chided by both her parents and, as an act of discipline, they would even stop her going to work.

As she lay in bed staring at the ceiling, she smiled softly to herself. She had had a lovely time that evening and knew her life was changing. After coffee at Lucky Restaurant, Sikander had taken her on a long drive and then, for a walk on Bandstand. They ended up sitting at Lovers Point, where Bandstand ended before meeting the sea. It was where couples hung out in the evenings. When Sikander brought her there, she had doubted his intentions. But they just sat there and talked, interrupted at times only by the cool sea breeze. He didn't make a pass at her or imply anything untoward, which further convinced her that she was in the company of a gentleman.

By the time the lovely evening had come to an end an hour ago, with Sikander dropping her at a distance from the colony gates, she had decided she wouldn't mind if Sikander kissed her. But Sikander had merely wished her good night. She had remained there for an extra few minutes, secretly hoping that he would. But he simply touched her hand telling her that she was getting late.

Vandana hadn't felt as alive as she did when she was with Sikander. She wondered what he thought about her. Did he feel the same way about her? What was he doing at that very moment?

Sikander was definitely thinking about Vandana as he drove through the posh Bandra suburb of Pali Hill with a bottle of beer in one hand. He wished he had noticed Vandana many years ago, when she was younger and more vulnerable. Now, she had grown into an intelligent one with a mind of her own, which meant he would have to work very carefully on her.

He parked his Maruti Esteem outside a mossy building opposite Zig Zag road in Pali Naka, and honked twice. A suspicious looking man in a crushed shirt and *lungi* appeared and after a brief business exchange, disappeared back into the dark building. Sikander finished his beer and looked up to see that the man had re-appeared with an anxious looking girl wearing a long skirt and a provocative, low-cut blouse. She looked nothing like Vandana but he needed any woman right now to complete his evening.

Sikander drove a short distance with the girl up Zig Zag Road and parked in the quiet shadows of Pali Hill. Throughout the act, all he thought about was Vandana.

# 13

VALENTINE'S DAY. A DAY FOR LOVERS, A DAY FOR celebrating love. I knew all about Valentine's Day and till today, had no one to share it with. True, In India, it was a recently lauded 'festival', thanks largely to commercial greeting card companies taking advantage of a mostly Western concept to enhance their sales... but to me, it was real. When I loved someone the way I loved Vandana, what better occasion to express my feelings to her? Especially since until now, I had only been an observer from the sidelines and all through my college years, had secretly, desperately, wished for someone who would share all the small rituals of this special day with me... someone I would finally buy a card for... and maybe even flowers! And now, after all this time, I had my special someone. Vandana. The problem was I didn't know the first thing about choosing a card, much less how I would actually give it to her. That was why I had to go to my guide, Sikander. Sikander would know just what to do and he would surely help me do it the right way.

I stepped into an Archies gift shop and carefully scanned the neatly shelved cards. In fact, I was so careful that before I realized it, I had been in the store for three hours.

I selected a different card around nine times, but before the cashier rung me up, I pulled the card back to select another one. He didn't get irritated though, as he must have figured that I was the kind of guy who really loved his woman.

When I brought my card to the cashier for the tenth time, he made it a point to commend me on my choice. I purchased the card and even left a tip for him. As I was leaving, I noticed him dropping it into the CRY donation box on the counter.

Outside the store, I admired my purchase. It was a musical card that sang 'I love you' as soon as it was opened. I tucked the card into my half open shirt and set out to find Sikander.

Neither did I know where Sikander lived nor did I have his mobile number. But I knew where he operated his cable business from and set off towards his shop on S.V. Road.

S.V. Road was the main road that connected Mumbai from one end to the other. The road changed names as it crossed Bandra suburb into town, but it was a vital, arterial road for all commuters.

In Bandra, S.V. Road comprised mainly of shops, commercial buildings and businesses, with residential buildings at periodic intervals. There were many old buildings that had been broken down to give way to high rises. An important political figure had announced that since the city could hardly expand horizontally, it should do so vertically. As a result, every second existing structure was either under construction or repair, while apartment buildings sprouted like concrete weeds in the little open space that remained. This was the main reason behind the omnipresent dust in the once clean air of Bandra.

The other contributing fact was the consistent digging of roads all year round. The same roads were gouged two or three times each year. First it was the road repair people. Then the electricity people. After which the telephone people did their bit, to check their phone cables. Now with the advent of piped gas lines running underground, Mumbai roads would see an added nuisance.

As a result of all this burrowing, the three-lane S.V. Road was reduced to half its normal width and the persistent honking of aggravated drivers became a permanent feature. I often wondered why all these authorities didn't combine their strategies and dig the road just once so that they could all complete their work at one go. But that would never happen as many different tenders had to be passed, and with each tender many government officials got richer.

I turned into a by lane which housed a row of auto repair garages. As I walked past the garages, I recognized Sikander's car parked in one of them. A mechanic was changing the tint on the windows of Sikander's Maruti Esteem.

I walked further down and came to the small shop that housed Sikander's cable operations. It was so carefully hidden between two garages that it could go completely unnoticed by anyone passing by. I was aware of its location because I had been there as a kid, when it used to be a magazine store. Sikander brought us there, a couple of times, and allowed us to take turns at *Debonair* magazines. I never forgot places.

The shop was divided into two levels. Each level was a little over five feet in height. I had to duck to enter it and remain hunched once inside. There was all sorts of equipment, TV screens, DVD players and video players. The place seemed to be a mess but I knew that it didn't affect the quality of the programmes that filtered into thousands of homes every day. There were four people operating equipment all with their backs towards the entrance.

"Where's Sikander?" I asked no one in particular.

An elderly man with a scowl on his face, turned around to face me. I recognized him as Sikander's father.

"Who are you?" asked Sikander's father. "Are you a customer here to make a complaint? Or are you a creditor come to reclaim his money from my son?"

I didn't expect Sikander's father to recognize me. He had last seen me many years ago.

"I'm his friend," I said.

"You tell me," said Sikander's father angrily. "That boy left the house this morning and I haven't seen him all day. I opened this business for him and he hardly comes here. That friend of yours has no sense of responsibility."

Sikander's father abruptly turned back to a TV screen. I stood there for 10 minutes looking at the back of Sikander's father's bald head before I stepped out. I decided to wait outside the shop.

A Hyundai Sonata was being driven rashly by a mechanic on the severely pot-holed road. The car would never be the same again. The mechanic would deliberately make some function of the car faulty to ensure its return to the garage for repair.

A loud non-threatening bang was heard in the air. It indicated that it was time for devoted Muslims to end their daylong fast during the *ramzan* month. I checked my watch. It was 6:25 p.m. The sun had set. I began to feel restless. I didn't want the day to end without my card reaching my desired destination.

Half an hour later, an *auto rickshaw* pulled up in front of the garage. Sikander got out looking very groggy. He caught sight of me and muttered something under his breath. I walked towards him.

"What is it?" asked Sikander brashly, while paying the *auto rickshaw* driver.

The *auto rickshaw* zoomed off. I took the card out from inside my shirt and handed it to Sikander. He clumsily opened the card and was greeted by the romantic song. He quickly scanned the contents of the card and looked up at me.

"What is this?" he asked again, angrily. "Why are you giving me a valentine card, you homo?"

"For Vandana," I replied slowly.

"Oh," said Sikander. He quickly broke into a smile.

"And you want me to give it to her for you, huh lover boy?"

"Yes," I replied.

Sikander looked at the card and opened and closed it many times.

"I must admit, Babloo. You have good taste."

I continued looking at him.

"But you have it all wrong," continued Sikander. "This is not the way to do it. This card says 'I love you' inside. It might scare her."

"Give it to her," I said, with an edge of finality in my voice.

An oil-stained mechanic came up to Sikander and pointed towards his car, indicating that it was ready. Sikander surveyed the car and gave his approval. When the mechanic showed Sikander the bill, he pointed in the direction of his shop. He came back to me and opened the card.

"Ok Babloo," said Sikander, "I'll give her this card today. Just for you."

"Ok," I replied.

"Good," said Sikander.

From the store, Sikander's father could be heard shouting at the mechanic. Sikander paused to catch a part of it and then turned towards me.

"But Babloo," he said, "you haven't written anything inside. You can't give her a blank card."

"You write," I said.

"Now that's what I call trust. Will do."

With that Sikander got into his car and drove off with my card.

Shiv Sagar was a hugely successful South Indian chain of vegetarian restaurants all over Mumbai. With its superior quality of south Indian dishes, reasonable pricing and modest interiors, it had become very popular for a middle-class dining experience. For this restaurant, Valentine's Day was like any other day as it was mostly frequented by families. The only exception was a mismatched couple seated in a corner. Vandana couldn't figure out why Raghu had insisted on a corner table again.

The romantic couples would be at more youth-oriented places like Café Coffee Day or Barista, which would be decorated to celebrate the occasion. But Raghu didn't understand that. For him, bringing her to Shiv Sagar was his way of proving that he had taste. Vandana was secretly relieved because the last thing she wanted was anyone, even if he or she didn't know them, to think that they were a couple.

Vandana had blindly agreed when Raghu had suggested the place. He himself mentioned that he would have rather taken her to a Café Coffee Day but it was not safe. A political party had condemned Valentine's Day saying that it was a tradition of the West; in India it was not decent or acceptable. They issued a public warning that anyone who tried to celebrate it would face severe consequences. No one took them seriously, till the afternoon news reported party workers breaking down a greeting card store in the far suburbs. But like always, Bandra remained unaffected by the happenings in the rest of the city.

The waiter brought them two menu cards. Vandana didn't even bother taking hers. From her last outing with the chauvinistic bastard, she knew that he would make the final order citing quality or health issues to disguise his chronic stinginess.

Raghu ordered a banana split ice cream with two spoons and smiled at her. Vandana returned his smile with a glare. She made it obvious that she detested his company but he didn't seem to get it.

She had underestimated her mother. Her mother did call and check with Swati. Luckily, Vandana had prepared Swati for the possible cross-check but knew that this could just be the beginning of her mother's sniffing at her heels. Her mother seemed to have sensed that something was amiss.

Instead of giving her mother a chance to make educated guesses, Vandana decided to create a balance. So when her mother told her that Raghu wanted to take her out on Valentine's Day, she immediately accepted.

She was secretly hoping that Sikander would ask her out but gave up hope when he didn't call the entire day. As she was getting ready to leave, he called. And she was delighted. But she was honest about the fact that she had to go out with Raghu first.

Sikander said that he understood. That bothered Vandana. She was hoping that he would be jealous. She figured that either it was a bad sign or he was actually a very mature person. Vandana leaned towards the latter.

Sikander had told her to ditch Raghu after they finished from Shiv Sagar. He said he would be waiting for her in his car outside Café Mocha, on Hill Road. Vandana couldn't wait for the evening with Raghu to get over. She knew she had to try and be as sweet as possible because their mothers spoke frequently, and they would definitely discuss the events of the evening as told to them by their respective children.

The banana split, accompanied by two spoons, was placed on the table between them. Vandana looked at it. In the centre of the plate was a thick six-inch long banana adorned with various flavours of ice cream. Vandana was grossed out. This guy was sick.

"Have a bite," said Raghu.

"What?" she snapped in disgust.

Raghu was taken aback by her tone. Vandana felt bad. She realized that she was just being silly and he genuinely hadn't ordered the banana split to be suggestive. She picked up a spoon and took a bite. But she didn't touch the banana and stuck only to the ice cream. It actually tasted pretty good.

"Vandana, today is a very special day for us," said Raghu in between bites of ice cream.

"Why?" she asked, knowing what was coming.

"Because today is Valentine's Day. It's the day you tell your girlfriend how you truly feel about her."

The way he said it made it sound like a text book answer. He had probably just read that somewhere, she figured.

"So?" asked Vandana, concentrating on her ice cream.

"So, since you're my girlfriend..."

"Wait a minute," interrupted Vandana, "I'm not your girlfriend. I'm here because our parents wanted us to be here."

Raghu produced a huge envelope from below the table and held it towards her. She merely glanced at it and went back to her ice cream.

"Vandana," he said excitedly, "this is for you. Please take it."

She took it with one hand and kept it by her side.

"You don't have to wait to get home to open it," he said anxiously. "Please open it now."

Vandana was irritated. This guy would just not let her be. She picked up the envelope and removed the card. It had a huge heart in the centre when opened, with the line – My heart goes out to you. And below that Raghu had added – "I love you" and signed his name.

It was a sweet thought but Raghu had wasted it on the wrong girl. She did appreciate the gesture though.

"Thanks Raghu," she said, "that's very sweet."

"You're welcome," he said. "So what have you got for me?"

She put her spoon down and looked at him.

"What do you mean?"

"On Valentine's Day, a couple gives something to each other to show their love, even if it's just a rose," he explained. "So what are you going to give me?"

"Raghu," she said sternly, "people give things like that to each other only when they're in love. We are just getting to know each other, ok?"

He sulked silently. Vandana finished the ice-cream quickly and asked for the bill.

"You can't pay for this," he protested. "It's the guy's duty to take his woman out."

"Who's paying for it," she said dryly. "I just asked for it."

The waiter brought the bill. Raghu paid for it counting his money five times before putting it down. Vandana couldn't believe her eyes. It was only 35 rupees. And he didn't even leave a tip.

They got up and walked outside. Vandana tried to flag down an *auto rickshaw* but all the ones passing them were occupied.

"Why do you want to waste money on an auto," Raghu said, "the 214 bus goes straight home. Come this way."

"I am not going home," she said firmly. "You go ahead."

"Where are you going?" he asked.

Vandana was on the verge of losing her cool. Who the hell was he to demand answers from her? She knew she had to try and control herself.

"I'm going to a friend's place," she said calmly. "It's in the other direction."

"Ok. I will come with you. I would like to meet your friends," he said.

"No, you will not meet my friends," she scolded, but then immediately changed to a feigned polite tone. "We're just a bunch of girls meeting."

Luckily a vacant rickshaw stopped. She had to end this outing on a good note.

"Thanks a lot Raghu. I'll see you soon," she said sweetly, before the *rickshaw* sped off.

Sikander could make out that Vandana liked him. But he wanted to make sure that she fell in love with him. Only then he knew he could get her to do anything for him.

This Valentine's Day was a crucial day for him. He decided that if she agreed to meet him today, it would mean that she did want something more than a friendship. But he had no idea how to come across as romantic.

Babloo's Valentine Day card had come as a blessing in disguise. He looked at the card again. It was truly impressive and would definitely communicate the message to Vandana, without him having to verbalize it. When it came to being affectionate, he was always at a loss for words, especially when he didn't mean any of them.

His car was parked outside Holy Family Hospital just a few metres from Café Mocha. He looked at the blank card, trying to think of meaningful words to fill it with. Even though the card itself would communicate enough, he knew he would have to write something to make it personal.

He scratched his head, but couldn't think of anything. Frustrated, he scribbled the first thing that came to mind. "The card says it all, need I say more?" He looked at what he had written and felt proud of himself. Never before had he given a card to any woman. He hadn't needed to, as they all had surrendered easily. But Vandana was different. She was intelligent and smart and would see through insincere words. He had been careful enough to appear genuine. And it seemed to be working.

He was careful though not to write his name. Once he got what he wanted, he liked to move on without a trace.

He was fantasizing about Vandana's beautiful body when a sudden knock on the window brought him back to reality. It was Vandana. Sikander quickly summoned a smile and got out of the car.

"Hi Vandana."

"Hi Sikander. Sorry I'm late."

He took a moment to look at her. She was wearing a sleeveless T-shirt with a long denim skirt. He hoped that the slit in her skirt would work to his advantage.

"Of course not," he replied, with a wave of his hand. "I don't mind waiting. Especially when I know I'm going to meet you."

She smiled. But she was standing under a shadow in the dimly lit street so he wasn't able to decipher whether she was blushing. He would need to keep watch for any signs that would make his conquest easier.

"Come on, let's go inside Café Mocha," she said.

"I went inside and it's very crowded," he lied. "We would have to wait for at least an hour before we get a seat. I have another idea."

"Ok," she smiled, "Surprise me."

He opened the door of the passenger side for her and she got in. He got in behind the wheel.

"So where are you taking me?" she asked eagerly.

"I thought you wanted to be surprised."

"Oops. Sorry!" she laughed.

Sikander drove past Hill Road up the steep slope of Mount Mary. He played a special CD of love songs and allowed it to blare through the open windows, announcing the mood in the car to indifferent onlookers. Vandana was smiling happily throughout.

Sikander searched for a secluded place to park but there were people everywhere. He drove to the end of Mount Mary and then down Kane Road. It was the same story there.

As they drove through Bandstand, Vandana started talking about her day at work. Sikander only heard half of what she said, he was growing frustrated at being unable to find an inconspicuous spot. He finally gave up and lazily angle-parked by the sea face between two cars, in a line of cars parked facing the sea. Fuel was expensive and there was no way he was going to waste any more driving around. Besides, he figured that his new tint was good enough to keep them concealed from the people around when he decided to get into action. And no one would notice the windows getting fogged up in the night light.

"Why have we parked here?" she asked.

"I thought we could sit by the sea and talk."

"Ok," she agreed and rolled the window down.

"Why are you putting the window down?" he asked, trying to conceal his frustration. "The AC is on."

"The sea breeze is lovely. We don't need the AC."

Sikander resigned himself to fate and rolled his window down.

"So what's the surprise?" she asked eagerly.

He thought for a second and then turned to face her.

"Vandana, I have to be honest with you," he started sincerely. "I really enjoy spending time with you. And I am glad that you came out with me today."

"I'm glad you asked me out," she said looking deeply into his eyes.

"Vandana, I feel I've found a good friend in you. And I feel happy being with you. I cannot explain it. But when I don't see you, my day feels incomplete."

She blushed.

"I never thought that I could feel this way about a girl," he continued. "The time we spend together just never feels enough. I want to see you more and more."

Vandana couldn't believe her ears. She had been hoping that Sikander felt that way about her and he did.

Sikander couldn't believe himself. He had never coughed up such impromptu bullshit and was proud of himself.

A constable walked past their car and peered inside. Disappointed that there was no action going on inside that would earn him a quick buck towards a fine, he walked away.

"What are you trying to say, Sikander?" asked Vandana.

Sikander took out the card and gave it to her. She looked surprised. As she opened it, the song that played brought a sudden smile to her lips.

"This is lovely, Sikander. I never thought that I would get a Valentine Card from you. I didn't know that you felt the same."

Jai Babloo, thought Sikander.

"The same?" asked Sikander.

She nodded. He looked into her eyes. She held his gaze for a moment before turning away to look at the calmness of the moonlit sea. Sensing this as the right moment, he moved in closer, held her face softly and planted a kiss on her lips, before backing off slightly to see her reaction. Her eyes were shut, eyelids slightly fluttering. He kissed her again and this time she opened her mouth and invited his tongue in.

He kissed her passionately, holding her face with both his hands. Her hands lay by her sides. Their tongues met in sync with the slow movement of the waves outside. He lifted one hand off her face and moved it down her smoothly waxed arm. She moaned slightly and locked lips with him more purposefully. He gave into the moment for a few seconds, and then moved his hand over hers crossing it to rest on her leg. He caressed her leg slowly, increasing momentum slightly, when his progress was abruptly hampered by a quick motion of her hand pushing his hand away.

"What are you doing?" she whispered.

"Trying to show you that I love you completely," he whispered back.

She took his other hand off her face and sat upright in her seat.

"What happened?" he asked.

"Take me home, Sikander."

"Why, what did I do wrong?" he asked desperately. He was completely aroused and didn't want to stop.

She remained silent and looked ahead expressionless.

What was with this girl, thought Sikander. He was agitated but didn't want to blurt out anything that he would later regret. He knew it was his fault. He should have played it slow, but his desperation had got the better of him. The feel of her soft lips, her lovely fragrance had captivated him completely. This girl would take more time and he felt he should have been sensible enough to guage that.

They drove back in silence. When he dropped her outside the colony gates, he didn't even say good night. As Vandana walked into the colony, tears rolled down her cheeks. The one man she felt had truly liked her for the person she was, turned out to be just like the rest. Her dreams were shattered.

## 14

THE BANDRA STATION RAILWAY OFFICE WAS LOCATED next to the Ticketing Counter on Platform 1. The office was purely administrative in nature and housed the air-conditioned cabins of the Senior and Junior Railway Officers. The railway clerks sat on old wooden desks in the huge open area which merged with the waiting room.

The loud, arrhythmic beats of both trains and travellers, easily found their way into the open area. The employees here had no relief from the stifling Mumbai heat except for the slow, revolving floor fan that whirled in their direction for a few seconds every minute. Flies were frequent visitors and came in droves whenever tea or biscuits were brought in.

The desks were placed strategically in the open area in accordance with the seniority of the clerks. The more senior or favourite ones were seated closer to the air-conditioned cabins, giving them a whiff of the cool draft whenever a cabin door opened. Amar's desk had been in the same spot by the main entrance, all through his tenure. But now, with his improved status on the personal front, his desk overtook other, more deserving clerks and was moved, overnight, closer to the cabins, indicating an unspoken conferring of seniority – courtesy Shekhar Gupta.

Now, whenever Shekhar would call for tea, he would order an extra cup and invite Amar in, to join him. This would happen around four times a day. Sometimes Shekhar would even invite Amar to join him for lunch.

It was afternoon and Raju, the peon, stopped by Amar's desk to inform him that Mr. Gupta was waiting for him for lunch. Amar immediately took his lunch *dabba* from under his desk and walked across the short space to Shekhar's door. He straightened his shirt, wiped his sweat with an already damp handkerchief, and knocked.

"Come in."

Amar went in and Shekhar stood up to greet him. He motioned for Amar to sit down on the long couch. In front of it was a large coffee table on which Shekhar's lunch had already been laid out.

"Come Amar, please sit."

The recent favourable turn of events had changed the way Shekhar addressed Amar. First it was Srivastav. Now it was Amar.

"Let's see what Sudhaji has made for lunch today," said Shekhar.

"Nothing special, Shekharji. Just *sabzi, chapatti, dal* and rice."

"Call me Shekhar," he said.

Shekhar picked up the container of *dal* and sniffed at it apppreciately.

"Sudhaji has magic in her hands. This smells so good."

"It's just normal *ghar ka khana*," said Amar matter-of-factly.

The peon brought in a bottle of mineral water with two glasses. Amar's new change in status had made his filtered, tap water days a thing of the past.

They served themselves from both tiffins. Amar took a bite of the *bhindi* from Shekhar's lunch box. It was fairly average.

"Madhuji is a great cook," lied Amar. "This tastes so good."

"Yes, but nothing compared to Sudhaji's food," said Shekhar, through a mouthful of *dal* and rice.

They continued eating in silence for a few minutes.

"So where's Babloo?" asked Shekhar. "Wasn't he supposed to start coming to work last month?"

"Yes he was," said Amar. "But now that you're family I can be honest with you. That boy has refused to work here. I am so worried, I just don't know what to do with him."

The entire colony never spoke directly about Babloo having any problems. Neither did Shekhar now.

"What does he want to do?" asked Shekhar. "I am sure he has

some interests. Tell me and maybe I can do something."

"No, there's no use," said Amar. "He doesn't have an interest in absolutely anything. You have done enough by creating a job for him here."

"That's the least I can do for you, Amar," he said. "Your family is like mine. Your problems are my problems. Please remember that the job is always open for him. I wish I could have offered something better but as you know, all the other positions are government posts and have certain requirements."

"No, no Shekhar," said Amar, "you have done enough."

"So how's Raghu's work going?" asked Shekhar.

"He's still under training. He will take on his permanent position from the beginning of May."

"Good. That boy is on the right track. He will do very well in life."

Amar beamed proudly as he finished the last of his meal.

"Amar," said Shekhar. "You must have some *kheer*. Madhu made it especially for you."

Amar took the proffered *kheer* and put a spoonful in his mouth. He didn't fancy sweets too much but couldn't refuse Shekhar.

"So, I was meaning to ask you Amar," said Shekhar carefully. "Have you and Sudhaji decided on a wedding date?"

"Shekhar, whatever you and Madhuji decide."

"Raghu and Vandana can keep getting to know each other. But we feel that we should announce a wedding date. Of course, you mentioned that you wanted Raghu to get settled at his job first. We respect that. But everybody's asking about it, so we need to have something in mind."

"Shekhar, you must have thought of something," Amar said. "We will respect anything you and Madhuji think is right."

Shekhar had finished eating. He wiped his hands with a napkin and looked up at Amar.

"We were thinking that the last week of May will be good. By that time, both Raghu and Vandana would have become better acquainted with each other and Raghu will be settled in his job."

"But Shekhar," expressed Amar with concern, "won't it be too hot in May to have the wedding?"

"Well, yes it will," smiled Shekhar, "but don't worry about that. We will have the wedding ceremony and reception at Siddhartha Hotel. It has a good air-conditioned hall and I know the owner very well. Then we can have a small party in the colony lawns."

Amar thought about this. Siddhartha Hotel was a well-known three star hotel nearby on S.V. Road and would definitely prove expensive. Shekhar sensed Amar's apprehension.

"We will take care of all the expenses. That is our responsibility."

Of course it is, thought Amar, you are the girl's father.

## 15

I STEPPED INTO THE STATIONARY 8:35 A.M. Churchgate local. The train commenced its journey from Bandra, so if I got there early, a seat in the soon-to-be-crowded train was assured.

I found a window seat in the men's first class bogey and quickly occupied it. In this compartment I wouldn't have to stick to sweat-drenched shirts or be subjected to bad breath, unlike in the second class. However, once the train began getting crowded, people would try and create more space on the hard cushioned seats and I knew I would get squeezed further into the steel interior. That aspect of Indian mentality, to create space out of no space, cut across all train compartments.

Mornings were peak business hours for beggars. Indians were superstitious and in the hope of starting their day on a good note, would drop coins into the waiting palms of beggars. That made begging a lucrative profession, especially in trains where it would be difficult to dodge such scroungers. I had once followed a beggar around all day, pursuing him through trains, stations, platforms, and I had calculated that the beggar had made 300 rupees that day. That was more than the earnings of the common man toiling away long hours in a daily wage position.

A blind beggar carefully climbed into the train, using a wooden cane to create space for his next step. He found his way to the seating area and positioned himself in front of me, reciting blessings, saying that good things would happen to me if I were to display some generosity. I didn't encourage begging. But I didn't ignore the beggar. I stared point blank into his pitch-dark glasses. Within a minute he was gone.

I needed a change from my usual theatres in Bandra. So today I had decided to go into town to watch a newly released film that marked the debut of the nation's new heartthrob. The film was a super hit and the new actor was the latest hero in the hearts of film-going women and on the front of hairdressing salon windows. I had wanted to watch the film on the first day itself but the movie had run full house and the black ticket rates peddled by touts were beyond my budget. Eros Cinema in Churchgate was playing a morning matinee show of the film and I was positive I would have some luck on a weekday.

The train compartment was filled to capacity now. As the train started crawling away from the platform, a group of four college kids jumped into the moving train. Once inside the compartment, they high-fived each other and cast victorious glances around. They pushed their way inside and stood close to where I was seated.

One of the boys tried to nest his backpack on the luggage railing above my seat. The bag slipped and lazily fell on my head.

The boy said, "Sorry Uncle."

The other boys giggled like a bunch of schoolgirls.

I looked at them but gave no outward reaction. I was trying to focus my thoughts on Vandana and how she must have reacted to the card. The boys had disturbed me. I reprimanded them with a stare and returned to looking out of the window.

The morning breeze brought in a stench as the train passed Dharavi, touted as the biggest slum complex of Asia. There was talk of developing the land into high-rise buildings and commercial complexes, which would change the skyline of Mumbai. I had read that there were close to a million people living there who would need to be relocated on their terms. Space in Mumbai was scarce, and like all other governmental plans aimed at the greater good of a greater number of people, I knew that this one too would stay stuck in the planning stage forever.

The train pulled into the bedlam of Mahim Junction. My thoughts were still centered on Vandana. What must she be thinking, now that she knew how I felt about her? Would she be awkward about it or did she feel the same way about me?

My mind embarked on a Q & A session.

*Was the card good enough?*

*Of course it was!!! She must have really liked it!*

*Then how come she hasn't told me anything?*

*Give it some time, Babloo. You are the best...*

The bag on the rack above fell on my head again. My friend suddenly disappeared.

"Sorry Uncle," the boy said once more, as he bent forward to retrieve the bag and put it up again. The other boys chuckled.

I stared at them hard. They all looked back, making faces at me, trying to break my icy expression. Soon they looked away and resumed chatting amongst each other.

The sound of *bhajans* from a group of office-going people, on the other side, immediately mingled with the train babble. Passengers turned in their direction, some smiling, others irritated. I figured that the group singing must have gotten acquainted with each other on this local and travelled together every day. There were many such groups, who in order to break the monotony of the commute, indulged in various group activities, which even included playing cards.

I shifted in my uncomfortable seat. There was no leg space and I was pushed further in as people tried to make space on the long seat. I didn't fancy being confined to the same place for too long and was glad when the train pulled into Mahalaxmi Station indicating that I was just three stops away from Churchgate.

Sikander had proved to be a good friend, I thought to myself. I was sure that he must have said the right things about me, and Vandana must have been very impressed when she opened the card. I had waited for her in the colony that night after Sikander was going to meet her but saw no sign of her.

As the train pulled into the chaotic familiarity of Churchgate Station, the bag dropped on my head again. The same college boy looked at me apologetically. In unison all the boys said, "SORRY UNCLE" and laughed hard as they alighted.

I rubbed my head and felt a bump. I noticed the boys passing my window as they were walking on the platform. The same boy stuck out his middle finger at me and said, "Spin on it."

I felt a silent rage consume me. I looked at my watch. It was 9 a.m. I had an hour to pass before the show.

I got off the train and walked briskly till I spotted the group of boys. I followed them at a safe distance as they exited the station and passed the landmark Satkar Restaurant into A Road.

I pursued them for the entire length of the busy road till they entered the gates of Jai Hind College. I had attended college for six years, and knew that the morning classes in Mumbai colleges were reserved mostly for 12th Std. students. The heavy backpacks and geeky demeanour of the boys on the train indicated they were students of the science stream; their lectures would go on till mid-afternoon. Commerce or Arts students usually didn't carry a backpack.

I headed back in the direction of Churchgate Station, towards Eros Theatre. Students were rushing past me, probably trying to make it in time for class. They were dressed very simply and they didn't seem the type that was interested in the glamorous life of college. Many of them would study hard, make good careers and do well in life. I was reminded of my own college days. I had been a sincere student and had attended all my lectures, but my life had turned out differently. And now I was rushing too, but in the opposite direction, to catch the morning matinee of the new Hindi blockbuster.

A stall outside Satkar restaurant, known for its inexpensive, quality sandwich ice creams, caught my attention. I made a quick stop and ordered a mango sandwich ice cream. But when the server's fingers touched the wafer biscuits that held the delicious ice cream together, I flinched and walked away.

There was a huge crowd of students hovering outside Eros Theatre. Most of them had backpacks and were in line for tickets. These were probably the non-serious, science students who had bunked lectures to watch the film.

The line was long and eager movie buffs were waiting patiently. Most of them were looking anxiously ahead hoping the ticket counter wouldn't shut by the time their turn arrived. I took my place at the end of the line and became a part of the meandering stream.

By the time I reached the head of the line 45 minutes later, the ticket counter was still open.

"There are only front seats in the stalls available," the man said.

"One," I said, as I paid the man.

By the time I found my seat directed by a flashlight managed by an usher, 15 minutes of the film had already been reeled. This didn't bother me. I had watched enough Hindi films to learn that filmmakers deliberately started the engaging part only half an hour after the commencement of the film as they knew that in a place like India, people never arrived on time.

I enjoyed the film thoroughly. When the hero and heroine came together in a song, I imagined myself with Vandana in the same scenario. I lightly smiled to myself as I thought of us exchanging the same dialogues in the same situations.

The film had all the makings of a blockbuster; great songs, amazing locations, comedy, romance, action – everything that the audiences loved. Moreover, the light-eyed hero had all the trappings of a superstar. His being the talk of the nation was justified.

The story was simple enough for me to be able to understand and enjoy the cinematic proceedings. The action scene at the end was well-choreographed and kept me writhing in the seat, waiting for the hero to beat up the bad guys. I loved watching justice being meted out in Hindi films.

When I walked out of the theatre, squinting in the sunlight, I felt energized and charged. I was all set to seek my own justice. I jaywalked across the streets till I found my way back to A Road. At 2:30 p.m. sharp, I was outside the gates of Jai Hind College. I waited patiently, hoping that I hadn't missed the group of college boys from the train. Maybe they had lab practicals that day which would keep them in for an extra hour.

I remained planted in the same place outside the gate as students kept passing me, going in and out of the college campus. A puny security guard appeared in my line of vision.

"Why are you standing here?" he asked. "*Chalo*, go from here."

I kept staring at him.

"Go from here. Get lost," said the security guard, more firmly.

I kept staring at him.

"Go from here, I said!" He now raised his *lathi* threateningly.

Before I could react, the security guard was called inside by a peon. He put his *lathi* down and mutely disappeared into the interiors of the college.

It was four o'clock by the time three of the group of four boys from the train emerged from the main college building. One of them saw me and pointed in my direction. They all started laughing, including the boy who had repeatedly dropped the bag on my head.

All three of them remained standing a few feet from me, looking in my direction while whispering to each other in low tones. I kept an eye on the boy who had dropped the backpack on me. I walked towards him and the boy's smile faded away.

Within a second, the boy felt a strong punch straight in his stomach, which left him gasping for breath. The other boys stepped back as this boy fell to his knees. He looked up to see my outline blocking out the sun as I stood over him.

"Laugh," I said dryly.

The boy looked up at me disbelievingly. He scanned around for assistance, but his friends had stepped back to a safe distance, joining the crowd of bystanders that had just gathered. The security guard had returned but remained seated on his stool.

"Laugh," I said, in the same tone.

The boy slowly tried to smile as another punch of mine caught him on the side of his mouth.

"Oh shit! Oh shit!" shouted one of his friends, now mustering the courage to come closer.

Those two punches brought on an unfamiliar adrenaline surge that tingled through my blood; a rush that awoke my senses and made me feel alive. I mentally basked in this amazing new sensation as I ran full speed towards Churchgate Station. At the station entrance, I saw the blind beggar from the train standing by the corner *paanwala,* smoking a cigarette while reading a magazine.

I had originally planned to wait at Churchgate station so that I could spot Vandana when she came to take the train. But after the episode at Jai Hind College, I deemed it safer to rush straight to Bandra on the Virar Fast.

I was standing under the big clock above the Bandra station entrance as it struck 9 p.m. I had been keeping an alert watch for more than three hours, but no sign of Vandana.

Fatigue crept into my body as I abandoned my post and started walking in the direction of home. As I entered the colony gates, a Maruti Esteem came straight towards me at full speed. I recognized it as Sikander's car and stood still. The car came to a stop just a foot away from me. Sikander was behind the wheel. Mahesh, Madan and Pravin's heads popped out from the other windows.

"Get out of the way," shouted Sikander jokingly.

I looked dumbfounded. Sikander smiled sneakily at the others. They reciprocated his mischievous expression. Sikander got out of the car and playfully jumped in front of me.

"Hi Babloo," he said cheerfully.

"Did you give her the card?"

"Yes I did, sir."

"What?"

"What what?" asked Sikander.

"What?"

"You mean what happened?" asked Sikander.

"Yes," I replied.

"She liked the card a lot, Babloo."

"Ok."

"She thought it was very sweet."

"Ok."

"See Babloo, she liked the card a lot, but then there wasn't enough time for me to ask how she felt about you in return. So I will need some more time, ok?"

I remained silent.

"Ok?"

"Yes."

"Good, now get out of the way," ordered Sikander, with a sudden change of tone. "I have to go."

"Where?"

"What do you mean by where?" asked Sikander angrily. "Since when did I have to start giving you answers? Move!"

"Can I come?" I asked, moving to the side.

Sikander snickered as he got in the car. "You want to come with us?"

"Yes," I said.

Mahesh, Madan and Pravin who until now were chatting with each other, fell silent. They looked at Sikander for his reaction.

"Ok, get in," said Sikander.

Mahesh leaned forward from the back seat. "Are you sure?" he asked. "He might tell somebody."

"Don't worry," said Sikander. "He doesn't talk to anyone. Besides, he will be good entertainment for us. You'll see."

The back door opened and I slid in with Mahesh and Madan. They were sipping from beer bottles concealed in brown paper bags. Mahesh offered me a sip. I didn't react.

"Have some *yaar*," said Pravin from the front seat. "The alcohol is very expensive there."

The "there" turned out to be a beer bar called Caravan on Linking Road. As they got out of the car, a valet parker saluted the others in recognition. A midget in uniform opened the main door to the bar.

I contemplated going in and then weighed my options. If I went home now, my family would still be awake. I would have to confine myself to my bedroom and wait patiently till the frequency of passing trains reduced, so I could go to sleep. Or I could hang out with my friend Sikander.

The other guys had already entered but the midget still held the door open for me. He looked at me expectantly. But all he received from me was a pat on his head as I walked into the shady looking place.

I had witnessed the scene inside in many Hindi films. But the real experience was something else. There were many girls dressed in backless *ghagra cholis* dancing on the floor in the centre, to popular Hindi film songs. I had never seen so many glamorous and beautiful women in one place.

The dance floor was surrounded on all sides by tables seating eager patrons. Most of them were nursing some form of alcohol while giving all their attention to the dance floor. The patrons were all males. If any man wanted attention or a special dance from a particular bar dancer, he would lock the girl into a stare and wave a note at her. She would take that as a cue and briefly dance just for him, to earn the note. The brief attention that the patron would get for just one note would never be enough, so he would soon be ready with his next one.

The bar girls were just dancers. There was no stripping or touching involved. As a rule, no male patron was permitted to step on the dance floor. If anyone did, the waiters doubled up as bouncers and quickly put the person in place.

Sikander, Madan, Mahesh and Pravin sat at a table with a full view of the disco-lit floor. But I was transfixed at the entrance with my eye on one particular girl. I wasn't attracted to her but found a strong resemblance to popular actress Soundarya Ghai, though the dancer was much shorter. She felt my gaze on her and quickly turned her full attention to me, giving me some of her best moves. She danced and moved her hands seductively across her body, still locked in my stare. On seeing no effort on my part to reach for my pockets, she turned away from me looking for another benefactor who would wave money at her.

Sikander called out to me. My eyes were still glued to the dance floor. Pravin came over and brought me to the table.

"See someone you like?" smiled Sikander, as I seated myself.

"No."

"Oh come on," said Mahesh, "we saw you staring at the short chick. Did she give you a hard on?"

I remained silent.

"This is not the colony," explained Sikander. "This is one place where you can keep staring at a chick and no one will mind."

I kept looking at the Soundarya clone. If I couldn't take my eyes off this girl, I wondered what would happen if I ever saw the real Soundarya Ghai in person.

"You got any money, Babloo?" asked Sikander.

I gave Sikander a brief glance and then turned my attention back to the dance floor.

"He's not having any fun with my money," said Mahesh. "I told you not to bring him."

"Relax," said Sikander.

The dancers on the dance floor noticed money changing hands at our table. Three of them quickly started pelvic thrusting in front of us. The waiter came by and took our order. Sikander ordered three beers.

"The one in the red is mine," said Sikander. "Look at those breasts. They're so big."

The others nodded in assent.

"I like the one in the yellow and pink," said Mahesh. "See see, she's looking at me."

"We all know who Babloo likes," said Sikander.

They looked at me and laughed in unison. I was still staring at the dance floor.

The waiter brought our order. Sikander handed him the money. I noticed that Sikander hadn't taken any money out of his own pocket. Within minutes, the waiter brought Sikander a stack of 10 rupee notes. He gave some to Mahesh, Madan and Pravin but kept most of it for himself.

He took one 10 rupee note out and looked at the girl in red. She was moving wildly to a fast-paced song. Most of the patrons' eyes were on her. She saw Sikander's 10 rupee note but turned and danced in the other direction, where a man held out a 50 rupee note.

"I'm sure she's a whore," said Sikander, in between sips of his beer. "This money was not enough for her. That other guy throwing money at her has booked her for the night."

The others nodded in agreement.

But it was a misconception that bar girls were prostitutes. They actually didn't need to sleep for money since they made a good amount of cash every day just by dancing. Most of these girls belonged to decent families but were in this profession as a means to support their families. Some of them had ailing parents while others had sisters to get married off. Most of them had the same story. They came to Mumbai from small towns or villages in search of work. But the lure of easy money brought them into this profession. Now, they led glamorous lives – the seasoned ones living in their own flats and driving their own cars. They mostly lived in the far off suburb of Mira Road where their true identity would not follow them home at the end of the night.

"Hey Babloo," shouted Sikander, over the loud music.

I was now standing by the edge of the dance floor. I was in doubt. The bar dancer looked so much like Soundarya Ghai that I thought that maybe it really was her. I hadn't seen the actress in a film for close to a year. Maybe she had changed careers and moved into this profession. Maybe, in reality, she was not as tall as she looked on screen.

The Soundarya clone came to life with the playing of a popular song from one of Soundarya Ghai's films. Even though this was sufficient evidence, I needed to be sure. The place was essentially dark with the exception of the flashing disco lights and illuminated dance floor. I needed to get a closer look.

I stepped on the dance floor amidst gasps from all around and found my way through the other dancers till I was standing right in front of the girl. She stopped dancing and looked up alarmed. Within seconds, I felt a pair of hands grasp my shoulder but I shrugged them away. I was trying to concentrate but the hands came back and this time held me firmly, trying to pull me back.

I spun around, and with one hand pushed the waiter in the chest. The waiter lost his balance and staggered backwards till he fell on a nearby table breaking a few glasses and plates in the process. I didn't realize my own strength.

All the dancer girls quickly rushed to a door at the other end of the room. Within seconds, another pair of hands found a firm grip on my shoulders – then another and another. They held me and tried to move me towards the entrance but I started swinging at them wildly.

"Shit!" exclaimed Sikander. "This guy is a madman!"

"I told you we shouldn't have got him here," said Mahesh.

"Shut up," said Sikander. "Let's get out of here quickly before they come after us."

They got up quietly and walked out of the bar.

Two more waiters joined in and one of them punched me in the stomach. I didn't even flinch. My stomach was hard from my daily workouts. But another, harder punch forced me down to the ground. I didn't give up and tried to stand up to face my opponents.

Two waiters quickly got a hold of my legs and two others of my arms. They carried me to the door as the other patrons gaped in amazement. I was transported outside the main door and put firmly on the ground.

"Should we call the police?" one of the waiters asked the manager standing next to him.

"No," the manager replied. "We don't need to attract attention here."

The manager looked down at me. I simply stared back at him.

"You stay out of here, you understand?" he warned. "If I ever see you here again, you will be lying in some gutter and your parents won't be able to recognize you! Do you understand?"

The manager stretched a hand out towards me. I didn't like touching anyone or being touched. But I took the outstretched hand as I was in pain now and could use the assistance to get up on my feet.

I stood up and faced the manager. He looked at me closely.

"You look like you're from a good family," he said calmly. "You shouldn't be coming to places like this. Go home Beta."

A small crowd had gathered outside the bar. As per the instructions of the manager, the waiters whisked them away. I remained standing there.

"Go home. Forget about what happened. Don't come here again, ok?"

I stood staring at him.

"Ok?" asked the manager.

"Ok," I replied and walked away into the night.

# 16

"YOU HAVE TO GIVE UP YOUR JOB VANDANA," Madhu said firmly.

Vandana had just walked in after a hectic day at work and was seated on the couch, looking disbelievingly at her mother.

"I have spoken to your father about this and he thinks so too."

Vandana turned towards her father. He acknowledged with a slight nod but didn't meet her eye. He was watching a report about the developing tech industry in Bangalore, which Vandana knew he had no interest in.

"Tomorrow you will tell your boss that you're quitting and then stop going to work from the day after," stated Madhu.

Vandana felt the tears coming to her eyes but she held them back.

"Shekhar, tell her," Madhu said, turning to Shekhar.

Shekhar turned hesitantly to Vandana.

"Your mother is right," he said delicately. "Maybe it's a good idea for you to stop working."

Madhu's expression changed to one of annoyance.

"What do you mean by maybe?" she demanded. "Is that all you have to say? Tell her what we discussed."

Shekhar looked at Vandana and then turned the television off.

"Beta, we feel that work is taking too much of your time. You need to spend more time with Raghu and get to know him before you get married."

The mention of Raghu and marriage in the same sentence made Vandana flinch. She looked at her father with disappointment. She felt like she didn't even know this man.

"And why do you even need to work?" he continued, taking on a more cheerful tone. "Enjoy your life. Go out with Raghu and have fun. You wanted experience in the advertising world and you have got that."

*But I haven't even made a career in advertising yet,* she wanted to shout. Arguing was hopeless and she knew that it would fall upon deaf ears.

"Beta, I know that this may come as a disappointment to you," her father explained. "But marriage is more important. In the years to come, you will realize that you made the right decision."

"If Raghu wants you to, then you can work after marriage also," her mother added.

Raghu, the guy who would not even let her order what she wanted at a restaurant, would let her work?! That was a joke. If only her parents knew. But even if they did, they would never understand.

The way Vandana saw it, she had no way out now. Her fate was sealed. She had seen some hope in the form of Sikander but he turned out to be a slime ball. He wanted her for the same reason other guys did.

Even if her parents had arranged this mismatched alliance for her, she couldn't fathom losing her freedom. Her work was her only outlet, away from this madness. It wasn't the most ideal job but the way she figured, a majority of the population wasn't satisfied with the work they did. At least her job gave her a reason to be out of the house and see the world, no matter how small her world was.

That night in bed, Vandana refused to cry and pity herself. She had never imagined she would have to give up her dreams, without even coming close to them.

She still believed that good people always got the best in life. And she knew her heart was in the right place. If this was what her parents had decided for her, she would respect it. If destiny had now turned against her, she hoped it would one day be in her favour and all her dreams would come true.

The next day Vandana reached the office earlier than usual. Office hours started at 10, but most people sashayed in only after 10:30. If anyone asked, they usually blamed it on the transport – "There was an accident on the road," "Someone pulled the chain of the train," "My car had a flat." Vandana always arrived on time, but no one had seemed to notice.

She switched on her computer, opened the MS word application, and started typing, but couldn't get past the first line. She wanted to mention a valid reason in the letter so that she would not have to give an explanation to Firoze. He may be the scum of the earth as far as she was concerned, but he was still her boss and she wanted to leave on a good note.

After several minutes of thinking and rethinking, she decided to mention she was resigning on grounds of personal obligations. If Firoze asked her to explain herself, she would be honest about it and tell him that she was getting married. It wasn't something that she was very proud of but it was the truth.

As Vandana proceeded to type her resignation letter, tears welled up in her eyes. This was not the way she had expected things to pan out in her life. She had imagined falling in love with someone special, bringing him to the office and introducing him to everyone. His dynamic personality would drive women to jealousy and men to envy. But she couldn't even imagine bringing Raghu to her office. The very thought embarrassed her.

Vandana had imagined resigning under different circumstances – for a higher and more responsible position with a multinational advertising agency. And it would be then that Firoze would realize her hidden potential and bemoan her loss. He would offer her a better position and higher salary to lure her to stay. All wishful thinking, she realized.

Her resignation would just be a standard procedure. No one would really miss her. Swati would find another alibi. Firoze would hire an attractive secretary from the secretarial school and maybe she would succumb to his demands. Vandana knew she would be forgotten in no time. And once married, she would be lost in oblivion. She burst into tears and put her head down on the desk to find solace in her own arms.

The telephone rang. She quickly wiped her tears. It was nearing 10 o'clock and other dedicated employees like her would soon start pouring in. She looked at her face in her small hand-mirror. Her mascara had not smeared. She packed the little mirror back into her purse and prepped herself for the last call she would ever officially answer as receptionist with the company.

"Hello. Thank you for calling AdMagic, this is Vandana, how can I help you?"

"Vandana?"

"Yes?"

"Hi Vandana, this is Sikander."

Vandana was stunned into silence. Many days had passed since the Valentine's Day episode. She had made it clear to him that she never wanted to see or speak with him ever again.

"Vandana, please don't hang up. Please just listen to what I have to say."

Vandana remained quiet, anxious to hear what he had to say. He had revealed his true colours, she thought. What could he possibly have to say?

"Vandana, I want to say I'm sorry. I mean that's the expected thing for me to say after what happened. But the truth is that I'm not sorry. I know that what happened may have shocked you and you have probably lost respect for me. Vandana are you there?"

"Yes," she said softly.

"See Vandana, please believe me when I say that you are the most beautiful person I have ever met.

"In my mind, I felt very close to you. When you agreed to meet me on Valentine's Day, I can't tell you how happy I was. Vandana, at least say something so I know you're listening."

"I'm here," she said coldly.

"So on Valentine's Day, when we kissed, I felt so close to you that I didn't realize what I was doing. It just felt natural. When two people care about each other, they don't take permission from each other for everything. It just happens naturally. What I'm trying to say is that I didn't realize what I was doing. If it helps, I want to say I'm sorry. Vandana, I love you very much and really want to see you again. Vandana, please meet me once and let me explain myself."

"Is there anything else you have to say?"

"No... I just want to..."

Vandana slammed down the receiver.

She quickly signed her resignation letter and went into Firoze's cabin and placed it by his wife's framed picture on his desk. Then she went back to her own desk and collected all her things. Before walking out of the office, she took one last look at the place which had been her second home over the past few months. She figured that this company had given her no good memories so there was no reason to leave on a good note.

As she walked down the stairs, she passed Firoze who was walking up. As he wished her good morning, she felt his hand brush against her butt. She gave him a tight slap and left the building. Now she felt she had closed the chapter on the right note.

I whiled away most of the day walking by the railway tracks trying to figure out Vandana's reaction to the card.

Did she like me the way I liked her? Was the card effective in communicating my feelings to her? Another Q & A session went on in my head. When this tired me mentally, I exhausted myself physically by racing with the trains between Bandra and Khar Station. For some reason, I felt a surge of energy and power running on the railway tracks.

I returned home at 10 o'clock that night to find my parents watching some silly soap opera on television. I wasn't hungry so walked straight into the bedroom. Raghu was lying on his bed wide awake, staring at the ceiling. On hearing me walk in, his eyes flickered in my direction for a brief second and then went back to the ceiling.

I changed into my shorts and T-shirt in silence and lay down on my bed. We both lay in silence for a good 10 minutes until Raghu turned towards me and spoke.

"I'm getting married you know."

I turned to look at him. I couldn't believe the words I had just heard. According to Indian tradition, it was the elder brother who got married first. Raghu would have to wait till I got married, whether he liked it or not, I thought to myself.

Raghu turned back to stare at the ceiling. I kept looking at my idiotic brother. I was wondering which girl, in her right mind, would agree to marry him. I couldn't wait to see his reaction when he learned of Vandana and me. Our parents who never gave me any attention would soon realize their elder son's worth when they learned of the girl I was going to spend the rest of my life with.

"I can't believe it," said Raghu. "I mean I never even thought that I would get married to such a beautiful girl. I just can't believe it."

I was not even paying attention to him. I was lost by then in my visions of life ahead with Vandana. The conversation was distracting me.

"Ma and Papa want the wedding to take place in May. But I don't mind getting married tomorrow. I'm so excited."

Raghu's words reverberated in my ears. Ma and Papa had been planning Raghu's marriage all along without any regard for their elder son. They had proved that they were unfair and biased parents. But all that would change soon, I thought with a smile on my face. It was just a matter of days before Sikander found out Vandana's response to my card. Or maybe if I bumped into Vandana before that, she herself would tell me.

Raghu turned towards me. "So do you want to know who I'm getting married to?"

"No," I replied.

"You're not going to believe it," said Raghu excitedly.

I thought about it. Who could he possibly be getting married to that was giving him a reason to be so excited? Was it an actress or a model? As far as I was concerned, even the *sabziwali's* daughter wouldn't spare a second glance for my wimpy brother.

I didn't like getting into conversations with Raghu. He spoke to me only when he thought it convenient and was otherwise very rude. Now that he was excited and probably didn't have anyone to share it with, he had decided to have a conversation.

"So do you really want to know," asked Raghu again, eagerly. "You won't believe it."

I knew that I wouldn't get sleep for a while but I really wanted to go back to my thoughts. I also knew that my brother was very irritating and would go on and on until he broke the news to me. And so I just wanted to get it over with.

"Ok. Who?" I asked dryly.

As Raghu said her name, two trains crossed each other right outside our window drowning out his voice completely. I didn't hear anything but just said, "Ok" and turned the other way. At least now Raghu would let me go to sleep.

## 17

*HOLI*, THE FESTIVAL OF COLOURS, WAS CELEBRATED with huge pomp and splendour in the railway colony. It was the one day when all the residents, casting their prejudices aside, would come together in good spirits. *Diwali* was also celebrated with equal excitement but not everyone could afford expensive fireworks, which would bring out the status difference between the residents of Block A and Block B.

In the railway colony, the festivities did not even touch upon the actual meaning behind the festival. It was more to do with catching up with fellow residents, spraying and painting them with colours and eating specially catered snacks thereafter. For the more ambitious who wanted to end the occasion on a 'high' note, a *bhaang* counter was set up in one corner.

By Mumbai law, *Holi* was only to be celebrated till noon, after which the use of colours was illegal. Every year, there were reports of someone losing an eye or worse to spurious paints and colours.

As always, the Mumbai trains remained unaffected by the festival. The frequency of running trains was less compared to that on an ordinary working day, but nonetheless my eyes opened to the sound of the first train scraping across the steel tracks outside my window. The sound was painfully unendurable, reminiscent of nails scraping across a blackboard.

I lay awake and contemplated my plan of action for the day. Playing holi down in the colony was out of the question. I detested being touched by anyone and *Holi* was the one day when people took the liberty of smearing colour on people they didn't even know. I knew that I would end up hitting someone before recognizing them under their colour coated face.

The catered food was always an attraction, but the residents forgot all etiquette when it was time to eat. They would all dip their hands into the same platter and just looking at that made me sick. Till about two years ago, my parents persuaded me to join the family for *Holi* since, like the other residents, they had made a monetary contribution towards the event and wanted to derive full value for their money. But the last time, I ended up pushing a colony elder into the muck and slapping two kids when they tried to smear my face with colour. Since then, Ma and Papa never asked me to accompany them.

I lay in bed listening to train after train till sunlight found its way into my dingy bedroom. The loud banging of the musical *dholaks* from the colony echoed through the air, indicating that the residents in the colony were ready to play *Holi*.

I watched Raghu as he changed into a white kurta paijama. He left the room without saying a word to me and joined our parents in the living room. I heard the rest of my family chatting excitedly for a few minutes before the main door opened and closed. I immediately got out of bed and frisked into the living room. I had the whole house to myself.

I switched on the TV. A *Holi* song filled the screen. I quickly jumped into the shower and a few minutes later, returned in a towel to stand in front of the television. I flipped channels incessantly but found nothing interesting to watch. Within minutes I became restless, abandoned the remote and walked around the house till I found my way into the balcony. A band of three were playing *dholaks* in the centre of the lawn while the colony residents were still pouring in, scattering themselves across the compound.

I changed into my blue shirt and blue jeans and walked out of the door. Once I reached the ground level, instead of turning left towards the celebration, I headed right towards the tracks.

Vandana had enjoyed playing *Holi* during her school days. But once she came of age, she kept away from the colony celebrations, preferring to go over to a friend's house to play *Holi* in a smaller group. The last time she had played among the uncivilized colony residents, it took her days to get the *gulaab rang* out of her hair and off her face.

From the window of her living room, she looked down at the garden trying to recognize the building residents who were running around with painted faces, attacking in groups the residents who arrived fresh on the scene. A slight laugh escaped her lips when a passing elderly lady started shouting at a group of jeering kids armed with *pichkaris*, when one of them sprayed some water on her spectacles.

"Vandana, you're not ready yet! Hurry up, the whole colony is already down!"

Vandana turned to look at the excited face of her mother. Madhu was draped in an expensive pink sari. The colony would not take mercy on it.

"I'm not coming Mama. You and Papa go. I'll watch from here."

"No Beta. You must come. Even Raghu is coming and they're expecting you. Hurry up and get ready."

"Mama, I'm not coming," said Vandana firmly.

Madhu's cheerful expression turned somber.

"You have to come. What will Raghu's parents think? Your father is already downstairs and will get upset if you're not there." She paused. "Come for a little while. Just say hello to everyone and then come back. Now hurry up."

Vandana sensed the edginess in her mother's tone. She disappeared into the bedroom and within minutes reappeared in her best salwar kameez, reserved for special occasions, to tick her mother off.

The beautiful garden in the centre of the colony was multicoloured as were the people walking around in it. The persistent drumming of the *dholaks* echoed throughout the colony making it sound like a call to war. Now someone seemed to be setting up a microphone in front of them, amplifying their music into cacophonous sounds.

As soon as Vandana emerged from her block, a group of men and women, whom she could barely recognize, attacked her, chanting "*Holi Hai*". They were rough on her, smearing her face with all kinds of colour. The men took a little more time with her. When they were done, they retreated looking for their next target.

Vandana closed her eyes and opened them carefully ensuring that no colour had entered them. Madhu had joined the rest of the ladies, her pink sari now tarnished. Vandana saw Raghu at a distance, smiling at her gleefully.

Madhu was now greeting Raghu's parents and exchanging token smears of colour with them. Vandana walked over to a few empty plastic chairs which were at a safe distance from the main action. As she sat down, some children came and sprayed water on her with *pichkaris*. Vandana had some wet *rang* on her hands and playfully smeared the kids who didn't resist and wished her "*Happy Holi*" before leaving.

Vandana was now enjoying the scene. Everyone was chatting animatedly with each other and having a good time. It was one of those days when everyone blended in and there were no secluded groups gossiping among each other. That would happen the next day.

Vandana sensed Raghu's eyes on her. She was hoping he wouldn't come over and sit with her. She dreaded the day when people would see them together as a couple. Now she wished she hadn't come down at all and was thinking of a quick exit strategy. But when she saw Raghu walking in the other direction to speak to some colony elders, she decided to stay a little longer.

Vandana was lost in her thoughts when she sensed someone occupying the seat next to her. She looked to her side and saw Sonal smiling through coats of colour.

"Hi Vandana didi."

Sonal was much younger than Vandana and looked up to her as her role model. Vandana too enjoyed talking to Sonal from time to time. But ever since she had started work, she hadn't seen Sonal in months.

"Hi Sonal. It looks like they didn't spare you. I wouldn't have recognized you."

Sonal giggled.

"So how's college treating you?" asked Vandana. "Having fun?"

"Yes," replied Sonal, "I'm having lots of fun, not in college but outside college."

"That's nice. So you have a good group of friends now?"

"Yes Vandana didi. I have some good friends. And I have a boyfriend too."

"Oooh," teased Vandana. "Looks like someone has grown up! Does he study with you?"

"No no. He's not from my college. But he's very good looking and a nice person. Vandana didi, you won't tell my mother, no?"

Vandana was taken aback by this. She hated the fact that Sonal didn't consider Vandana part of her generation.

"Of course not! Don't be silly! Why would I tell your mother?"

"Can I tell you a secret then?"

"Sure."

Sonal bent closer to Vandana. "I'm in love with him. I want to marry him."

Vandana felt bad for this naïve little girl. She was barely 16 and misled into believing she was in love. The guy would merely take advantage of her and this poor little thing would eventually get hurt. But then it would make Sonal stronger and sensible, Vandana thought.

"You're too young to think about marriage, Sonal. Just enjoy yourself and focus on your studies!"

Sonal was about to say something but got interrupted by the loud squeaking sound that the microphone made as it was being adjusted. Everyone fell silent. Sonal's father, Tripathi was behind the microphone, tapping into it.

"Hello everyone! It's great to see everyone back here together!"

He tapped into the microphone once again to confirm that he was being heard. The thumping sound echoed all over the colony.

"This function has been made possible by everyone's contributions. I am pleased to announce that we have collected 20,000 more than the required amount, which shall be utilized in planting a flower bed in the colony."

Everyone clapped. Vandana looked around at all the stupid people who were clapping as if being dictated by prompters. How would a flower bed benefit anyone? If the extra funds were to be utilized correctly, something should be done about the water shortage in the colony. At a time when most of Mumbai had water round the clock, this place was still behind the times despite being a colony built by the government for government employees.

"I am pleased to also announce that the catering today has been generously provided by our respected Mr. Shekhar Gupta. Shekharji would like to say a few words."

Her father always made an extra effort to be a hero in front of all these tacky people and Vandana could never understand why. He was behind the microphone now, waiting for the uncoordinated claps to die down.

"Hello friends. I hope everyone is enjoying themselves."

No response. People listened to her father only because of his position. He had average public speaking skills.

"I have an important announcement to make. In fact there is some wonderful news that I would like to share with all of you."

Vandana's face turned red. It was a confused expression of anger and embarrassment. She was hoping that her father wouldn't say what she thought he was going to say.

"I would like to share with all of you the wonderful news of the impending marriage of my daughter Vandana with Amar Srivastav's son, Raghu. And all of you are invited!"

An applause followed, accompanied by stares in Vandana's direction.

"You're getting married, Vandana didi!" exclaimed Sonal. She hugged Vandana's stiff body.

The *Holi* colours on Vandana's face hid her tears well. She had maintained her distance from the colony residents all these years. But now by announcing this in front of the entire colony, her father had instantly made her one of them. Within minutes, colony members came over to wish her. She managed to maintain a courteous smile. She thought that she could find a way to come to terms with the whole situation, but each moment made her despise it even more.

The murmuring was interrupted by a Maruti Esteem with music blaring through its open windows. Sonal nudged Vandana excitedly.

"My boyfriend."

Vandana's eyes followed the car as it parked at a distance. She recognized the multi-coloured figures of Sikander, Mahesh, Madan and Pravin. She felt sorry for Sonal. She was a cute kid-sister with a good heart and deserved better than one of these colony loafers. Vandana didn't even bother asking her as to which one of them was her boyfriend.

The boys headed onto the grass and greeted everyone with colours. After that, they headed straight for the *bhaang* counter and gulped down several glasses each. Mahesh whispered something to Sikander, who turned and looked in Vandana's direction. Vandana got up and walked towards her apartment block. She had no intention of being part of the gathering anymore. She didn't care if the residents gossiped about her leaving abruptly. If she was lucky, they would think she was just being shy.

She stopped outside the door to her apartment and inserted her key in the lock.

"Vandana."

She turned around startled. Sikander was standing on the top stair, leaning across the aged wooden banister, panting.

"Vandana, I know that you're angry with me," he said between breaths. "Will you please listen to me?"

"What do you want?"

"Vandana, I am truly sorry," he said earnestly. "Please believe me. I never intended to hurt you. I really like you a lot and understand your not wanting to talk to me. It's all my fault. I'm not like that at all."

Vandana looked at him impatiently. She wished he would get this over with soon. After what had happened down in the colony, she just wanted to sit at home and cry.

"I just want to ask you for one favour," he said sincerely. "And I will respect whatever you say."

"What?" she asked dryly.

"It's my birthday on the 25th. And I would really like to spend it with you. If you never want to see me after that, I won't pursue you any further. But it would really make me feel nice if you would come out with me for a cup of coffee. Please."

Vandana didn't say anything.

"You don't have to answer me now," said Sikander. "I'll be waiting for you outside Barista on Bandstand. Saturday the 25th, at 7 in the evening. It would make me really happy if you came."

Vandana didn't reply. She entered her house and closed the door behind her.

By the time I reached the tracks, my face was painted black. A group of urchins had attacked me on the way with oil paint, smearing my face completely till I fought them away. Initially I let them have their *Holi* fun, but when their touching my face began bothering me, which was within seconds, I kicked one of them hard on the shin. One of the others got a punch straight on the chest. They cursed me while they ran away but I didn't bother chasing them. I just wanted to be alone.

I took the outer track, which saw a lesser frequency of trains. I walked at a steady pace towards Santacruz station. When I reached, I sat on a solitary bench on the platform and observed my surroundings. As a rule, no colours were permitted inside the station. But there were small puddles of *gulab rang* all over the platform. No one seemed to respect the law in this city.

After resting for a good 10 minutes, I got up to head back and took the outer track once again. The outer track was isolated and at a safe distance from the busier lines in the centre.

I had been exercising regularly and had managed to toughen up my body considerably. Every night, I practiced my punches against the weak walls of my room. The satisfaction that action gave me had me craving for more.

The main issue clawing at me now was Vandana. I wanted to make her proud of me somehow. Even if she did like me and enjoyed my company, what had I achieved? I understood that women liked achievers. And now I wanted to strive to be one. But I didn't know how.

A good job in a respectable company didn't seem like a possibility, considering that I had been unsuccessful in finding one all this while. I was not bright in academics nor could I ever become a sportsman or a film star. So how could I make myself look like a hero in front of her? A Q & A replaced my tumultuous thoughts.

*What is my sense of purpose?*

*You will find out*

*What am I meant to do?*

*It will find you.*

*What if I end up a loser all my life?*

*You won't Babloo. Trust me.*

I realized I needed a sense of achievement, not for myself but for Vandana. Being a good person was not good enough. I would need more, to win over a beautiful person like Vandana.

I walked past Khar Station. The tracks were empty now and no train had passed for several minutes. In the far distance, popular Hindi songs blared through crackling loudspeakers. People were celebrating all over Mumbai.

I noticed a three and a half-legged stray dog limping alongside me.

I tried to shoo the dog away with some stones, but it kept following me, wagging its tail.

Suddenly, a piercing scream filled the air. I thought I had imagined it. I turned to look at the dog. It had also stopped in its tracks, seemingly stunned. The scream came again, cutting through the loud music. I felt a growing sense of alarm.

The dog quickly turned around and hobbled away. I stood still. The scream was a girl's and she sounded in trouble. The music was too loud to figure out the exact source. I closed my eyes and concentrated. My senses were sharp and I had to make them work for me. Someone was in trouble and I was determined to find out what had made this girl let out such a high-pitched scream.

She screamed again. A chill ran down my spine. It reminded me of a helpless scream in a C-grade horror film, in which a girl was being attacked by some monstrous creature. I kept my thoughts in control. I now had an idea of which direction the scream came from. I just had to hear it once more to get the exact direction.

I waited for a few minutes. I had almost given up hope when it came again, this time so shrill that it pierced me instantly and forced my eyes open. I ran quickly in the direction of the scream, behind a row of chawls. I had to climb over a fence and jump a wall. I was now in a narrow, deserted *gully*. The scream seemed even closer.

The next scream took me past the gully into the centre of a commercial market place. A shop sign indicated that I was on the east side of Khar. All the shops were shut. There wasn't a soul in sight. I stood in the centre of the street and looked around for some sign of disturbance.

I heard the sounds of a car door slamming, accompanied by another scream. It was coming from an alley up ahead, roughly a 100 meters from where I was standing. As I rounded the corner, I saw the rear bumper of a white Hyundai Santro car. I quickly ran past it and the source of the commotion came into view.

Three men were standing in a semi-circle over a young woman lying sprawled on the ground. She was covering her face with her hands, alternately crying and screaming. Her purse lay by her side and there were dozens of papers scattered all over. The man in the centre was holding up a bottle of clear liquid in his hand, waving it in her direction.

He emptied a few drops of the liquid onto one of the scattered sheets of paper. Within seconds, the liquid melted the paper with a hiss. It was acid. I knew what acid was. I had seen a Hindi film in which a man threw acid on a woman's face which disfigured her forever. "Please," the girl sobbed. "Let me go, Shamsher. I'm sorry."

Shamsher looked around in frustration. A black bandana was wrapped around his head. He was six feet tall, dressed in a well-tailored black Pathani suit outlining his muscular physique. His menancing eyes caught sight of me.

"Hey, who the hell are you?" he demanded.

I was around 10 feet away from him. I had to think of something to say. Shamsher had a bottle of acid in his hands and I knew I had to be careful.

"Get out of here, you black joker."

I caught my reflection in the tinted window of the parked car. My face was painted jet black. It made me look like some evil character from a comic book.

Shamsher kicked the girl with his foot and she yelped in pain. He then turned all his attention towards me.

"I told you to get out of here, you *chutiya*," he said.

I didn't move. The leader looked frustrated.

He motioned to his two accomplices.

"Get him out of here."

The two guys moved towards me. In the background, the girl was crying profusely. She seemed to have no energy left to scream.

The two guys didn't seem to be confident because they were careful to stay in step with each other. Just like Bollywood henchmen who always attacked in pairs. The two guys came within two feet of me and stared into my expressionless face anxiously.

I could have stayed there just staring at them. But the leader was harassing the girl in the distance, moving his foot around violently in her skirt. He still had the bottle in his hand so she was still protecting her face while whimpering in the pain that his foot caused her.

The two men gained more confidence as I backed away from them. I retreated deliberately to give them the impression that they were in control. Then, when they least expected, I would spring my weapon on them. The element of surprise. I mentally counted – 1...2...3.

In a quick motion, I yanked one of the guys' heads with both my hands and slammed it onto the bonnet of the parked car. The impact was so hard that the car shook slightly. There was no sign of blood on the guy's face as he passed out by the front tyre.

The other guy looked at his partner in crime lying unconscious. He then turned towards me and advanced angrily. But on seeing my blackened face up close, he quickly retreated and stood behind his leader.

"What the...?" asked Shamsher puzzled.

He stepped back and saw his crony lying on the street. He took a few steps towards me, then holding the bottle a safe distance away from his body, flipped the contents in my direction. A short spray flew out of the bottle but most of the contents hit the ground between Shamsher and me. A few drops fell on my shirt. Since my shirt was loose, the acid did its job on the lower part of my shirt which had come untucked, and didn't find its way to my skin.

I was angry now. This was my favourite shirt and I had made sure that no *holi rang* got on it. Now this guy had gone ahead and made some holes in it. The leader retracted his arm to toss the bottle again but doubled over in sudden pain as a sharp kick from me caught him in his gut. He shouted in pain but didn't let go of the bottle.

I punched the leader's arm and the bottle fell out of his hands, ricocheted off the alley wall and bounced back onto the bonnet. The acid came pouring out, sizzling on the metal, making the loud celebration music in the air sound like a background flute recital.

Shamsher stood horrified as his eyes alternated between his car and my darkened face. I took a boxing stance and held that position. Shamsher winced in pain as he tried to move his arm. I gripped his collar, and raised my fist. But instead kneed him in the groin. Shamsher went down in silence, staring at me in agony.

The last guy witnessed it all in silent horror. He backed away as I turned in his direction. He seemed too frightened to run away.

"Take them home," I said, looking him straight in the eye.

The guy stood frozen in terror.

I bent down near the girl. She looked at me, still crying in fear.

"Please," she said, using her chubby hands to protect her face. "Please don't."

Her long skirt was pulled up to her thighs, exposing her bare shapeless legs. My memory quickly darted back to a Hindi film, in which the hero was in a similar situation. I instinctively straightened the girl's skirt and stood up.

The girl burst into fresh sobs and cried profusely. I looked down at her questioningly, wondering why she was still crying now that she was out of harm's way. Girls can be so silly sometimes, I thought to myself.

The other guy was still leaning against the shutter witnessing the whole scene silently. Finally, after 10 minutes, the girl wiped her tears and made an attempt to stand up. She straightened her skirt further and duck-walked around collecting the scattered papers. I made no attempt to help her. I was exhausted and wanted to go home now.

After composing herself, the girl walked towards me.

"Will you please walk me to the main road?" she asked, looking at my grimy face searchingly. "There are no *autos* here and I don't feel safe walking alone."

"Yes."

"Who are you?" asked the girl, as we walked through the shanty marketplace. Businesses were closed, vegetable vendors' stalls stood empty as did abandoned hand carts, and the only sign of life was a group of stray dogs sniffing at an open municipality trash bin.

"What's your name?" she asked.

I looked at her. Her big eyes were highlighted with *kajal*, now partly smeared. A huge red *bindi* sat like a bulls-eye on her forehead, perfectly aligned below the middle parting of her straight, shoulder-length hair. Her loose kurta and long skirt could not quite conceal the fat around her stomach. But she had something very pleasant about her, which clashed with the rowdy look of the guy who had threatened her a few minutes back.

Surprisingly she didn't have any *holi* colour on her.

"Why don't you tell me your name?" she persisted, looking at me intently.

I stared straight ahead.

"Listen," she said, "you just saved my life. If you hadn't come in time, God knows what would have happened."

I thought about this. If I hadn't arrived in time, she would have either been raped or disfigured by acid – or maybe both.

"What's your name?" she asked again.

I remained silent. I didn't want to reveal my name because I didn't know her. And she could get me into trouble. I was glad that my face was painted black. Now even if she saw me later on, she wouldn't recognize me.

"Where did you come from?" she asked.

I was getting irritated now. She was asking too many questions. I decided to reply, but not give away too much.

"From the railway tracks," I said.

Her glum expression slowly gave way to a smile.

"Oh, so you're a hero who came from the tracks," she said thoughtfully. "You wear black face paint to conceal your identity."

I wanted to tell her that a group of urchins had smeared oil paint on my face, but didn't say anything.

"You don't have a name," she continued, "or don't want to give your name. And behind that face paint is a different person altogether."

I was trying to understand what she was getting at. I couldn't figure it out. Now she appeared to be babbling to herself, using her hands as if creating an imaginary picture in the air.

"So let me see if I got this right," she said. "You have no name, no identity. You came from the railway tracks to serve justice. You're like a superhero, just like those superheroes from the American movies. And your name is...uh... RAIL MAN! You protect the railway tracks and your purpose is justice! Wow, what a story!"

I thought about this. What was this girl saying? Had she gone crazy?

But then I let it sink in. Meeting this girl in this situation had happened for a reason. Perhaps to make me realize what my true purpose was? She interrupted my thoughts.

"Rail Man, you didn't ask me anything about what just happened, who those guys were... why they were harassing me?"

I was deep in thought. I was thinking about what the girl had said earlier. But I forced myself to snap out of it to listen to her.

"That guy, Shamsher, used to be my boyfriend," she explained. "I don't know why I fell for him. We were going around for a few months. But then he started getting possessive and all. He started hitting any guy I would even talk to. What world did he think we were living in? Anyways, so I told him it's not happening. Then he went totally psycho on me. He started stalking me, calling me, threatening me. He even started making crank calls to my parents. But I didn't take him seriously. Then today morning, as I was getting back from work, he caught me alone with his friends. And well, you know the rest. Now, thanks to you, I don't think he'll ever bother me again."

I wondered what kind of job she had if she worked all night. She looked neither like a beer bar dancer nor a prostitute. In fact, she spoke eloquently and came across as a well-educated girl from a decent family.

"So tell me something about yourself," she said, turning towards me. "Who are you?"

"I am Rail Man."

She laughed. "Well, if you're not going to tell me who you are, at least allow me to introduce myself. My name is Shoma Banerjee."

We turned a corner and the main road came into view. There was plenty of activity on the road – *Holi* was on, in full-swing. Some street urchins ran towards Shoma with coloured hands. I raised a fist, and they cheerfully took a diversion. I looked at my watch. It was 8 a.m.

I flagged down a passing *rickshaw*, playing a peppy Marathi song. Surprisingly, it stopped. The rickshaw driver asked us where we wanted to go. Depending upon our direction of travel, he would decide whether he wanted to take us as passengers. But I put his meter down and gave him no choice.

"How do I get in touch with you, Rail Man?" asked Shoma.

"No," I said.

Shoma was taken aback. She probably didn't expect me to be so abrupt. But diplomacy wasn't one of my traits. She broke into a smile.

"Thanks a lot, Rail Man," she said, while getting into the *rickshaw*. "You're a true hero. And the bravest man I ever met."

She tapped the driver and the *rickshaw* pulled away and merged with the regular traffic. I remained standing there, her last words resonating in my head. She had helped me recognize my sense of purpose. So I hadn't helped her; she had helped *me*.

## 18

I AWOKE WITH A START, TO THE SCREECHING OF THE DAY'S first train as it came to a halt at Bandra Station. It was the day after *Holi*. I looked at my watch. 4:30 a.m. I got out of bed and dropped to the floor to do my push-ups. Raghu was still fast asleep, his snores disturbing the peaceful silence between the departure of one train and the arrival of the next.

My body ached after my 10-minute workout. I lay back on my bed to rest, and stretched.

I thought about the incident that had transpired the previous day and my conversation with Shoma. I needed answers and turned inwards, to my only friend.

*Did I do the right thing?*

*Yes you did.*

*Is this what I am meant to do?*

*You did the right thing. You saved a girl. Doesn't that make you feel good, Babloo?*

*I don't know.*

*Don't you feel a sense of achievement? Doesn't that make you feel like a hero, Babloo?*

Before I knew it, I was asleep.

When I woke up, it was broad daylight in the room and the rumbling of the intermittent trains indicated that it was a busy time of day. I looked at my wristwatch. 10:30 a.m. I hadn't slept so late in years.

I got out of bed and stretched. My body was well rested and I felt an urge to venture out. I headed into the kitchen for a glass of water and saw that there was no one at home.

I looked around for the newspaper, then remembered that the printing presses had been shut yesterday on account of *Holi*. I switched on the television and surfed through the channels till I settled on a Star News bulletin. The bulletin mentioned something about a major economic deal being chalked out between India and a foreign country. The newsreader was giving her opinions about the deal. I shook my head in disapproval. The news reporter's job was to simply report the news, rather than offer an opinion. I was about to change the channel when the bulletin abruptly moved into an indoor studio. A reporter wearing a suit smiled into the camera from behind a newsdesk.

*"In our special story, we have the first hand experience of Holi crimes by a victim, who is a reporter for* MiD-DAY. *Shoma Banerjee was heading home in the early hours of the morning after completing a late night assignment. She was attacked by a group of inebriated men who threatened to throw acid on her face. The reason for attack was unknown..."*

I sat up surprised. Shoma hadn't told me that she was a press reporter. But then, I hadn't asked.

I understood the true reason behind the incident being withheld. If Shoma had disclosed her previous association with the assailants, it would forever tarnish her reputation, which would go against her when her parents would try to get her married. That's if she wasn't married already.

*"... but a hero emerged from nowhere and fought the assailants in the nick of time. We have Shoma Banerjee here with us in the studio to tell her story as it happened."*

The camera panned to the left to include a dolled-up Shoma wearing long earrings.

*"Thank you for joining us today, Shoma,"* said the newsreader, turning to her. *"Tell us what happened."*

*"I was being harassed by a group of hooligans who caught me on the road and forced me into an alley,"* said Shoma, wide-eyed with excitement. *"I tried to fight them, but it was hopeless. They threatened to pour acid on my face."*

"What was the purpose behind the attack, Shoma?"

"No motive, I think," said Shoma thoughtfully. "Just a group of drunk hooligans looking for some fun."

"And then?"

"And then out of nowhere, a man emerged and fought them. He gave them the beating of their lives..."

"Who was he...?"

"He didn't reveal his name. His face was covered in black paint so I couldn't really see what he looked like. He said he came from the railway tracks."

"Was he someone you think knew you?" asked the newsreader. "How did he find you there?"

"I was scared and was screaming for a good 15 minutes," said Shoma dramatically, "and he heard me and came and saved me."

"You must have been terrified. You must have been screaming very loudly for it to have reached the railway tracks."

"Yes I was. And no one from the area came to my rescue. But this man came from nowhere, saved me and walked me to an auto rickshaw."

"Then he must have told you something about himself. Who was he?"

"He didn't really talk. But for me he was a superhero. The way he looked. The way he acted. He didn't want to reveal who he was because he didn't want credit for his good deed. He did it from the goodness of his heart."

"Did you go to the police after that, Shoma?"

"No, I didn't need to. Justice was served by Rail Man!"

"Rail Man?" asked the newsreader, confused.

"Yes. That's what I call him. He emerged from the railway tracks. So I call him Rail Man. A true hero!"

"Well, that's an interesting story Shoma. Thanks for bringing it to

*Star News first.*"

"*It's my pleasure. I want people to know that there is goodness out there, a hero who is out to save the world selflessly.*"

"*Do you think you will ever see Rail Man again?*" *asked the newsreader, smiling.*

"*If I am in trouble and by the railway tracks, maybe I will. But if you're out there and watching this, Rail Man, thank you so much. Thank you for saving my life.*"

"*Thank you Shoma.*" *The newsreader turned to the screen. "That was* MiD-DAY *reporter Shoma Banerjee, a potential victim of a violent crime, saved by a real life hero, whom she calls Rail Man.*"

The feature changed to the sports news. I got up and started walking restlessly all over the small house. A flurry of thoughts ran through my head. I meandered from the living room to the bedroom to the kitchen to the balcony, back to the bedroom and so on. Suddenly, I stopped in front of the inadequately lit mirror above the undersized washbasin.

As I peered at myself in the mirror, I felt I was looking at another person. A man who hadn't thought twice before saving a woman's life. A man who was being proclaimed a hero. Shoma had said that I did it from the goodness of my heart, when I actually had no clue what prompted me to enter a dangerous situation that didn't concern me. If the acid had fallen on me, I probably wouldn't be alive or even if I survived, I would be carrying a body with rotten flesh for the rest of my life. I had risked my life and hadn't thought twice about it because, unconsciously, my prime concern had been justice.

Under normal circumstances, no one would have understood my intentions – like the time I hit the milkman, the colony thought that it was prompted by my mental condition or uncontrollable anger. But when my face was concealed with black paint, my noble intentions and goodness of heart were recognized. I was praised on national television as a hero.

Realization dawned on me that Babloo was my mask, but Rail Man reflected the person I truly was. Rail Man was my means to attain a sense of achievement and make Vandana proud of me.

I darted into my bedroom and searched for the clothes that Rail Man had worn the previous day. After tossing stuff around frantically, I found them in their usual place, hanging on a hook behind the door. I noticed the huge, even hole created by the acid on the lower part of his shirt. My jeans had acquired black patches on them.

I took them off the hook and held them up against the sunlight. They trembled slightly in my hand as a passing train lightly shook the room. This would be Rail Man's attire when he set out to save the world, I decided. Now for the black paint...

In another block in the colony, realization dawned on someone else in another way. Vandana had just finished watching the news report on Rail Man on Star News. How could such a selfless person exist in this day and age, who would do such a heroic deed without even trying to claim credit for it? Vandana was sure that it was some publicity hungry lunatic who would eventually come in front of the camera to be recognized. In today's world no one did anything without an ulterior motive, she thought.

Thoughts of Rail Man lasted in Vandana's head just for a few minutes. After that, depressing visions of her bleak future took over. She was bored sitting at home and couldn't think of anything productive to do. Her other option was to go shopping with her mother and Mrs. Srivastav, which didn't interest her in the least.

All Mrs. Srivastav spoke about was her son Raghu. She kept suggesting that Vandana and Raghu should spend more time together. That morning, before her mother and Mrs. Srivastav left, Vandana had successfully convinced them that she and Raghu didn't need to meet often since they were getting married and she would rather Raghu concentrate on his work than have the added pressure of devoting enough time to her. They were both impressed.

Vandana had secretly hoped that AdMagic would call her back to work. But slapping one's boss would hardly merit future prospects in any organization, she realized. After the previous day's engagement announcement at the colony *Holi* party, Vandana dared not set foot out of the house, to avoid the embarrassment of being congratulated by any colony member she ran into.

She opened her Robert Jordan novel to the dog-eared page. But instead of focusing on reading, she started thinking about Sikander and his audacity to come up and talk to her after what he had done. The fact that he did own up to his mistake indicated that he didn't have an ego and genuinely wanted to rectify the situation. He sounded sincere but what he did could never be rectified as far as she was concerned. He had crossed his limits.

Or was she being too hard on him? Was it she who had sent out the wrong signals? Did her anxious non-verbal reactions encourage Sikander to do what he did? Was she also to blame?

No, thought Vandana. She had never done or said anything to encourage Sikander to get so physically intimate with her. Vandana was very conscious of her actions and the way she carried herself. And she hadn't crossed the line. She leaned back on the couch and turned her attention back to the novel. Now she would follow her destiny blindly.

The doorbell rang. Vandana's eyes opened with a start. She had dozed off. She looked at the clock. It was 5 p.m. She rubbed her eyes, straightened her jeans and T-shirt and headed for the door.

She opened the door sleepily to a smiling Raghu. He was wearing a faded white shirt sloppily tucked into a pair of black trousers. He looked like a waiter from a low-grade restaurant.

"Hi Vandana," said Raghu.

"My mother is not at home. She went out with your mother. They should be back in the evening."

Vandana had blocked the doorway completely.

"I know," smiled Raghu. "Ma told me. She called me in the office and told me that you were home alone. She told me to come back early and spend time with you till they returned."

Vandana could not hide her displeasure on hearing this. How

could they already start controlling her life like this?

Vandana dropped her hands in resignation and went inside the house. Raghu followed her and closed the door behind him.

She sat down on the couch and picked up her novel. Raghu sat on the adjoining single-seater couch facing her.

Vandana was infuriated. The very person who she was hiding from had now come into her territory to invade her privacy. Why didn't he just get it? As long as he didn't get on her nerves, she knew she would be able to get through the evening.

"I would like a cup of tea."

Vandana looked up. Raghu had taken off his shoes and was sitting comfortably with his feet up on the coffee table.

"What?" asked Vandana, not sure whether it was a request or a command.

"I would like a cup of tea," said Raghu. "I usually take a cup of tea when I come back home from office."

*This is not your home, you idiot. Go and make it yourself.*

"Everything's in the kitchen," said Vandana, looking back at her book. "Please help yourself."

"I don't know how to make tea," said Raghu.

*Stupid Mama's boy.* Vandana banged her novel down on the table and got up. Who the hell was he to bark orders at her?

She headed into the kitchen and noisily proceeded to make tea. She heard the television being switched on. Raghu seemed to be making himself comfortable in her house.

"I like my tea light with lots of milk," called Raghu, from the adjoining living room. "And some biscuits would be nice too."

Vandana deliberately made the tea strong and added less milk. She rummaged through the kitchen shelves and found some stale biscuits. She carried the cup of tea in one hand and the biscuits in the other, without a tray, and banged them in front of Raghu on the coffee table. He looked pleased.

"Where's your tea?" asked Raghu taking his cup, his joint eyebrows furrowing enquiringly.

"I don't drink tea. I prefer coffee."

"Coffee is a South Indian beverage. You should drink tea. You will like it when you taste Ma's tea. She makes it very well."

I'm sure she does, thought Vandana. And I'm sure you don't even go to the bathroom without her permission...

Raghu took a long sip, making a loud, rasping sound. He grimaced and put the cup down.

"This is not how I like my tea."

"This is how I make it Raghu," she said firmly. "Take it or leave it."

Raghu quickly picked up his cup. He took another sip.

"I can't taste the sugar."

"You were the one who said that sugar is not good. If you don't like it, put it down."

"No Vandana. You have made it. That makes it sweet enough."

How corny could he get? Vandana would have preferred it if he just kept quiet. She went back to her novel.

There was a good five minutes of silence. Vandana looked up and saw Raghu staring at her T-shirt. She looked down at her T-shirt and saw the outline of both her nipples pressing against her T-shirt. She wasn't wearing a bra. She never wore a bra at home.

"What are you looking at?" she asked angrily.

"Your T-shirt," he said honestly.

"What about it?"

"I like it."

What was there to like about it? It was a plain white T-shirt with nothing written on it.

"I know what you're looking at," she said curtly, "and it makes me uncomfortable."

He quickly turned to the television and increased the volume. Of all the channels on cable, Raghu had selected a local Mumbai news channel. The TV stations were catching onto the flavour of the day – Rail Man. The Khar Police station incharge, Inspector Anil Satpute, was being interviewed in Hindi but replying in Marathi. He looked visibly hassled.

*"Inspector Satpute, why is it that on a public holiday like Holi, a day which has seen a lot of crime in the past, there were no police officials in Khar East?"*

*"There were police officers patrolling the area,"* said Satpute angrily. *"They were patrolling the main road and have registered many cases. The police have been doing their job."*

*"Then why is it that a girl was screaming at the top of her voice and none of your policemen rushed to her rescue? A man walking on the railway tracks 500 meters away heard her screams. But the main road is less than 200 meters away."*

*"Listen, I know you're doing your job,"* said Satpute exasperated, *"but we know how to do ours. There was a lot of noise on the main road. They didn't hear her. I don't know. I wasn't there."*

There was a finality in the Inspector's voice, but the off-camera interviewer continued.

*"One last question, Inspector. What do you have to say about Rail Man? Who is he? How does it feel that he did what the police force was supposed to do? The whole city is calling him a hero!"*

The inspector banged his fist on the desk in front of him.

*"He is no hero! He is a criminal. He broke the law and took it in his own hands. He beat those boys up. I have just come back from the hospital. One of them has a skull fracture. We will look for this lunatic Rail Man and press charges against him."*

*"You will arrest the person who saved the girl's life? And what about the boys who were trying to harm the girl?"*

*"Listen, there is no proof. The boys have denied the allegations and the girl has not yet filed a case against them but is talking about it in the press. So how can we arrest those boys? No further comment."*

*The reporter tried to probe further but the Inspector got up from his desk and headed into the next room. The camera followed him to a point but was blocked by a constable. The interviewer appeared in front of the camera and gave her version of the interview.*

Raghu lowered the television volume and turned towards Vandana. He bit into a biscuit and his face gave way to a sour expression. He put the uneaten half on his plate.

"This Rail Man is such a joke," said Raghu. "He has nothing better to do."

At least he has more guts than you, Vandana wanted to say. You can't even show courtesy towards a woman you're going to marry. And this guy risked his life to protect a person he didn't even know.

"I hope they arrest him, clean his face and put him to shame," said Raghu.

"Really? So would you have rather the girl got raped and disfigured?"

"There must be something else behind the story," said Raghu. "If she were from a decent family, she wouldn't be out all night. She probably deserved it."

Vandana looked at him in disbelief. She could have argued her head off and put him in his place. But she would just be wasting her time. This man obviously was not sensible enough to even have a conversation with, let alone a debate. But she had to say something.

"The girl was saved and that's what's important," stated Vandana. "That girl could have been me. Then what would you have said?"

"A girl like you wouldn't be out all night," he said defiantly.

Go to hell, thought Vandana. Why was she even talking to him? She went back to her novel. They sat in silence for 10 minutes after which Vandana's father returned from work. She was grateful for the diversion and went into the bedroom, closing the door behind her.

She sat up in her bed and looked out of the window at the distant railway tracks. Rail Man must be out there somewhere. She wondered what he was like in person. Vandana kept painting a picture of him in her head, but then erasing it to form a new one. She decided that she would like to meet him. He was a true hero, unlike any other guy she had seen or met.

# 19

TV CHANNELS WERE PROCLAIMING RAIL MAN AS A
superhero. For me, superheroes were in a different league altogether,
just like the ones in Hollywood. I had never intended to become one
but now I would have to live up to it. Destiny had chosen me in an
unusual way to carry out a certain responsibility and I would have to
do it to the best of my ability.

All the American superheroes had some special senses which
enabled them to arrive at the scene of crime in the nick of time. But
how would Rail Man find crime? Or how would crime find him?

I realized I needed a strategy. I was Rail Man. Rail Man's home
territory was the railway tracks. But the railway tracks stretched from
one end of Mumbai to the other. How would I cover the entire
length of the tracks and be at the right place at the right time?

I knew I would have to be careful. I had watched the news and Rail
Man was gathering publicity by the hour. The police had launched a
manhunt with the assistance of the Railway Protection Force to
apprehend the "crazy criminal." I decided that for starters, Rail Man
would have to stick to the railway tracks outside the colony so that I
could run back to the safe confines of home if required.

I had spent the entire day at Santacruz market, shopping for the right
kind of black face paint. I figured that it would be safer to shop away
from home since no one recognized me here. I had been to both
hardware stores and stationery shops, but when I read the
instructions on the paint containers I saw that they were not meant
for the skin, let alone the face. The other options, such as house
paint, would never come off and water colours would never stay on.
Rail Man would need something more solid.

I was heading back through the busy Santacruz station road
when a flimsy make-up shop caught my attention. Instinctively, I

walked towards the shop.

The shop had a counter which was manned by an old man. He was swatting flies when he noticed me in front of the counter. The man put his swatter down and looked up at me.

"Yes," asked the man, "what can I get you?"

"Face paint."

The man smiled. "What colour?"

"Black."

The man retreated back into the store and returned with a small boxed packet.

"Here," he said, "black pancake."

I was puzzled. I had heard of pancakes as a part of breakfast but never for the face.

"I need face paint," I said.

"What do you need it for?" asked the man.

"To paint the face." Some people just didn't get it the first time, I thought to myself.

"Then this is what you need," said the man, with forced cheerfulness. "It is black pancake. Actors use it all the time. Just smear it onto the face and it stays all day. Then wash it off. Simple."

I thought about it. It sounded perfect.

"How many do you need?" asked the man quickly.

"How much?" I counter-questioned.

"60 rupees a box."

"Give me 10," I said taking out the money from my secret pocket.

City crimes were so frequent that their media impact lasted only for a day or at the most, two. Then they were replaced by a new headline. But a week had passed since the *Holi* incident and Rail Man was still the talk of the town. This was one of the few instances in which a senior person of the press was the direct victim of a crime and she was not going to let the people of Mumbai forget about it.

A full-length, front page article had appeared in *MiD-DAY*, the city's widely-read afternoon daily. In it, Shoma had called Rail Man "the superhero that Mumbai needs." The article was so impressive and well written that I had to read it five times to understand it completely.

Shoma had compared Rail Man to political greats such as Mahatma Gandhi who had fearlessly awoken the patriotic spirit in every Indian and successfully guided the country to independence from the British rule. Every ordinary Indian has a chance to do something great for their country, but they were either too scared or too self-absorbed in their own lives. She went on to say that Gandhiji and Rail Man had taken their chances and every Indian should be like them.

The TV media had come up with a cartoon sketch of Rail Man. Usually such sketches were created for criminals but this was the first time it was created for a superhero.

The politicians had a different take on the entire incident. They put further pressure on the police to bring "this cartoon character" to justice. Maybe they couldn't tolerate media attention being taken away from them. As a result, heavy police vigilance had been installed at the suburban railway tracks. Any suspicious character was searched and interrogated but the police came up with nothing. They were further criticized and then overnight, were recalled to handle more serious matters. And the issue died down completely.

During this time, I spent my days either in the movie hall or sitting by the sea face on Carter Road. My thoughts alternated between Rail Man and Vandana. I had not seen Sikander in days but was sure that my friend was doing my work for me. I hoped that Vandana felt the same way about me. And I was almost certain that my secret identity as Rail Man would help me further.

My thoughts took me to Bandra Station and I waited outside. This was the time that Vandana usually came home. I waited the entire evening as I had on previous days, but there was no sign of her.

That night, I sat patiently on my bed while my family was having dinner in the living room. I usually ate leftovers from the small refrigerator after they had finished, as I preferred eating in peace.

I changed into Rail Man's clothes and kept a packet of the black pancake in my pocket. My family had finished dinner and were chatting excitedly, at the dining table. I decided to skip dinner, rather than get trapped in their derisive remarks, and noisily walked out of the house, heading purposefully for the tracks.

The trains were running at great speed. I was careful to walk at a safe distance from the tracks. I covered the entire distance from Bandra to Vile Parle, but neither did I hear any cries for help nor did I see a situation that demanded Rail Man's intervention. I gave up and jogged from Vile Parle back to Bandra towards the railway colony.

I took one last look around before entering the colony. But all I heard was the sounds of the trains moving speedily past my line of vision. It wasn't a day for Rail Man, I thought, as I called it a night.

# 20

SIKANDER WAITED RESTLESSLY IN HIS CAR PARKED outside Bandra station. He fiddled with his stereo system while glancing impatiently at the gates of the railway colony. He hated being made to wait. Usually he was the one who kept women waiting.

Finally she appeared. Dressed in a mini-skirt, like Sikander had told her to, Sonal looked very attractive and inviting. He shifted in his seat in anticipation.

He wished that Sonal could get out more often. He knew it would save him a lot of money on prostitutes. But the fact that she had managed to leave her house at 9 in the night, that too in a mini-skirt, instilled in him a fleeting sense of admiration for her.

She hugged him as she slid into the seat beside him.

"Hi *jaanoo*," she said, planting kisses on his face. "I love you so much. I missed you."

"I missed you too," he said quickly, putting the car in gear.

They drove towards Juhu. Within 10 minutes, they found themselves stuck in a huge traffic jam. Sikander took it as an opportunity to indulge in some foreplay and save time.

"Tell me sweetheart," he whispered in her ear, as his hands were finding their way below her skirt. "How did you manage to get out of the house in such a sexy mini-skirt? What did your parents say?"

She giggled and then moaned. "I stepped out in jeans and then changed on the staircase. I told my parents that I'm going to Vandana's house. Are you proud of me?"

The thought of Vandana made Sikander suddenly more aggressive. He quickly pulled her T-shirt off.

"What are you doing, Sikander?" she exclaimed. "We're in the middle of traffic!"

"I know, love," he smiled sneakily. "I just want every memory with you to be exciting."

Suddenly there were horns blaring. Sikander looked ahead and saw that the traffic was moving.

"Shit," he said and took his hands off her.

He drove into a secluded by-lane in Juhu and parked.

He turned towards Sonal who was half-naked and immediately started fondling her breasts. She caught his hands immediately and pushed them away.

"What happened baby?' he asked.

"This is all we do," she said, finding her voice. "You pick me up, we make love and then you drop me back. Where's the romance?"

"What do you mean, sweetheart? This is romance. This is the ultimate romance for two people in love."

"No, it isn't," she said, putting her shirt back on. "You never take me out for a film, or dinner. That is romantic."

"But sweetheart," he said placatingly. "You have problems getting out of the house. I would love to take you out but you can't be seen with me. That's what you said."

"Have you ever asked?" she asked curtly.

That was true. He had never asked.

"I told you that I have problems being seen with you inside the colony, not outside."

"I'm sorry sweetheart. I really love you."

She simply stared ahead.

"I'll make it up to you," he persisted. "I'll do whatever you want from now on."

She smiled and turned towards him. "Really?"

"Yes sweetheart, really. Now please let's finish off what we started. The night won't be complete until I make love to you."

She hugged him and guided him towards her. He lifted up her

skirt and pulled down her panties. Sikander entered her forcefully and in a matter of minutes, it was over for him. But she let him go only after kissing him passionately.

The silence between them was broken by a loud tap on the car door. They quickly separated and saw the source peering into the window. It was a policeman. Behind him stood his police jeep with the engine running.

He tapped again. Sikander zipped up his pants while Sonal wore her clothes as quickly as they were taken off. Sikander rolled the window down.

"Get out of the car," ordered the policeman.

Sikander got out. Sonal remained seated in the car, shaking with fear. The last thing she wanted was having her parents come pick her up from the police station. She saw Sikander talking to the policeman, gesticulating with his arms as he explained himself. Sikander took out his wallet and placed something in the policeman's waiting palm. Within minutes the policeman and his jeep were gone.

Sikander got back behind the driver's seat. He didn't say anything. It was obvious from his frown that he was seething with anger. This girl had cost him two nights of a good time. Plus she was getting too demanding. As he put the car in gear and drove off, he decided he would never see Sonal again.

Rail crime was reported every day in the newspaper's crime section. But I didn't come across any suspicious activity in the vicinity of the tracks in Bandra. The crimes were happening at farther stations or right in the trains. A gang of chain and purse snatchers had been reported on the local trains at Borivali, but I couldn't take the risk of being seen so far from home.

I was now walking along the tracks in Bandra in the dawn hours of Friday. Instead of lying awake in bed, I had decided to utilize this time in furthering my purpose. The trains were running at full schedule as daylight broke.

A huge stench filled my nostrils. A group of men were squatting on the other side, unloading themselves for the day. I quickly walked ahead. When the freshness of the morning filled my nostrils again, I slackened my pace.

I was on the east side of Bandra now. I carefully crossed the tracks, to the other side, and found myself on a secluded side road. A milkman on a cycle passed me. The road was too narrow for a car to drive through. I sat down on the side of the path, against a wall. I was tired and hadn't slept well all night.

I put my head between my arms and rested them on my knees. I needed a power nap and then something to eat if I was to get through the day.

I awoke with a start. I heard a pair of heels running past me. I let it pass and tried to sleep again. But within seconds, I heard a more aggressive set of heels whizzing past me shouting abuses. I managed to catch the glint of a sword, a knife and other weapons in their hands as they rounded the corner and disappeared. Then it became silent again except for the sounds of the passing trains.

I stood to full attention and stretched out. My legs had fallen asleep but I managed to limp in the direction of the running men, soon breaking into a sprint. I rounded the corner and the only path was a straight *gully* ahead. I covered the distance in huge leaps till I reached a T-junction.

One road led to a fence that partially concealed the railway tracks. The other path led into an old three-storied building. That was the obvious direction since there was no way that the group of men could have crossed the tall fence by the time I got there.

I ran towards the building but stopped outside the rusted gate for a quick second and took the black pancake out of my pocket. With the cotton inside the packet, I smeared my face evenly and quickly checked myself in the side mirror of an Ambassador car.

I carefully packed the pancake back into my pocket and ran into the building compound. On the way, I picked up an idle brick. As I entered, a window banged shut on the second floor. This was followed by more sounds of windows shutting till the colony looked completely uninhabited. From Hindi films, I knew that these were the reactions of people wanting to shut themselves away from a monstrous act about to be committed. I had reached my destination.

I heard a commotion from inside the building and ran towards it. A small, balding man in a safari suit was being held up by a dangerous-looking man in a *pathani* suit against the wooden door of a ground floor flat.

"Hey!" I shouted.

They all turned around. One of them started laughing and the others joined in. There were four of them and each one looked more dangerous than the next. They all had weapons clenched tightly in their fists.

They left the man and walked towards me. I stood still. They stopped five feet away from where I stood. I kept the brick concealed behind my back.

"Too bad you saw us," said one.

"Looking at your appearance, no one is going to miss you," said another, still laughing. "*Bhai*, let me finish him."

One man nodded. He must be *Bhai*, I figured. The laughing man advanced lazily and pointed his sword at me, the blade touching my shirt. I slowly counted under my breath...1...2...3. In a quick motion, I brought the brick out and smashed it on the laughing man's forehead. His laughter changed to a smile and then to no expression as he dropped his sword and fell to the ground unconscious.

The other men rushed towards me and I quickly turned around and ran. They had geared themselves for a fight and I knew that my trusted weapon, the element of surprise, would not work just yet. If I ran outside the gate, they would chase me. If I managed to escape, what purpose would I have served? And Rail Man's purpose was to serve justice.

I changed my direction using the parked cars in the compound to keep a safe distance from them. With the help of a parked car against the wall, I climbed the bonnet onto the roof and heaved myself over the 10-foot concrete wall. I landed on a long stretch of marshy land filled with 2-foot-high, wild grass. I felt around the turf. My hands found a broken bottle. I was careful now not to lose my weapon. If the brick hadn't smashed, I wouldn't have had to run. I leaned against the wall and waited.

A full minute passed before one of the men idly climbed over. He hung on my side, his legs dangling in the air, and was about to drop when I grabbed his legs and pulled him hard, bringing him crashing down. Before the man could regain his senses, I smashed the broken bottle on his right temple. The bottle didn't crack but his skull did before he passed out.

Within a minute, the second guy started coming over. He was calling out, "Irfan, Irfan." Then he said to his side of the wall, "He's not replying *Bhai*. I think he's chasing that crazy guy."

"You go," barked *Bhai's* voice.

The man quickly dropped himself to the ground. He turned around in time to see my bottle swinging at him. He ducked in time. The bottle hit the wall and smashed into pieces.

"*Bhai*, the crazy guy is here," he shouted. "I'll take care of him."

We circled each other carefully. The man felt in his pocket and produced a *rampuri* knife. With a quick flick of the wrist, he flashed it open and swung it at me. The knife sliced into my sleeve and a thick line of blood trickled down my forearm. I looked at my shirt and got angry. I hated it when anyone damaged my favourite shirt.

I threw myself at the man, not giving him enough time to swing again. The man's back smashed against the wall and the knife fell from his hand. I held him there with one hand clutching his neck, and with the other hand, punched him repeatedly on his face and stomach. The man tried to hit back but he had no room to deliver his punches with force. I kicked him on the groin. The man dropped to the ground in pain. I kept kicking him wildly on his face, stomach and back till he passed out.

I waited for *Bhai*. 10 minutes had passed but no sign of him. Either he had run away or he was still there, silently waiting for me. I looked down at my arm. The wound was stinging now but luckily the knife hadn't cut deep.

I wanted to go home and rest, but first I had to make sure that the victim was in safe hands. That was Rail Man's responsibility.

I threw a stone over the wall. I heard some activity, which sounded like the shuffling of a pair of feet. That meant that *Bhai* was still there.

"Come here if you have drunk your mother's milk, you blackfaced coward," shouted *Bhai*.

I looked to both sides. My eyes rested on some old tyres around a 100 meters away on my side of the wall. I silently ran towards them.

I stacked some of the tires against the wall and climbed over the wall with ease, taking a muddy wine bottle with me.

I landed in another building complex. I ran the entire length of the wall and then turned left till I reached the exit gate. A uniformed watchman shouted at me as I darted out.

I was now on the same road that led to the three-storied building. I entered silently and saw *Bhai* with a hockey stick in his hand. He was facing the wall, with his back towards me, and hurling abuses.

I walked straight in *Bhai's* direction. He turned around and saw me when I was just 20 feet away. There was a look of alarm on his face.

"Where are my men?"

I remained silent.

"Where are my men?" he demanded angrily. At this time, a resident opened a window but quickly closed it.

"They are resting," I said slowly.

"What do you want?" asked Bhai uncertainly, now in a softer tone. "Who do you work for?"

"I am Rail Man."

Bhai saw a deadpan look in my eyes. With the black paint, I must have looked even scarier.

"Listen, we have taken the *supari* of Patel," said Bhai carefully. "I am willing to share it with you…uh…Rail Man."

I had come across the word *supari* in many Hindi films. It meant a contract to kill.

I kept staring at *Bhai*. He tried to avert my icy glare but couldn't. His expression immediately changed to one of anger. With a war cry, he rushed towards me. All this while the wine bottle was concealed behind my back. When Bhai was just five feet away, he was greeted with the smashing of the bottle on the side of his head. The sound of the hard impact resonated in the entire building. *Bhai* fell to the ground and made no further attempt to move.

I dropped the bottle and ran towards the building entrance. The victim, Patel, was lying in a pool of blood. I felt something rushing up my throat but nothing came out. Covering my mouth with one hand, I banged desperately on all apartment doors of the ground floor with the other hand, but no one responded. I ran frantically outside the building and shouted but no response from any of the shut windows.

I rushed back inside and tried lifting Patel. He was a small man and I could hold him up in the first attempt. His face and clothes were bloody. I could hear him breathing heavily. He was alive.

I checked his clothes to see where he was bleeding from. On opening the first few buttons of his safari suit, I saw a stab wound stare back at me from his chest.

The sensible thing for me to do would be to run straight home and get away from the crime scene. But the right thing for Rail Man to do was to take this bleeding assault victim to the hospital. And now I was Rail Man.

I lifted Patel onto my shoulders and walked out of the building. A *rickshaw* had just parked outside and the occupant was paying the driver. When the driver saw me carrying a lifeless, bloody person, he quickly started the three-wheeler and raced outside the building taking the occupant with him.

I jogged outside the gates with the added weight on my shoulders.

I managed to take a quick look at my watch. It was 6:30 in the morning. I bolted towards the sound of traffic. As I rounded the corner, I saw a *rickshaw* parked on the side. The driver was snoozing in the front seat.

I carefully placed Patel in the backseat and sat next to him. Then I shook the driver awake. The driver woke up with a start. He saw us through the rear view mirror and jerked his head around.

"What is this?" he shouted. "Get out! Get out!"

With a quick motion of my hand I caught the rickshaw driver's neck and squeezed. The driver coughed. I held my grip.

"Drive," I ordered.

"Who are you?" he asked.

"Rail Man." The expression of alarm on the driver's face eased. He nodded his head and started the *rickshaw*. To be safe, I held my grip on the driver's neck. As we joined the steady flow of cars on the main road, a police jeep and ambulance passed us.

We reached the emergency ward of Bhabha Hospital in Bandra, in a record time of 12 minutes. I lifted Patel out of the *rickshaw* and started walking up the ramp, amidst stunned onlookers, when a doctor crossed our path and ordered a nurse to get a stretcher.

Within minutes, the unconscious Patel was put on a stretcher and he disappeared through double doors. There were many people in the waiting area and they all looked anxiously at me, the black-faced man with longish hair.

A child whispered to her mother, "Rail Man."

The word spread and soon a circle formed around me. I turned to head out but was blocked by a nurse.

A young, pleasant-faced doctor came rushing out of the double doors.

"Who brought him here?" he asked the nurse.

The nurse silently pointed at me.

The doctor looked at my black face. But he had no time to make character analyses.

"What happened?" asked the doctor.

I wanted to relate the whole incident to the doctor, but all the words jumbled up in my head.

"He was stabbed," I said.

"I know," said the doctor impatiently. "But who stabbed him?"

"I don't know."

"You will have to wait till the police get here," said the doctor. "They will need your statement."

The black pancake on my face probably hid my alarmed expression.

"No," I said.

"Excuse me?"

"No!"

I turned around and ran. I was relieved to see the *auto rickshaw* driver waiting. I got in and was surprised to see that the seat was sparkling clean. No sign of blood. The *auto rickshaw* driver beamed at me through the rear view mirror. We pulled out of the hospital compound and got lost in the Mumbai traffic.

"I have heard about you," said the *auto rickshaw* driver. "You were all over the news. I know who you are."

I stared at him. The driver averted my stare to concentrate on the road.

"We need people like you in this city," continued the driver, with mocked concern. "This city has gone to the dogs. No safety. No security."

I kept staring at him.

"Tell me something, Rail Man," said the driver. "Why are you doing this?"

I remained silent.

"By the way, where do you want to go?"

"Bandra Station railway tracks."

"Ok."

We drove in silence for awhile. Then the driver spoke.

"I can keep all of this a secret. I won't tell the police anything, if you tell me who you are. Just show me your face."

The driver smiled at me. I returned his smile with an angry glare.

When we reached the Bandra station road, I guided the driver to turn left into a gully. The driver parked the *rickshaw* and got out along with me.

He looked at me and started laughing.

"You know, you're a cartoon. Come on, tell me who you are."

His laughter turned into gasps as I clasped his neck with a solid grip.

"Don't tell anyone," I said, staring into his eyes.

A few bystanders came closer but I kept my grip.

"I promise, Rail Man," choked the driver, "I won't tell anyone."

I immediately released his neck and ran towards the railway tracks.

My family was having breakfast in the living room by the time I got home. I entered the house silently, wiping my face clean on the way, and went straight into my bedroom. I took off my bloody clothes, tucked them under my bed, and changed into a red shirt and another pair of blue jeans before walking out of the house again. It was 8 o'clock in the morning and Dr Desai's clinic would open in half an hour. I figured I would need a tetanus shot and maybe some stitches for my knife wound.

## 21

THE SITUATION THAT RAIL MAN HAD ENCOUNTERED was dangerous and I realized that I could have got myself killed. For some reason, that didn't deter me and I felt more charged than ever.

I followed the news on TV but there was no report of the incident. I went to the Bandra Station newspaper stand and looked through all the dailies. No reports. The only major headline was a proposed increase in fuel prices.

I realized I couldn't go on like this. I couldn't be Rail Man all the time. Apart from Vandana, Rail Man was all I seemed to be thinking about these days. I needed another identity and all these years being just Babloo had given me no identity at all.

All superheroes had a real life image and a day job. They were normal people in everyday life. I figured I needed a real job.

It was a busy afternoon outside Bandra Station as I pondered on how to solve this problem. I had tried looking for a real job but hadn't been able to find one. What kind of job could I get now?

Again a Q & A session began in my head. Within minutes, I snapped out of it and headed towards my father's office.

I walked straight to my father's desk. Papa was concentrating on a file open in front of him. I waited patiently for a few minutes. When Papa turned the page, he looked up and saw me towering over him. He closed the file and folded his arms.

"What is it?" asked Papa.

I simply stared at him.

"Babloo, don't waste my time. What happened? Why are you here?"

"I have come to work."

"What?"

"I have come to work."

Papa's lips twitched into a slight smile but he quickly controlled it.

"So you're saying that you want to take that office boy job?"

I stared at my father.

"Babloo, answer me," Papa said, in an irritated tone.

"Yes."

"Are you sure?"

"Yes."

"Wait here. I'll be back."

Within 10 minutes, Papa was back. I hadn't budged. I was standing in the same place and position. The other clerks in the office all had their eyes on me.

"Come with me," said Papa.

I followed him a few steps to a cabin that had GUPTA and some initials imprinted on the glazed glass. Papa opened the door and I followed him inside.

"Hello Babloo," said Mr. Gupta, from behind the desk.

"Hello."

"Your father tells me that you have come to work with us. Take a seat."

Papa and I both sat down.

"So how are you Babloo?" smiled Mr. Gupta. "Where have you been? I didn't see you on the day of *Holi* either."

I was busy being Rail Man and serving justice, I wanted to say.

"I was busy," I replied.

"Ok," said Mr. Gupta. "So are you excited about your brother's wedding?"

I was far from excited. I felt sorry for the poor girl whose life was going to get ruined forever.

"You're not excited?" asked Mr. Gupta.

I remained silent.

"Babloo, answer Mr. Gupta," prompted Papa.

"I want to work," I stated.

"Ok," said Mr. Gupta animatedly. "That's good news. I have kept the job open for you. It's good that you want to work and help your father."

I'm not doing this to help my father, I wanted to say. I am doing this for Rail Man.

"So when would you like to start?" asked Mr. Gupta.

"Now," I replied.

"That's the spirit! Go outside and I will send Sawant to come and talk to you."

I remained seated.

"Babloo, go outside."

"But I want to work."

"Yes, you will work," said Mr. Gupta patiently. "But this is my office. This is where I work. You will have to go outside because your work is outside."

I got up and went outside. I was happy that I had solved Rail Man's biggest problem. Now, in my mind, Rail Man was a true superhero.

Sawant explained my responsibilities to me, which involved basic office work – making photocopies, transporting files from one desk to the other and occasionally running errands. In return, I would get paid 2,000 rupees per month, plus benefits. I asked Sawant whether the benefits included my own place of residence. Sawant laughed but I didn't find it funny. Rail Man needed his own house.

Sawant attempted to give me my uniform but I made no effort to take it. He disappeared for a few minutes and then came back and told me that Mr. Gupta had said that I didn't need to wear a uniform as long as I dressed decently.

My first day saw me signing many documents as per new employee procedure. I signed differently each time but the clerk didn't seem to notice. On one document, I had started signing as Rail Man but quickly realized my mistake and crossed it out.

Towards the later part of the afternoon, I was assigned my first errand to make photocopies of an important document. I managed to figure out the copier machine and finished my first task successfully. Rail Man's first real job assignment had proved successful.

I proudly took the copies back to the clerk who had assigned the task to me. When the clerk asked for the original, I realized that I had left it in the copier machine. He started scolding me in front of the rest of the office. But I kept staring at him and he stopped his ranting abruptly.

By the end of the day, I was tired. I left after Papa did and returned home much later at night after catching the 6 p.m. show of *Lady Daku* at Nandi theatre.

It was a dark, C-grade film about a female dacoit who used sex as a weapon. The woman was pathetic looking and looked even more repellant when she took her shirt off. Her stomach competed with her breasts in filling up most of the screen. What I couldn't understand was that if she was an armed dacoit, why did she have to use sex as a weapon? But the theatre hall was filled to capacity which indicated that the film was successful in its target market.

I reached home to be greeted by a total change in atmosphere. Ma seemed happy to see me, and Papa invited me to join them for dinner. But I was smart enough to understand their change in attitude towards me.

All these years I wasn't good enough to be treated as part of the family. Now why should one job change everything? I was not doing the job for them. I was doing it for Rail Man.

Besides, I wasn't hungry. I had filled myself with three sealed packets of popcorn in the cinema hall. I changed into my shorts and T-shirt and lay on my bed. The trains would not let me sleep for hours but Rail Man would have to stay indoors. The police would be looking for him.

I closed my eyes and let images of Vandana fill my mind. I let my thoughts take me to that familiar park bench with Vandana sitting by my side. That scene went on for hours till I fell asleep and my natural dreams took over.

# 22

THE NEXT MORNING RAIL MAN WAS ALL OVER THE NEWS. I got a whiff of it when I passed a group of colony residents chatting. Everyone was talking about Rail Man. They were listening to others' opinions and offering their own.

I stayed down in the colony for an hour hoping that I would see Vandana passing by. But I didn't. Where could she be? I decided that I would wait for a few days and then ask her father. I hoped that she hadn't taken my card the wrong way and was deliberately avoiding me.

I wanted to find Sikander and ask him what was going on. But that could wait. There were more important issues to attend to. Vandana wasn't going anywhere and Sikander had nowhere to go. I rushed back up to my house and snatched the morning paper from my brother's hands at the breakfast table.

"Hey!" shouted Raghu.

I took the paper and went to the balcony. This time the feature on Rail Man had hit the front page. It wasn't the main headline but it was still on the front page which featured only issues of national importance. Rail Man was really a superhero!

I read the article a couple of times. The article mentioned the entire incident in detail. Apparently, Patel had recovered and not only given the police a statement but had also addressed the press and given them the details.

Patel had no recollection of Rail Man but the doctors had related to him how, and under what circumstances, he was brought to the hospital. He expressed his gratitude to Rail Man.

Patel was a jeweller by profession. Apparently he had received extortion calls but hadn't given in to the threats. As a disciplinary measure, he was stabbed and left to die as an example to other extortion victims in the jewellers' community.

The injured assailants had been arrested from the scene, but were presently undergoing treatment under strict vigilance. They were admitted to Bhabha Hospital, the same hospital to which Patel was taken initially. The attackers had all suffered serious injuries. Patel was quoted, "They could suffer nothing less. After all they were beaten up by a superhero."

Patel went on to state that he and other members of the community had complained to the police in the past but were not offered any assistance. Now they were happy that some action had finally been taken and were grateful to Rail Man for that.

Patel's last quote in the article said, *"Rail Man, if you're reading this, I cannot even tell you how grateful my family is to you. As a token of appreciation, I would like to offer you a reward of three lakh rupees."*

My eyes popped out. Three lakh rupees was a lot of money but I knew that I couldn't reveal Rail Man's identity for any amount. I folded the paper and threw it on Raghu's face on my way to the bedroom. I quickly got ready and headed out for my second day at work.

All the news channels carried reports on Rail Man and the heroic way in which he saved Patel. One channel had employed actors and had created a dramatized reconstruction of the entire episode.

Vandana sat amazed in front of the television. An ordinary man, unarmed, had beaten up four men, single-handedly. It took more than strength to do that. It took guts to even face four armed men.

Vandana watched the entire dramatization – the way Rail Man had hit the first man, who had a sword, with a brick. He had then cleverly dodged the other three through parked cars and leaped over the wall. It took shrewdness on Rail Man's part to use the wall as a means to fight them one by one as they jumped over the wall to catch their only witness to the attempted killing. Rail Man was not only strong but also smart – two qualities that Vandana dreamed of in her ideal man. However he was very violent. He had cracked two of these mens' skulls.

Vandana changed the channel to another news channel. The Commissioner of Police was addressing the press. He maintained that Rail Man had interfered with the police department's work.

*"The Police department has always been successful in controlling crime in the city. Statistics show that over the years, crime has decreased and Mumbai has become a safer place. The police are doing their job. As soon as a criminal activity is reported, the police have always reached the scene on time."*

*"What do you have to say about Rail Man? Why is it that..."*

*"See, this person is a criminal. He has committed a crime by taking the law into his own hands. I strongly urge the media not to glorify him. He is not a role model but a dangerous element whom the police will eventually put behind bars."*

*"Sir, don't you think he should be rewarded? He has prevented two crimes."*

*"The first thing that a responsible citizen must do to prevent a crime is call the police, not take the law into his own hands. By doing so, he has become a criminal."*

*"Who do you think Rail Man actually is?"*

*"I have organized a special team to track this man. My experience tells me that he is a frustrated, jobless youth who is seeking his 15 minutes of fame. We have some leads on him and we shall do our best to catch him."*

*"What will the police do when they catch Rail Man?"*

*"He will be tried in a court of law like any ordinary criminal."*

Vandana changed the channel again. Filmmaker Manish Dutt was giving his views on the situation in a special talk show. He said that he admired the guts of this youth and would like to make a film on his story. At regular intervals, public reactions were being recorded on the street. College kids were wearing T-shirts adorned with black painted faces.

Vandana lowered the volume of the television. She found it all so silly – but at the same time exciting.

The doorbell rang. Vandana went to answer it. It was Raghu's mother. She had started making herself comfortable in the Gupta household and dropped in at all hours of the day.

Vandana regretted having quit her job. She wished she had been much stronger and stood up to her parents.

"Hello Beta," said Sudha, kissing Vandana on the forehead.

"Hello Aunty," replied Vandana.

"Where is your mother?"

"She's in the kitchen."

"Make yourself comfortable, Sudha," Madhu called from the kitchen, "I will be out in a few minutes."

"Do you need some help?" responded Sudha, seating herself on the couch.

"*Nahi, nahi*" said Madhu. "I am just finishing up."

Sudha turned her attention to the television. There was a caricature of Rail Man being displayed on the television screen.

"Such nonsense, this," said Sudha. "The media has nothing better to do. Some silly, retarded guy goes running around, pretending to be a superhero. He must be mad. He should be put behind bars.

"I wonder what our police is doing," Sudha continued. "They should catch this madman and punish him severely. It is not safe for decent people like us to step out of the house with a maniac like that on the loose. He should get a job, something respectful, like my Raghu. I am so proud of him."

"And what about Babloo?" asked Vandana immediately.

Sudha was taken aback and fell silent. Vandana always wondered why Mrs. Srivastav never spoke about Babloo. And at her parents' behest, Vandana never asked about him. But she didn't care anymore. Babloo had a good heart and as far as she was concerned, was a far better human being than his idiotic younger brother.

"Yes and Babloo too, of course." said Sudha.

"Aunty, how come you never talk about Babloo?"

Sudha looked down.

"What is there to talk about, Beta? Raghu's father and I don't know what to do with that boy. He does his own thing. He never listens to us. We have left his destiny to God. Even though he has just started working as an office boy at your father's office, we have no expectations of him. We know that he is not capable of anything."

"What do you mean, Aunty?" said Vandana defiantly. "Have you ever tried to understand him? Have you ever asked him what he wants to do?"

"What is there to ask, Beta? He has problems and we all know that. We have brought him up but beyond that, we cannot do anything for him. He himself does not want to do anything with his life."

"But isn't he trying Aunty? He even has a job now. He must have some dreams. How would you know if you don't even ask him?"

"What dreams can he have? His duty as a son is to fulfill his parents' dreams. Just like Raghu. He doesn't understand these things."

Vandana's mother came silently into the room and stood behind Sudha. She widened her eyes at Vandana. That was Vandana's cue to keep silent.

Vandana decided not to pursue the topic any further. It was obvious that Babloo was neglected. He had no support from his parents which was probably the reason for his lack of confidence.

She looked at the time. It was 5 p.m. She excused herself and went into the bedroom and within minutes, reappeared in a well-fitted, white shirt and tight dark blue jeans.

Both mothers were discussing their views on Rail Man. It was probably a hot topic in almost every household nowadays.

"Where are you going, Vandana?" asked her mother suspiciously.

"Just going out to get some fresh air," replied Vandana. "I'm going to Joggers Park, for a bit. I'll be back in time for dinner."

"Why don't you wear a *salwar kameez*?" asked Sudha. "You look so good in those."

Vandana controlled her anger. Who did this woman think she was to tell her how to dress? Vandana ignored her and averted her mother's glaring eyes. She walked out of the door, closing it behind her.

"Madhu," said Sudha, turning towards her, "do you think it's right to let Vandana go out dressed like that? She would attract a lot of attention. I hope I'm not coming across the wrong way."

"No, Sudha," said Madhu smiling. "Don't worry. Vandana is a well-brought up and sensible girl. This is how all youngsters dress today."

Sudha realized that she may have crossed the line and regretted having said anything. She wanted to play her cards right. She quickly turned the conversation to the safe topic of wedding preparations.

"Bandstand," Vandana instructed the *auto rickshaw* driver.

The date was 25th March, Sikander's birthday. When Sikander had spoken to her outside her door on *Holi*, he had seemed sincere and apologetic. She had decided that he regretted what he had done and he was not a bad person after all. She was the forgiving type and after putting much thought into it, she figured that everyone makes mistakes.

Besides, she knew that her fate was sealed and she would never be able to have a relationship with Sikander. But, at this point, she was very lonely and just needed a friend. Sikander was easy to talk to. He seemed to be on her wavelength and she did enjoy his company.

Besides, it was his birthday. The fact that he wanted to spend it with her proved that he needed a friend too. Vandana decided to let bygones be bygones and to start on a new note with Sikander – a note of friendship.

She was lost in her thoughts as the *auto rickshaw* turned into Bandstand. As usual, there was a small crowd gathered outside a majestic bungalow on the sea face. This was where film star Riyaz Khan lived. Every evening his fans would gather outside his house, hoping to get a glimpse of their favourite star. Sometimes, he came out and waved at his fans. This gave them something to remember and talk about for years to come.

Vandana knew that Mumbai was star crazy and that the media was responsible for it. The perfect example was the publicity that Rail Man had garnered. The city needed a new headline everyday to make their daily life seem worthwhile.

The headline would first appear at home in the morning newspaper. From there it would be carried by word by daily commuters on their way to work. At the workplace, it would be discussed at periodic intervals and during the lunch hour. By evening, the headline would have lost its charm. The next day would see something new. It was a vicious, never-ending circle.

But the scoop on Rail Man was different. Like many others, Vandana had been wondering who this person was and why he did what he did. His identity was mysterious and she had always been curious about the unknown. That was one quality that made her a typical *Mumbaikar*.

The sharp sun didn't seem to dissuade the Bandstand residents who were beginning to fill up the promenade. Vandana closed her eyes and breathed in the fresh sea breeze. It was intoxicating and calmed her senses immediately. The place had a positive effect on her and she was certain that the evening would go well.

The *auto rickshaw* pulled up outside the Barista coffee shop. About 10 feet away she saw Sikander's car parked. She looked at the time. It was ten to six. Sikander had come early.

Vandana paid the *rickshaw* driver and walked up the three steps into the open patio of the coffee shop. The place was crowded. All the seats were occupied with extra chairs pulled up at some tables. Vandana looked around but there was no sign of Sikander. She looked inside through the glass doors but couldn't spot him there either.

She went back to the road and looked at Sikander's parked car. It was definitely his car. But where was he? She carefully crossed the busy street and found her way onto the promenade. She found a clean area to sit on, which would give her a clear view of the coffee shop.

Men ogled at her as they walked past. She attracted attention wherever she went. But Mumbai was not like the West where guys would come over and speak to a girl. If it had been like the West in this respect, Vandana would have known a lot of people.

A well-dressed, decent looking, middle-aged man came up to her.

"Excuse me Beta, could you tell me how to get to Lilavati Hospital?"

"Sure," replied Vandana. "Go down Bandstand and take a right at the end. Follow the road to Bandra Reclamation and ask someone there."

Vandana knew that in a city like Mumbai, this was the only way to direct someone. The city was not well planned and there were too many by-lanes to give precise, complete directions. The best way was to give clear directions to a known point from where another helpful person would take over.

"Thank you, Beta," he said, but remained standing there. "My wife is very ill and I need to buy these medicines." He produced a piece of paper. "My ATM card isn't working so I can't withdraw from the bank till Monday morning. If you could help me out with 500 rupees, I'll send it back to whatever address you give me. God will bless you."

Growing up in Mumbai had acclimatized Vandana to such con men. Beggars came in many categories with different stories. This man took the cake, Vandana thought. Lilavati Hospital was one of the most expensive hospitals in the city. One needed to pay a huge deposit to be admitted and medicines were billed to the patient's account like most other hospitals. This man should have thought his story over.

"I don't have any money with me now. I'm sorry."

"Anything, Beta. Even a 100 rupees will do."

"I'm sorry, Uncle. I cannot help you out."

"God will bless you. My wife needs this medicine."

"Uncle, please leave me alone. I'm sorry I don't have any money."

This man was being polite to her so her good nature dictated that she reciprocate in the same tone. But she sensed her courtesy was being taken advantage of.

Suddenly Sikander appeared from nowhere and stood between the man and Vandana, facing the man.

"Hey Uncle," said Sikander sternly, "back off. No money here, ok?"

The man quietly turned around and walked away. He accosted a couple seated on a bench a few feet away.

"Looks like I came just in time," smiled Sikander. "I saved you from getting broke."

"What do you mean," exclaimed Vandana. "I wouldn't have given him any money."

"Sure you would have. You're a very nice and sensitive person. Anybody can figure that out just by looking at you."

Vandana broke into a smile. Sikander somehow always knew the right things to say.

"Happy birthday!" she said.

"Thanks. But please don't ask how I old I am."

"I won't," she laughed.

An awkward silence took over. They caught sight of a couple walking hand in hand past them. Sikander turned towards Vandana.

"Vandana,' he said. "Thanks a lot for coming today. It really means a lot to me."

"Come on," she said, nudging him. "I'm not going to let you spend your birthday alone."

"Thanks. Does that mean that you've forgiven me?"

"Yes. Maybe I overreacted. Maybe I gave you the wrong impression. As long as you understand I'm not that type of girl, we're ok."

"As long as you can trust me again, we're ok."

"Don't be silly! Of course I trust you."

"So friends then?" he asked.

"Always friends," she replied.

"The place is crowded," said Sikander, looking in the direction of Barista.

"Yes it is," she agreed.

"It's going to take some time till we manage to get a table."

"Let's go somewhere else," suggested Vandana. "We can't spend your birthday just waiting around."

"I'm sorry Vandana. But I'm not spending my birthday at Café Seaside!"

"Oh shut up!" she said.

"Where do you want to go?" he asked, as they sat in his car.

'Sikander, it's YOUR birthday! Where would you like to go?"

He started the car. "I don't know. Let's drive around for awhile. When one of us sees a good place we'll stop, ok?"

"Sure," she replied. "But we have to agree on something."

"What?"

"Wherever we go, I'm paying. That's my birthday gift to you. And I want no argument about that."

"Ok, ma'am."

They drove around for a while through Pali Hill, Carter Road, Bandstand and Mount Mary. They passed many familiar cars which seemed to be on similar, endless drives.

Vandana marvelled at the posh buildings and bungalows in Pali Hill. Many movie stars and affluent folk lived in this locality. Tall trees shaded the entire area giving it a sense of serenity. There were few people on the road, mainly out for evening walks. Vandana enjoyed the drive thoroughly till Sikander brought the car to a halt against the wall of a building in a quiet lane at the end of Pali Hill.

"Why have you stopped?" she asked curiously.

"The car heated up. I just need to keep the engine off for a while."

"You want to take a walk then?"

"No Vandana. I'm really tired. Let's just sit here for a bit and then we'll find some place in Pali Naka where we can get a coffee."

"Ok," she said cheerfully.

Vandana noticed that Sikander hadn't switched the ignition off.

"Sikander, won't the car get heated if you keep the AC on?"

"No," he said. "It just heats up when the engine is running."

Vandana didn't really find his answer convincing.

He adjusted his body so that he was facing her.

"So, where's my birthday present?" he asked.

"I'll treat you. I told you that I'll pay wherever we go."

"You didn't even wish me properly. You just gave me a handshake. How about a hug? It doesn't even feel like my birthday."

Vandana thought about this. A hug wasn't an unreasonable request. That was the most natural way to wish someone on their birthday.

She leaned towards him and hugged him. She withdrew after a few seconds but he held on to her. He pushed her back on her seat and was suddenly half on top of her.

"Sikander!" she screamed. "What are you doing?"

"I just want my birthday present, baby!"

He adjusted the lever next to her seat so that it instantly reclined to a 180 degrees. Now he was lying on top of her.

"Get off me, Sikander!" she warned.

"Why baby? Don't you want to finish off what we started?"

He proceeded to kiss her. She decided that she wouldn't cry. But she wouldn't give in either. She wasn't the naïve and vulnerable person he probably perceived her to be.

"I thought we were friends," she reasoned, tears welling up in her eyes, as she turned her head from side to side averting his kisses.

"Of course we're friends," he said between breaths. "Even friends have fun with each other. Come on baby."

She felt the bulge in his jeans pressing against her inner thigh. Why had she put herself in this position? She should have just been a good girl and stayed home. Putting up with her mother's nonsense was a small price to pay in comparison to this. Now she just wanted to go home. She silently prayed to all her Gods to somehow take her away from here with decency.

Sikander was trying to unzip her jeans and had taken his hands off her shoulders. She used this to her advantage. With all her force she pushed him, and the back of his head lightly hit the windscreen. She quickly unlocked her door and tried to push it open. But it hit the wall and didn't open more than a few inches. Sikander had shrewdly parked so close to the wall that she couldn't get out.

"Did you really think it was my birthday? You women are so stupid!"

Sikander let out an evil laugh. There was little that Vandana could do in that cramped space. She felt around helplessly, fighting back her tears. Sikander heaved himself on her again, furiously working on unzipping her pants. Her hands found her purse. She opened it quietly and felt around inside it until her fingers caught hold of her deodorant spray.

"Sikander," she said softly.

He looked up surprised. His eyes were met with a blinding spray. He tried his best to avert it. But the cramped space didn't prove to his advantage either. He shouted and shrieked as she sprayed half the bottle at his face.

He sat back down on his seat and rubbed his eyes, muttering a string of abuses. Vandana looked for an escape but she was still trapped. She waited patiently till Sikander got a hold of himself. He turned towards her, squinting his eyes, and caught hold of her hair.

"Sikander," she said calmly, now feeling in control. "If you hurt me in any way, I will go straight to the police. The best thing for you to do now is drive me back home safely and I promise I won't tell anyone about this."

Sikander remained quiet for a few moments, as he pondered over her words. Then he abruptly started the car and pulled out of the lane. They drove back to the colony gates in silence. He stopped the car and looked down.

"What you tried to do with me, don't you ever try that with any other woman," she warned authoritatively. "And don't you ever even try to talk to me again."

He looked up at her angrily. He stepped on the accelerator before she could open the door and drove straight into the colony.

"What are you doing?" she shouted. "Please drop me outside!"

He went around in circles, brakes screeching at regular intervals. He knew this would attract attention.

"You thought you could get away so easily? Everyone's going to see you with me now. Your reputation is screwed, Miss Perfect."

Vandana was alarmed. It was past 9 o' clock now and no one was around in the colony compound. But people would surely come out to their balconies to see who was creating the commotion.

"Please drop me outside," she begged.

"Who do you think you are, you bitch?" he hissed angrily. "You're getting married to Raghu and you come out to meet me. And when I make my move, I'm the one who is indecent?"

Vandana felt a tear rolling down her cheek. He abruptly brought the car to a halt in front of her block.

"See," he smiled wickedly. "I am a gentleman. Front door service."

She wiped her tears but didn't get out. She made one last request.

"Please drop me outside, Sikander. Please."

"Get out of the car now or I'll get out and create a scene. You're nothing but a tease. You deserve to be married to someone like Raghu. Get out!"

Vandana silently got out of the car and walked into her block with her head down. She sensed the anxious stares from the balconies around the colony.

Sudha Srivastav stared down in disbelief as she saw Vandana entering her block from a car in which there was a boy behind the driver's seat. And she knew for a fact that the boy wasn't her son Raghu.

## 23

I LEFT HOME IN HIGH SPIRITS. JUST A FEW DAYS AGO I had begun going to work and I didn't hate it as much as I had thought I would.

No one really bothered me at my new workplace. Someone would assign me a task and I would work towards it. If I messed up, the peon Raju would correct it. As a result, Raju was always rude to me. I never figured out that I was the source of his mood fluctuations. The way I looked at it, if I were made to wear a uniform all day, I too would be in a bad mood.

As I exited the colony, I stopped in surprise in front of a huge Amul hoarding that hovered over the Sarkari Bhandar building. Amul was the premium brand of butter in India. Every month, the company came up with a humorous yet witty advertising visual that tied the current topic of debate in the country into their product.

The animated hoarding featured a man with his face covered in butter, standing against the backdrop of the railway tracks. The hoarding read 'THE AMUL MAN – THE REAL MAN'. I looked at the hoarding for a good five minutes but didn't seem to get the connection. I gave up and headed towards Bandra Station, the place where Rail Man worked.

I entered the office and noticed that I was the last person to arrive. Everyone was seated behind their desks performing their usual duties, which mainly involved reading through files.

I was determined to find out more information for Rail Man. The two incidents that he had been involved in had come his way, purely by chance. It was just about being at the right place at the right time. But Rail Man couldn't always rely on luck to help someone in distress. He would need to have prior knowledge. This is where his day job would help him.

I had come to this conclusion when I compared Rail Man to Hollywood's super heroes. Rail Man's real job was that of an office boy in the Bandra Railway office and I had to make that work for him. I had decided to try and find out more about the railway crimes in and around Bandra Station, to make his work that much easier.

I finished making copies in the first half of the day. It was lunch hour now. Ma had told me not to eat with Papa but to come home for lunch. She said it would be inappropriate for an office boy to be eating with a Senior Railway Clerk. As far as I was concerned, it had always been inappropriate for me to eat with my father.

I usually ate from a sealed packet of biscuits at a canteen on the railway platform. But today I decided to skip lunch and do some groundwork for Rail Man. I headed straight for the file cabinet room and looked around.

There were about 10 steel cupboards standing in a line on one side of the room. The other walls were empty and I figured that they were meant to accommodate more steel cupboards as files accumulated over the years.

I opened the first cupboard and a stack of files fell out. I picked up the first one and opened it. I couldn't make sense of the handwriting on any of the pages. The same was the case with the other files. I looked for key words that would probably point to some crime but found none. Frustrated, I left the files there on the floor and walked out of the room. It was Raju's responsibility to clean the mess.

I approached the desk of the junior clerk, Kamble. Kamble kept to himself but was always nice to me. He looked up smiling.

"Hello Babloo. Enjoying your work so far?"

"Yes," I replied.

"Good," said Kamble and he looked back at his desk. He was comparing two files and making notes.

Kamble sensed that I was still standing there. He looked up.

"Did you have a question?" he asked.

"Yes."

"What is it?"

"Some files."

"What files?"

"Files on crime."

Kamble thought for a second.

"What kind of crime are you looking for?" he asked.

"Railway crime."

"Oh," said Kamble. "Who has asked for them?"

"Gupta," I lied.

"Well, I'm not sure exactly what files you're looking for. Ask Mr. Gupta which files he wants to see. Then come and tell me and I'll look for them in the file room and take them to him. Or if he's looking for the latest update, I will order them from the Railway Police office."

"Ok," I replied.

Kamble looked confused as he saw me head out of the office, in the direction opposite to Mr. Gupta's cabin.

I walked out of the station to the adjoining Railway Police office. The office was manned by one inspector and two constables at the time. I made sure they didn't see me and went into a room where an elderly man in plain clothes was seated behind a desk. He was reading a file. I wondered why everyone in government offices read files all the time.

"Hello," I said.

The man looked up at me, grunted and went back to his work.

"Hello," I repeated.

"What do you want?" barked the man, irritated. I noticed the man's nose hair protruding from his bulbous nose.

"I want files," I said.

"This is not a stationery shop," said the man sternly.

"I want railway crime files."

The man eyed me closely.

"Who are you?"

"I am from the railway office."

"Do you have an identification card?"

I had just received my identification card the previous morning. It indicated that I was a Government employee. My designation as an office boy was not mentioned anywhere. I took the card out of my shirt pocket and handed it to the man. He merely glanced at it.

"So you're from the Bandra railway office and want the latest reports on incidents reported on the Bandra railway territory. I haven't seen anyone from your office in months. It's good that the administration department is finally taking some interest in our work."

The man quickly got up and took a file out from a cupboard.

"Here. This has all the reports over the past two months. Who has asked for these files?"

"Mr. Gupta."

The man's voice took on a civil tone.

"Please tell Mr. Gupta that Krishna More has sent his regards. If he has any questions, please tell him to call me anytime."

I picked up the file and headed towards the door. Instead of walking back towards the office, I set off in the direction of my house, armed with my new, prized possession.

Sudha sat opposite Madhu in Madhu's living room. Madhu was filling her in on the building gossip. Sudha wasn't paying attention as she was waiting for the right moment to voice her concern over what she had witnessed the previous night. Vandana was sitting in the next room with the door closed.

"Madhu," said Sudha finally, "something has been bothering me since last night. And I feel I should tell you first before you hear it from someone else."

"What is it Sudha?" asked Madhu concerned. She was wary of conversations that started like this.

"Last night I saw a boy dropping Vandana home in his car."

Madhu was shocked but didn't show it.

"I was just concerned," continued Sudha. "She told us that she was going to Joggers Park alone. Then why did a boy drop her home?"

"I didn't know about this," said Madhu honestly. "I'll have to ask her."

"This has really been bothering me, Madhu. The whole building saw her getting out of that boy's car. I couldn't see his face. I thought maybe you would know."

"Don't worry, Sudha. He must be an old college friend of hers who gave her a lift home. Vandana is a very sensible girl."

"I know she is. I just thought that I should tell you. It has been bothering me. I wasn't able to sleep last night."

Madhu noticed the disturbed expression on Sudha's face. It was a genuine look of concern. There was no hint of suspicion.

"Sudha, you're like my sister," said Madhu soothingly, "and we're like family now. Our matters are your matters. Let me put your mind to rest now. Vandana!"

Vandana opened the door and entered the living room. She smiled at Sudha and looked at her mother inquiringly.

"Where did you go last evening?" demanded Madhu.

Vandana looked at Sudha. This woman must have definitely witnessed the car fiasco last night and brought the news to her mother. This lady seemed to have nothing better to do.

"I went to Joggers Park," said Vandana innocently.

"Who did you go with?"

"I went alone Mama. Why?"

"Sudha Aunty told me she saw you coming home with a boy."

Sudha looked away immediately. She had been hoping that Madhu would handle the issue tactfully without making her look like the bad person.

"Yes I did. So?"

"Who was he?" asked Madhu abruptly.

"I bumped into Ritesh, you know my old friend from college. And he dropped me back home. Why?"

"See? I told you," said Madhu, turning towards Sudha. "Nothing to worry about."

Vandana looked straight into Sudha's eyes. How dare this woman come into her home and try and create problems? If she was sensible enough, she would have not told Vandana's mother about it.

Vandana turned around and retreated to the bedroom, closing the door behind her. She looked through her phone book and tried to locate Ritesh's number. Her mother was unreliable now. She was very capable of calling Ritesh and finding out, even though she had never met him.

There was a knock on her bedroom door. She had expected the knock a few minutes later. She told her mother to come in. Madhu sat down on the bed as Vandana closed the phone book and put it on the side.

"Why do you sit here alone all day?" asked Madhu.

"What can I do Mama? Sudha Aunty is here all the time. I can't even roam around freely in the house anymore."

"Beta, she's a part of the family now. You can come and sit with us. In fact, most of the time we're discussing the wedding plans."

*That's the main reason I don't want to sit with you.*

"I'm fine here Mama. Really. Now tell me, what is it that you really want to talk about."

Madhu glared at her daughter. Sometimes Vandana could see right through her.

"Why were you out with a boy yesterday?" asked Madhu, with a sudden change of tone.

"I was not out with anyone. He dropped me home. I told you that!"

"Yes, but why did you take a lift from him? Were the *auto rickshaws* on strike or something?"

"Mama, what's wrong with taking a lift?"

"You are going to be married, that's what is wrong," said Madhu angrily. "A small thing like this is bad for your reputation. Do you understand? Sudha told me that the colony people have already started talking about you and that boy."

"Tell her to mind her own business."

"That's no way to talk about your mother-in-law! Show her some respect! She is only concerned about you!"

"She is not concerned about me, Mama. She is concerned about her silly son."

"He is going to be your husband."

"You want him more as a son-in-law than I want him as a husband," said Vandana defiantly.

"So are you saying that you're not happy with this marriage?"

"What do you think Mama? Of course I'm not happy!"

"Well, that's too bad. It's too late now."

Why am I even trying to reason with her, thought Vandana. Even her father didn't have a say with his headstrong wife.

Madhu got up from the bed. Before leaving she said, "You will hear about this from your father now," and closed the door behind her.

Vandana sat in the bedroom the entire evening. She heard her father come home. She heard her mother complaining endlessly to her father. But her father didn't come and talk to her. She knew that deep down he trusted her.

## 24

I SPENT THE NEXT TWO EVENINGS TRYING TO MAKE SENSE of the files on criminal activity in the Bandra Railway Police jurisdiction. It was all written in Marathi. I had studied Marathi in school so I could read the language but there were many technical terms that didn't make sense to me.

I read the first report over and over till I managed to understand it. It mentioned that there were frequent reports of stone-throwing from the slums situated by the railway tracks. There had been a few cases of serious injuries. The Railway Police had conducted serious enquiries into the matter with no success. Most of the incidents had occurred between 9 p.m. and 11 p.m.

I remembered the news report on television about the lady commuter who lost her eye as a result of stone-throwing. The thought still angered me now as it had when I had first seen it. Then, I couldn't do anything about it. But now Rail Man could. The files had proved useful after all.

It was 8 p.m., an appropriate time for Rail Man to start patrolling the area in question and catch the culprits red-handed.

I changed into a pair of jeans and a shirt and proceeded to do my push-ups. My muscles needed to wake up if they were going to get into action.

Pocketing the pancake, I headed into the kitchen. I wrapped some *sabzi* in two *chappatis*. When I turned around, Papa was standing there.

"Why can't you ever eat like a civilized person? Dinner will be served soon."

I tried to walk past him but the kitchen was too small for me to pass. I bent my head down and charged straight ahead. Papa moved to the side. He never knew how to react when I behaved like this.

By the time I reached the tracks I had polished off both the *chappati* rolls. There was room for more but I didn't want to fill my stomach. It would only slow me down. I proceeded to walk along the tracks towards Khar Station, where the huts in question were situated.

The trains were running at full capacity as people were still returning from their places of work. The sound of trains crossing each other was deafening and drove me crazy. But such sounds were not supposed to affect Rail Man. Rail Man always kept the larger picture in mind.

I reached the designated area. It was five past nine. I found a spot in the shadows and waited silently, staying alert for any signs of stone-throwing activity. Apart from the clatter of the passing trains and the sounds of television shows coming from a few of the tenements, I heard nothing.

For the next half hour, I kept looking up at the dark sky to see if I could trace any flying objects in the direction of the trains. Nothing.

By the time it was 11 o'clock I realized that this was not a day for Rail Man. I proceeded to head back in the direction of home.

As I neared Bandra Station, I saw the outline of two figures on the tracks walking towards me. The headlight of a passing train revealed the two figures to be police constables. They directed their flashlight at me as they approached. I kept my head down and tried passing them but was blocked by the *lathi* of one of the constables.

"*Thamba*," said the constable.

*Thamba* was the Marathi word for 'stop'. I stopped.

"What are you doing here?" demanded the constable.

I remained silent. The constable let the beam of his flashlight dance in my direction.

"What are you doing here?" asked the constable again.

I remained silent.

"Have you been drinking?" asked the constable, in a louder voice. He moved in closer and sniffed. Then he stepped back. The other constable was silent and kept looking at his watch.

"Who are you?" asked the constable. "Where are you coming from?"

The second constable now spoke. "Forget it Rana. Let's go."

"No Bhosle," he replied impatiently. "*Saaheb* told us to question any suspicious person that may look like Rail Man."

"Forget it," stated Bhosle, in an irritated tone. "We have been looking for that cartoon all these days and have questioned so many people. After all those news reports he is not going to be stupid enough to walk around the tracks. Look at this guy. Do you think he could be Rail Man? Do you think he could beat up four people on his own?"

Constable Rana looked at me closely. His expression indicated that he agreed with Bhosle.

"Let's search him," said Rana.

Bhosle sighed.

"Put your hands up," ordered Rana.

I stretched my hands up in the air. Rana felt my shoulders and patted me down till he came to my shirt pocket. He removed my identification card and directed the flashlight on it.

"You're a government employee like us!" he laughed. "Look Bhosle, he works for the railways!"

Bhosle showed no interest in taking a closer look at the ID card.

"Come on. Let's go home. Our duty is already over. Why are you wasting time?"

Rana put the card back in my pocket. My arms were still stretched upwards.

"You can put your hands down now," laughed Rana. "What are you doing here?"

I put my arms by my side and felt the black pancake resting safely in my jeans pocket.

"I am going home," I said, enunciating each word slowly.

"You shouldn't be going by this way," said Rana, "especially with a madman like Rail Man on the loose. He just might catch you and beat you up."

I looked at Rana as he laughed at his own joke. As far as I was concerned it wasn't funny. Rail Man didn't beat people up for no reason.

"Since you've been walking here, have you seen anyone suspicious?" asked Rana seriously. "Have you seen Rail Man?"

I remained silent. I looked straight into Rana's face. He held my gaze for a few seconds. Then he broke into a huge laugh.

"Stop wasting time," said an agitated Bhosle. "Let's go. We're getting late."

Rana waved and walked ahead with Bhosle.

"You will always remain a constable, Bhosle," Rana was saying, as they walked away.

I waited for both the constables to merge with the night before resuming my walk home.

## 25

SUNDAY WAS USUALLY FAMILY DAY AT THE GUPTA household. The three of them would have a late, heavy breakfast followed by an afternoon nap. In the evenings they would go out for a film and then an early dinner.

But now Sundays were not the same in the Gupta household. Ever since *Holi*, the Srivastavs made it a point to spend the entire day with them. The families would sit in the living room all day and after lunch, would suggest that the couple go out somewhere. Vandana had always made an excuse and stayed in.

But she decided that from today onwards, she would do things differently. After the incident with Sikander, Vandana had reconciled to the fact that the only man she would have to depend on would be Raghu.

She felt no attraction towards Raghu. And not only did she not enjoy his company, she despised it. But when she thought about it, how many women actually were in happy marriages? How many women were married to men of their choice? In India, so many women had no control over their fate.

Vandana had relied heavily on luck to change things for her. But who was she kidding? A distraction in the form of the fiasco with Sikander had shown her that her fate was sealed. And her fate was Raghu.

She decided to change her outlook towards Raghu. After all, they were from similar backgrounds even though she was much more liberated. But in reality, she was still the daughter of a government employee. And at the end of the day, one got married to someone from a similar family background.

When she thought about it, Raghu was not a bad person. He was just an idiot. And it would be her responsibility to smarten him up. It was a golden rule that opposites attract. And Vandana and Raghu were polar opposites.

Vandana decided that from that Sunday onwards, she would be nicer to him and make a serious attempt to get to know him. Fate had decreed him to be her husband after all.

The two families had finished lunch and were sipping tea. Vandana had made the tea and this time made sure that Raghu's tea was blended with extra milk, the way he liked it.

"How do you like the tea?" she asked.

"Very nice," Raghu said smiling.

Vandana brought her own cup from the kitchen and sat next to him.

"So how's your job going Raghu?" asked Shekhar.

"Very good, Uncle," said Raghu, putting his cup down. "I'm going to start my permanent position from April 1st."

"Very good," said Shekhar. "That's very good news. Amar, now that Raghu will start his new job, maybe it's a good time to set the wedding date."

"You took the words out of my mouth, Shekhar," said Amar smiling, "the sooner the better."

"Madhu spoke to our pandit. Madhu, tell Amar what the pandit said."

"Amarji," said Madhu. "Our pandit said that the *kundalis* are a perfect match. He set the date for May 10th. But that depends on what your pandit says."

Vandana should have been surprised that her mother had gone to the extent of matching horoscopes without her knowledge. But these days, nothing about her mother surprised her.

"We don't need to consult a pandit," said Sudha. "Your pandit must have decided carefully. May 10th is fine with us." She turned towards Amar. "*Kyon ji?*"

"Yes, yes," replied Amar quickly. "May 10th is fine. Now we should start the preparations. There's a lot of work to do."

"Amarji, what do you think Sudha and I have been doing every day?" asked Madhu, shaking her head from side to side. "We have planned everything. *Kyon* Sudha?"

"Yes," replied Sudha happily. "You men just do the bookings and leave the preparations to us. We have the wedding cards also planned out. We have even spoken to a printer. We were just waiting for the date to be fixed."

"It's fixed now," said Amar, looking at his wife proudly.

"Madhu, we have a lot of work to do starting tomorrow," said Sudha excitedly.

"Of course," replied Madhu, with equal fervour.

Shekhar turned towards Vandana.

"Beta, if you both want to go out please go ahead," he said. "We old people will keep talking like this the whole day."

"I don't know," said Vandana. "Do you want to go somewhere Raghu?"

"I need to digest my food," he said smiling. "I ate too much. Do you feel like going anywhere?"

"Let's go for a movie."

"You have to go where she wants, Raghu," said Amar teasingly. "This is just the beginning. You cannot disappoint your woman."

"Look who's talking," said Sudha to her husband, sarcastically. "How often do you take me for a film when I ask you to?"

They all started laughing.

Sonal closed the door of her house behind her that same Sunday afternoon. She had told her parents that she was going to Vandana's house and this time she hadn't lied. She ran up the two flights of stairs that took her to Vandana's floor.

Vandana and Raghu were getting ready to leave when the doorbell rang. Vandana opened the door to a visibly upset Sonal.

"Hi Sonal," said Vandana smiling.

"I needed to speak with you Vandana didi," said Sonal impatiently.

"We were just heading out. Why don't you come back in the evening?"

In the past Vandana was used to Sonal coming to her frequently for advice. She was surprised to see Sonal at her doorstep after a long time. Vandana thought that it would be one of their usual conversations about her career, college or boys. That's all Sonal ever wanted to discuss.

"Vandana didi. It's really important. I need to talk to you now. Please."

Vandana sensed the urgency in her voice. She looked over her shoulder. Raghu had sat back down.

"Give me a minute," she told the younger girl. "I'll be right down."

"Ok."

Vandana closed the door and went back in.

"I'm sorry," she said to everyone. "I forgot that I was supposed to meet Sonal this afternoon. She just came to call me."

"Who, Tripathi's daughter?" asked Sudha.

"Yes," said Madhu. "She looks up to Vandana as an elder sister."

"Raghu," said Vandana. "Can we please do this some other time?"

"Of course, please go ahead with your friend."

"Thanks," she said. "Mama, I'll be back soon. Bye."

They all said bye to her. She went out the door and found Sonal standing near the stairs, with a frightened look on her face.

"What happened?"

Sonal looked up with tears in her eyes.

"Should we talk here?"

"Yes sit down," said Vandana, concern in her voice.

Sonal sat down on the staircase. Vandana sat beside her. She could sense something was wrong. She had never seen Sonal so upset.

"Is it about your boyfriend?" asked Vandana.

Sonal was looking down. "Yes."

"Did you both have a fight?"

"No."

"Do you like someone else?"

"No."

"Is he not nice to you?"

"No."

"Sonal," said Vandana firmly. "What is it?"

"Vandana didi... Vandana didi..." Sonal broke into sobs.

Vandana hugged her. "What is it Sonal? Please tell me. I'm getting worried."

"Vandana didi... I'm... I'm..."

"Yes Sonal? Come on tell me."

"I'm pregnant."

Vandana let go of her suddenly.

"What?!"

"Vandana didi, I'm pregnant," said Sonal softly.

"Oh my God! How did this happen?" asked Vandana disbelievingly.

"I don't know."

"Are you sure Sonal?"

"Yes didi. I took a home pregnancy test and it was positive."

"Sonal, these tests can be wrong sometimes."

"I took three. And all of them were positive."

Vandana looked at Sonal. She had always been an innocent and naïve girl. Obviously she had got mixed up with the wrong guy.

"Is it your boyfriend?"

"Yes didi. He's the only one."

"How could you be so careless, Sonal?" chided Vandana. "Didn't you use protection?"

"No didi. I didn't know. I didn't realize."

"Ok ok," said Vandana soothingly. "Have you told your boyfriend about it?"

"No. I can't tell him. He may stop loving me. He might break up with me."

Sonal broke into sobs again. Vandana looked at her in amazement. She never thought that Sonal could be so stupid.

"You have to talk to him," said Vandana sternly. "This is his responsibility. Who did this?"

"I don't know if you know him, didi. His name is Sikander."

Vandana froze.

"Do you really think I should talk to him, didi?"

Vandana was still in a daze. She didn't reply.

"Didi," said Sonal. "If I tell him do you think he'll marry me?"

Vandana snapped out of her trance and looked straight into Sonal's eyes.

"Forget it, Sonal. Don't even bother telling Sikander. He doesn't care. In fact, he might go around telling everyone about it and spoil your name."

"No didi. He's not like that. He's very nice."

"Don't be foolish," scolded Vandana. "What world are you living in? That guy has no conscience at all. For him, all women are merely objects. He tried something funny with me too."

"With you didi?" asked Sonal surprised. "But he told me he loves me."

"He probably says that to every woman just to have sex with her. Grow up Sonal!"

Sonal looked down. The disturbed expression came back on her face.

"What do I do Vandana didi?"

"This is what you're going to do," said Vandana slowly. "You're not going to tell anyone about this. Give me a few days to find the best way to solve this problem. But you're not to meet Sikander at all, ok?"

"But shouldn't he know?"

"No, he has no need to know. First we have to take care of this. Go home now and don't worry about anything. I'll take care of everything, ok?"

"Ok."

Sonal got up and kissed Vandana on the cheek.

"Thank you didi."

After Sonal left, Vandana remained seated on the stairs. Sikander was such a slime ball. She was glad that she had protected herself from him. She was not weak after all. But now she had to help Sonal.

# 26

VANDANA SPENT MOST OF THE NEXT TWO DAYS leafing through the Gynecologist listings in the Yellow Pages. She zeroed in on Dr. (Mrs.) Khot's clinic located in Mahim, which was a safe distance from Bandra. She fixed an appointment for that evening.

Next Vandana explained the situation to Sonal. Sonal was alarmed at the thought of seeing a gynecologist. But Vandana explained to her that since the pregnancy had been detected early, a surgical abortion would not be necessary. There were special tablets that needed to be taken orally and would be 100 percent successful in doing the job within three days.

Vandana and Sonal went to the gynecologist that evening. Dr. Khot seemed to be a hardcore feminist and showed full sympathy and support for Sonal's situation. She provided her with the required medication and assured her that there was nothing to worry about.

When they emerged from the clinic, Sonal finally broke into a smile. She hugged Vandana.

"Thank you Vandana didi," she said gratefully. "I don't know what I would have done without you."

"You don't have to thank me Sonal. Just promise me that you will be careful in the future. Remember what the doctor said."

"I will. I promise."

"And promise me that you will stay away from Sikander and guys like him."

Sonal did not hesitate. "I promise."

"Good. Now this is our secret. And we will never talk about this to anyone."

"Thank you didi."

"Come let's go home."

"Didi, I'm going to my aunt's house in town. I just want to spend some time away from home. I already told my parents about it. I'll take the bus from across the street."

"Ok Sonal. Come home sometime. Stay in touch."

"I will," said Sonal.

She crossed the street. Vandana remained standing there and waited for an empty cab.

Mrs. Srivastav was elated that her son's marriage was now a close reality. On Sunday, when the wedding date was finalized at the Gupta residence, Sudha had decided that she would go on Tuesday to the Siddhivinayak temple in Prabhadevi to pay her respects to Lord Ganesha for answering her prayers.

She had been stressed all these days. Even though Madhu assured her that the marriage was finalized, she had been doubtful about Vandana. Vandana had seemed disinterested in the whole affair. But on Sunday, Vandana was very warm towards Raghu. And with the confirmation of the date, Sudha knew that the alliance was definitely confirmed.

Tuesday was considered the most auspicious day of the week for devotees to visit Mumbai's popular Siddhivinayak temple. Sudha stood in the long line that would rapidly advance towards the golden idol of Lord Ganesha. VIPs and film stars usually didn't have to wait in line and went straight up, but no one complained. The common public believed that Lord Ganesha listened to His true devotees only, the ones who waited for him.

Sudha got only a brief 10 seconds face to face with the Ganpati idol but that was all she needed to thank Him for His grace. She prayed quickly to the mighty elephant God under her breath, till she felt a slight nudge from the person behind her indicating that her time was up. The traffic was easier on the way down the marble path of the temple and within minutes, she was outside, amidst the thronging crowds. She crossed the road carefully to the bus stop on the other side of the road, and stood in the contorted queue of eager bus commuters.

Her bus to Bandra arrived within minutes. People immediately broke out of file, Sudha included, and rushed towards the empty bus. Despite the jostling, Sudha found herself a window seat.

She closed her eyes and took in the warm afternoon breeze that wafted in through her narrowly open window, as the bus lunged forward. Life seemed good. She looked out of the window and marvelled at the new high-rises nearing construction coming up in Prabhadevi.

The bus drove down Cadell Road from where it took a right turn to Sitladevi Road in Mahim. As it turned, Sudha saw someone familiar in the distance, standing on the footpath. She kept her gaze till the girl looked up. It was Vandana! And she was standing outside the entrance of an abortion clinic! There were no buildings immediately nearby and it seemed apparent that she had just stepped out from the clinic. Sudha kept looking at her till the bus passed the clinic and Vandana disappeared from her view. After that, Sudha looked straight ahead in shock all the way to Bandra Station.

She walked into the colony in a daze. She couldn't believe what she had just seen. Her suspicions had turned out to be true. Vandana was a girl of loose character. Either Madhu's parents knew of their daughter's association with other boys or Vandana did things on the sly. Either way, Vandana was not good enough for her son.

Now Sudha was in a dilemma. Madhu and she had become very close. All these years Madhu had come across as an arrogant and proud woman to Sudha. But when Sudha got to know her, she had turned out to be a very warm and genuine person. How could she, Sudha, be the one to tell Madhu about her daughter? She knew what she had to do.

She would have to think it over in the next few days. It was a sensitive issue for any mother, Sudha would have to find a way to break the news to Madhu very gently. And she would need Amar for support. It was a family issue now. Madhu and Shekhar would have to hear this together. And Sudha would have to bring up the topic tactfully.

Vandana lay down in her bed and stared at the ceiling. She was relieved. Things had gone well. She had protected herself from Sikander and helped Sonal. And she emerged from this whole mess without bringing any shame to her parents. She was still Papa's good girl.

After a long time, Vandana felt relaxed. At first she had resented her parents' decision. But now she came to realize that they were right in finding a partner like Raghu for her. He belonged to a decent family and would always be civil with her. Sikander, on the other hand, had just wanted her for a temporary fix. She had been wrong about him all along.

Vandana decided that she would not only do her best to be nice to Raghu but would also try and fall in love with him. She had blinded herself, paying attention only to his negative points. Now she would focus on his positive traits. She would make sure that from now on they were a team. Even if it meant teaching him how to dress or about general courtesy, Vandana would make an effort to do it all. By the time their wedding date arrived, she would be proud to be with him.

Vandana put out the lights and prepared herself for a night of peaceful sleep, which she hadn't experienced in days.

## 27

I SAT IDLY ON THE OFFICE BENCH TRYING TO READ an article in *The Afternoon*. There wasn't much work for me that day.

I stretched lazily and looked up from the paper at the employees in the office. This was their life. There was probably a superhero in all of them, as Shoma had mentioned in her *MiD-DAY* article. But their destinies had not called upon them to recognize it. I was not only the fortunate one, but also the chosen one.

I turned my attention back to the article. I had to go back to the beginning because I couldn't remember the 3 paragraphs I had been reading over the past 20 minutes.

The article was written by a renowned city psychologist Bharti Magnani. She had created an entire character sketch for Rail Man. She mentioned that Rail Man must have undergone some tragedy in his life which had caused him to vent through violence. The article went on to say that he was among the city's frustrated, jobless youths who had proved unsuccessful in all aspects of life and grew up as a neglected child. It was not bravery or heroism, she emphasized, but a case of mental instability. As far as I was concerned, Bharti Magnani had got only one thing right about Rail Man – the part where he was neglected.

The next page featured an article captioned thus – 'Patel being harassed by Rail Men.' It read that ever since Patel had announced the award of three lakh rupees to Rail Man, many men with their faces painted black appeared at his door claiming to be Rail Man. Patel had to install two private security guards outside his door to keep the imposters at bay.

I leafed through the pages and found another article titled 'Celebrities speak about Rail Man.' All the celebrities' quotes ridiculed and condemned Rail Man, except for my favourite actor

Riyaz Khan who said "*I am a naqli hero. Rail Man is an asli hero.*" I smiled. Only a real hero recognized another real hero.

"Gupta *saaheb* has called you."

I looked up from the paper to see the scowling face of the office peon, Raju.

"Gupta *saaheb* wants to see you now."

Raju walked away but kept looking back to see if I was on my way. If I didn't reach Gupta's cabin within the next few minutes, he would summon Raju again with the annoying buzzer.

I tucked the paper under my arm. I would need to carefully read the psychologist's article again later. I got up and walked towards Gupta's cabin. I didn't knock on the door and went straight in. My logic was that if one was expected, there was no need to knock. Only those who weren't expected needed to give some indication of their arrival.

Mr. Gupta was seated behind his desk, talking on the phone. He gestured me to a chair.

"Sit down," he said, putting down the receiver.

I sat down. Mr. Gupta had a serious expression on his face.

"Did you go to the Railway Police office and request a file on my behalf?"

I remained silent.

"Krishna More, the head clerk of the Railway Police called me and told me. Did you take a file from him?"

"Yes," I said.

"Why?"

I remained silent. I couldn't trust Mr. Gupta with my secret identity as Rail Man. I was doing it partly to make Vandana proud of me, but every superhero had to keep his secrets safe. Even from close ones.

"Babloo, did someone tell you to get that file for me?"

"No."

"Then why did you ask for that file? I don't remember having instructed anyone to get that file."

I stared straight into Gupta's eyes. He looked away from my intense gaze.

"Babloo," Mr. Gupta said softly. "Why did you go and fetch that particular file? This is something serious and I need to know."

"I wanted to learn," I said honestly. I decided I wouldn't reveal more.

"Babloo, it's nice that you're taking an interest in your job," explained Mr. Gupta. "But there are some things that you're not supposed to do. It's against the functioning of the office. Since it involves me, I'm going to let it go because we're like family. If it were anyone else, he would have got into a lot of trouble."

I was puzzled. Why had Mr. Gupta said that we were like family? Had Vandana told her father how she felt about me?

"I would like you to give that file back to More," he added. "I expect you to do it by tomorrow morning. And I won't remind you again. Do you understand?"

"Yes," I said.

"Good. That's all."

I remained seated.

"You may go now."

I left the room still wondering -- why had Mr. Gupta said that we were like family?

After work, I jaywalked across the road into the familiar gully that housed Nandi Theatre. The movie playing was *Pyaasi Sherni* – Hungry Tigress. From the poster of the film, I understood that the story was not about an actual tigress but a woman who had the spirit of a tiger. And her hunger was for sex. Another C-grade film.

In case of Nandi Theatre the saving grace, apart from it being close home, was that it showed a different film each week unlike the Gaiety Galaxy Multiplex, which ran the same film for many weeks in a row. The film was boring but had a somewhat interesting plot. A village girl's family was killed in front of her eyes by bandits. After that, the girl was gang raped. She decided to take revenge and adopted the fiery spirit of a tigress. She changed her appearance and used sex as her weapon to lure each bandit into her trap before killing him.

I reached home in time for dinner, which I picked up from the dining table and took straight to my room. While I sat eating on my bed, I picked up one of the Railway crime files and started looking for the next assignment for Rail Man.

All the reports featured isolated incidents but nothing close to the recurring nature of instances of stone-throwing. I closed the file in frustration. This file had been of no real assistance. Now I couldn't even get access to more files. Rail Man had no choice but to wait for crime to come calling for him.

I thought about the possibilities. Maybe I could create a secret signal for those in distress to call Rail Man. I would have to figure that out.

I lay in bed immersed in my thoughts. I had no intention of going walking on the the tracks at least for a few days. The brush with the two constables had been a close call for Rail Man. It made me realize that I had to think smarter for the sake of Rail Man.

And I had to find Sikander. Maybe Vandana had told him something. I was now determined to find out.

# 28

VANDANA LOOKED AT THE CLOCK. IT WAS 6:30 in the evening. Raghu would be there any minute to take her out for coffee. And she was actually looking forward to it.

She had decided on a strategy to smarten him up. First she would teach him how important it was to talk sensibly and pay attention to his table manners. Then, she would encourage him to read interesting books. Later on, she would take him shopping and change his entire wardrobe. And all through their courtship, she would make him take her to fun places.

Vandana's parents were in the next room. The doorbell rang. Vandana had a smile on her face before opening the door. She was surprised to see Mr. and Mrs. Srivastav. Raghu was standing behind them.

There was no cordial greeting from Raghu's parents as they entered without waiting to be invited. Vandana was confused. Raghu passed her without even looking in her direction. She knew something was wrong.

Vandana's parents appeared in the room almost immediately and greeted them. Sudha maintained the stone-faced expression that she had at the door. Amar forced a smile and then let it fade when Sudha glanced in his direction.

Vandana remained standing at the door. She sensed that something was amiss and for a second, contemplated walking out of the door and getting away from the situation. But she stayed on the same side of the door and closed it.

"What a surprise!" Shekhar was saying. "Come Amar, Sudhaji. Come sit. Madhu, make some tea."

Madhu turned and started heading towards the kitchen.

"We haven't come to sit," said Sudha abruptly.

Sudha's icy tone made Madhu stop in her tracks.

"What happened, Sudha?" asked Madhu. "Is there something wrong?"

"Yes, there is something wrong."

"Please come and sit down, Sudhaji," said Shekhar carefully. Sudha remained standing there.

"Is there something about your daughter that you haven't told us?" asked Sudha demandingly.

"What do you mean?" asked Madhu, in an equally harsh tone.

Amar now spoke. "Sudha, please tell them what you saw."

Shekhar and Madhu looked at Sudha enquiringly. Raghu remained standing behind his parents. Vandana was frozen with anxiety, standing in the same spot by the door.

"Did you think that you could get your daughter married to our good son to cover up her wild ways?"

Vandana was scared now. There was no way they could have found out about what happened between her and Sikander. She saw her father controlling his anger by tightly gripping the edge of the sofa.

"Please say what you have to say," said Shekhar sharply.

"Sudha, please just tell them what you saw," said Amar calmly.

Sudha looked around at everyone including Vandana and then took a deep breath.

"I saw Vandana coming out of an abortion clinic."

Madhu gasped. Vandana felt the blood rushing to her face both in anger and in fear. There was no way Mrs. Srivastav could have seen her there. It was just not possible.

Shekhar and Madhu looked at their daughter. But she didn't look down. She had no reason to. Her father understood that look on his daughter's face. It was a look that meant she hadn't done anything wrong. Shekhar turned to face the accuser.

"You saw her standing somewhere close to an abortion clinic and presumed that she went there? How narrow-minded can you be?"

The anger in his voice was obvious. The last time Vandana had heard that tone in her father's voice had been years ago when she had returned home late from a party. His anger was scary. It surfaced once in a blue moon but once it did, it was best for people to steer clear of him. Amar seemed to be aware of this because he took a step back.

"She did go to the abortion clinic," retorted Sudha. "Either you're trying to cover up for her mistake or you have no control over her. She has brought shame to your family and you're trying to protect her? What kind of father are you?"

"SHUT YOUR MOUTH!" shouted Shekhar.

A look of shock appeared on Sudha's face. She had expected Vandana's parents to try and clear out the matter and plead with them. Then she would listen to their explanation and decide. This was not quite turning out the way she had expected.

"How dare you come into my house and talk that way about my daughter? Do you know who you're talking to? Do you have any idea what you're saying ?"

"I know what I'm saying," said Sudha, finding her voice again. "First I see your daughter coming home with a boy at night. Then I see her outside an abortion clinic! Do you even know what your daughter is up to?"

"Calm down, Sudha," said Amar, seemingly alarmed at the way this was going.

"We have brought our daughter up very well," said Shekhar angrily. "If she came back with a boy that doesn't mean that she did something wrong. If she was standing close to an abortion clinic, it doesn't mean that she went there."

"Please ji," said Sudha sarcastically. "What excuses! Did you even ask your daughter once what she is up to before shouting at us?"

"I don't need to ask my daughter," Shekhar retorted. "I trust her completely. I don't even need to ask her based on what some outsiders say!"

"Oh, so we are outsiders now?" asked Sudha sarcastically.

"You don't even deserve our daughter," said Shekhar, his face turning red with rage. "Thank God we realized in time before we gave our daughter to small-minded people like you!"

"It is we who got saved and found out about your daughter's reputation in time. Your daughter is not worthy of our son. She would never have been able to keep him happy!"

Madhu finally spoke. "Sudha, what are you saying…"

"Get out!!!" shouted Shekhar, interrupting his wife. "I never want to see your faces again. I am breaking this alliance!"

"Please stop this drama," said Sudha spitefully. "Stop shouting just to cover up your daughter's mistake. Who are you to break this alliance? After what I saw, do you think we would let our son's life get ruined? We don't want this marriage!"

Sudha stormed towards the door. Amar and Raghu followed her silently. Sudha stopped and directed a look of hatred at Vandana. Then she turned towards Shekhar and Madhu.

"Who are you to throw us out of your house? You think that this is the end of this? Wait till the whole colony finds out what your daughter is really like. You just wait and see."

"Sudha, wait…" Madhu tried to say.

"Let them go," Shekhar said to her sternly.

They opened the door and slammed it shut after them. The sound resonated for a moment as they all stood in silence. Vandana's mother suddenly rushed towards Vandana. She grabbed her daughter's hair and pulled it with all her force.

"See the disgrace you have brought us, you stupid fool. We gave you so much freedom and see what shame you have brought us!"

"Let her go!" shouted her father. Vandana's mother's fiery expression changed to one of shock and she let go of Vandana's hair.

"Shekhar," said Madhu pleadingly. "I will go and talk to Sudha tomorrow. She has been misled. Let her calm down and I will sort this out."

"Don't you dare do that," said Shekhar angrily. "After the way they spoke about Vandana, do you think I'll give my daughter to a family like that?"

"Shekhar, don't say that. You're very angry now. Please calm down. The marriage has been finalized. It will make us look bad if it breaks off like this. The whole colony will find out."

"I don't care about the colony," said Shekhar, in a calmer voice. He turned towards Vandana who now had tears streaming down her cheeks.

"Vandana, come here. Sit down next to me."

Vandana sat next to her father.

"Papa, I'm sorry," she said softly.

"You have to be sorry if you are guilty, Beta. And I know you well enough to understand that you haven't done anything wrong. But I have to hear it from you first." He put his arm around her. "Don't be scared. Did you go to the abortion clinic?"

"Yes Papa. But it wasn't for me. I went there with a friend of mine. Sudha Aunty obviously didn't see her. Papa, I promise you. I haven't done anything that would make you ashamed."

"Who is this friend of yours?"

"I can't tell you Papa. I promised her."

"I understand. Don't worry. You don't have to tell me. I trust you Beta."

He hugged her. Vandana sobbed in his arms. Madhu felt tears welling up in her eyes.

"Papa," sobbed Vandana. "I'm sorry if I created a mess. I'm sorry if I upset you."

"Beta, you didn't upset me. They did. I judged that family wrongly. God knows what would have happened if you got married into that family."

Vandana was still crying. She loved her father so much. She was so proud of him. He had proved himself not only as a man of honour but also a good father; a father who loved his daughter and would do anything to protect her.

"Forget it Vandana," he said soothingly. "Let them say what they want to say. At the end of the day, it's the truth that people will believe. Don't worry about a thing. Papa will take care of everything."

Vandana hugged her father tightly. She never felt as safe as she did now.

Madhu witnessed the scene silently. Her husband's words raised a sense of alarm in her. She was a well-respected woman in the colony. It mattered to her what people spoke about her family. She secretly hoped that Sudha wouldn't take this further.

# 29

OVER THE NEXT FEW DAYS, SUDHA KEPT HER WORD and went out of her way to let the colony know that the alliance between the two families had broken up. And she over dramatized the whole chain of events to ensure that the Guptas were projected in bad light.

The repercussions of Sudha's rampage hit the Guptas in many ways. Madhu's friends from block B slowly started distancing themselves from her. She wasn't invited to the usual afternoon get-togethers that she had actively participated in. Whenever she passed a group of residents in the colony compound, she could sense them talking behind her back. The most envied woman and her beautiful daughter were now the subject of ridicule.

For Shekhar, it was even more humiliating. He wasn't greeted with the usual warmth and respect he had grown accustomed to all these years. The biggest blow came when he was asked to step down from his long-held position of Chairman of the society. That was the ultimate sign that he had lost the respect of the colony residents. He soon reached the conclusion that the colony was not suitable for him and his family to live in anymore.

The friction between the families hit the Srivastavs as well. Amar had found a close friend in Shekhar and missed the lunches that they shared every other day. Amar was genuinely fond of him and was sad about the way things had gone. Shekhar had proved very kind and helpful and had even gone out of his way to secure a job for Babloo in the office.

But Shekhar proved to be a fair man. He showed no malice towards Amar in the office and treated him professionally when it came to work matters. Above all, he was still courteous and accommodating to Babloo and gave no indication of Babloo's job being in jeopardy. Deep down, Amar still respected him.

He was angry with Sudha for the way she had handled the situation. He wished he had gone alone and spoken with Shekhar about the matter. And he secretly hoped that he would again secure Shekhar's friendship irrespective of whether the alliance could be rekindled.

But he soon realized that the damage was irreparable when Shekhar requested higher command for an immediate transfer to Mira Road railway station. He cited "personal decisions" as his reason. Coincidently, there was an opening at Shekhar's level in the newly developed Mira Road station unit. Now it was just a matter of days.

I was unaware of the trouble brewing between the two families I was desperate to bring together with my own marriage to Vandana. I had yet to meet Sikander and get a report on her feelings towards me. Now I was really anxious to know. I kept waiting in the colony compound in the evenings since Sikander and the colony boys usually hung out there at that hour. But they never appeared.

Finally one evening, I was all set to go to Sikander's shop. As chance would have it, I caught a glimpse of Vandana entering her block with shopping bags in either hand. Instinctively, I ran to talk to her. I decided I would handle this myself.

I caught up with her on the second flight of stairs of her building. She turned around with a start when she heard footsteps behind her. I leaned on the stairwell panting, trying to catch my breath. She put her bags down.

"Hi Babloo."

I looked at her closely. The usual cheer and happiness was missing from her face.

"How are you Babloo? I haven't seen you in a long time," she said. "You must have been very busy. I heard about your new job."

"Yes," I said.

"Are you enjoying it?"

"Yes."

"Good."

She picked up her bags.

"I have to go now Babloo. You take care. Bye."

She turned and started walking silently up the stairs but stopped when she heard me following her. She put her bags down and turned to face me.

"Did you get my card?" I asked.

"What card?" she asked surprised.

"My Valentine's day Card."

"No Babloo. I didn't get any card from you."

"Sikander said he gave it to you."

"Babloo," she said softly. "Sikander gave me a musical Valentine's Day card but it was from him."

I was puzzled. That was my card. And Sikander was supposed to have given it to Vandana on my behalf. A Q & A session started in my head but I quickly silenced it. I needed to concentrate on the situation at hand.

"Babloo, I'm confused," said Vandana.

"That was my card," I said, looking her straight in the eye.

"But Sikander said it was his card."

"No, it was my card," I mumbled slowly.

"Why did you want to give me a Valentine's Day card, Babloo?

"Because I love you," I said confidently, in one breath.

Vandana was stupefied. She probably would never have imagined such words coming from me.

"Babloo," she said slowly, "do you realize what you're saying?"

"Yes." I did realize what I was saying. It was something I had wanted to say to her ever since I first saw her.

"I have always loved you, Vandana."

"Babloo, I'm sorry," she said apologetically. "Please don't feel that way about me."

"I love you," I said, now even louder. Vandana looked around to ensure there was no one nearby.

"Babloo, we're moving away from here."

"What?"

"We're moving away from here," she said again, slowly. "You will never see me again after tonight."

A look of alarm appeared on my face.

"Why?" I asked.

"Things have turned out that way," she said.

"What?"

"We're moving to our flat in Mira Road tonight," she said sadly. "And then soon my father will send me to my Uncle's place in America for a while."

"Why?"

"Because things have changed."

"Why?"

"We can't live here anymore."

I was confused. Suddenly my face lit up.

"Your dream has come true. You wanted to go to America."

Vandana sat me down and explained very slowly about how Sikander had given her my Valentine Day card as his own, about how Sikander had wooed her and she foolishly went out with him, and how he tried to rape her and she escaped. Then she went ahead and told me about how our parents had fixed up her marriage with Raghu and how it had ended. She was surprised to know that I had no clue about Raghu and her. I listened carefully and felt many emotions swirl inside me.

"Please don't go," I said sadly, once she had finished. "I love you. I will protect you."

"Babloo, you're very sweet. I will miss you a lot."

I remained silent. My mind was racing. There were a lot of things to do. First I had to deal with Sikander. He would not stand a chance against Rail Man. But this was my problem, not Rail Man's. Then I had to deal with my parents. I could not tolerate anyone hurting the woman I loved.

And after all that, I would have to come back and talk to Vandana again. I would confess to her that I was Rail Man. I would explain to her that I had done it for her. Then she would be very proud of me and would believe that I could protect and take care of her. And finally, I would ask her to marry me.

But I could do only one thing at a time. The first thing was to hunt Sikander down.

I looked up at Vandana. "Please don't go. I will come back."

With that I got up and raced down the steps.

## 30

"COME ON GUYS. COUGH UP THE MONEY."

Sikander was standing outside his shop with Mahesh, Madan and Pravin. The garages were shut and the street was deserted. It was ten minutes past nine at night.

"I won the bet," Sikander snickered at them. "Come on, give me the money."

"How do we know that you actually pinned Vandana?" asked Pravin.

"You want to get a blood hound to sniff my car seats?" asked Sikander sarcastically. "I won the bet. Now show me the money."

Mahesh and Madan dug into their wallets and produced two 500 rupee notes. Pravin made no similar effort.

"Pravin, pay up," said Sikander irritated. "I won the bet."

"I don't believe you," said Pravin.

In a quick motion, Sikander kicked Pravin between the legs. Pravin whimpered and fell to the ground. Sikander fished around in Pravin's pockets and extracted some loose 100 rupee bills.

"Never challenge the best," said Sikander, laughing loudly. He counted the notes carefully. When he looked up, he noticed me standing at a distance, in my own shadow created by the dim, overhead street lamp. I approached him steadily.

"Hi Babloo," said Sikander curtly, and looked away cursing under his breath.

"Why didn't you give Vandana my card?" I asked, staring straight into his eyes.

Sikander produced a fake laugh. "Man, I did give her your card. I can't help it if she fell in love with me."

"She did not," I stated.

"Listen Babloo," Sikander said rudely. "Don't mess with my head."

I remained standing there.

"And Babloo," said Sikander softly, "that woman is no good for you. She's a whore. She was going to get married to your brother. Then she made me screw her. Forget about her. I helped you man."

He extracted two notes from his prize money.

"Here," he said, offering me the money. "This is some of the bet money I won from screwing Vandana. This is your share. You are partly responsible for making it happen."

We were standing in the shadows. Sikander didn't see it coming. I hit him hard across the face with my knuckles. Sikander stumbled backwards, losing his grip on the money. The notes scattered all over the place. Pravin quickly scrambled on the ground to retrieve his money. Mahesh and Madan stepped back. I held my hurting fist with an expression of determination rather than pain.

Sikander quickly regained his balance.

"You psycho," he said, dazed. "I have been nice to you. Get out of here before I break your face."

I charged forward and hurled myself at him. I got a hold of his neck and pushed him onto the wall. Sikander shouted in pain and started coughing. I pressed harder.

"You tried to rape Vandana," I said, staring straight into the loser's eyes.

"Take him off me!" Sikander managed to shout at his friends.

I felt two pairs of hands pulling me away from him. They held a firm grip on me and waited for his reaction.

Sikander took a minute and caught his breath. He slowly stood up and looked around. He found a metal bar in the nearby garage and picked it up. Then he walked towards me holding up the weapon, ready to strike.

"Trying to mess with me, huh?" hissed Sikander. "You asked for it, retard. Now you're going to get it."

With that, Sikander swung the bar straight into my stomach. I felt the stinging pain but maintained my balance. Before the second blow reached me, I quickly moved to the side. The bar caught Mahesh on his side and he fell to the ground screaming. Madan looked alarmed and instinctively let go of me. Pravin got up to his feet. Almost simultaneously, both Madan and Pravin turned around and ran.

"Cowards!" Sikander shouted after them.

He proceeded to swing the bar wildly at me, muttering abuses. I dodged the first two blows. Sikander's third blow hit the windshield of his own car. It shattered. Sikander looked at it in frustration.

"Shit! Shit!" he shouted.

He threw himself at me. I caught him halfway and pushed him against the car. I held him there and punched his stomach hard. He remained standing. He weakly tried to protect his face. But my punches found their way to his face.

Within minutes, his lip started bleeding. He moaned in pain.

I continued to punch his face and stomach. He slumped to the ground.

I put my foot above his face. His eyes widened with fear. I brought my foot down hard on his right cheek. Slowly, he closed his eyes and passed out. I looked around. Mahesh had also disappeared.

I heard the muffled sounds of people running towards us in the distance. I quickly regained my senses and ran away from the scene.

Ma, Papa and Raghu were glued to the TV watching Ma's favourite daily soap opera. They heard the main door open but didn't take their eyes off the television. I walked straight into the living room and stood in front of them blocking their line of vision.

"Move Babloo," ordered Ma.

I remained standing there. I looked straight at Raghu who was sipping a glass of juice. He looked up to meet my gaze.

"You were going to marry Vandana," I said accusingly.

"Get out of the way!" ordered Papa angrily.

I moved out of the way. My family's attention turned back to the television. I felt my frustration mounting. They didn't seem to be interested in what I had to say and I had had enough.

In a sudden motion, I snatched the glass from Raghu's hand spilling juice all over. I threw it at the television screen but the screen didn't break. The glass shattered in pieces as it hit the ground. My family looked up at me in shock. For what seemed like the first time in years, I now had their full attention.

I didn't bask in it for more than a few seconds as I lunged forward and caught Raghu's neck. Raghu made no attempt to free himself, and made choking sounds, looking helplessly at our parents. Papa got up immediately.

"Let him go!" Papa shouted.

"You insulted Vandana," I said angrily to Raghu.

Papa used all his force and tried to pull me away. I let go of my grip on Raghu and pushed Papa with full force. He fell back into his chair startled.

By the time I turned towards Raghu again, I saw Ma standing between us.

"Babloo what are you doing?" she asked me gently.

"You all hurt Vandana," I said.

"No Beta," said Ma softly. "We had fixed her marriage with Raghu but we realized we made a mistake."

"But I want to marry her," I said.

Ma was taken aback with surprise. She looked at Papa who was red with anger.

"Babloo, that girl is no good," she said softly.

'*You* are no good!" I shouted.

Papa stood up suddenly.

"I have tolerated you long enough," he said angrily. "You are a useless person. All you have brought us is shame and disappointment and..."

He was interrupted by a wild shout from me. I picked up the coffee table and threw it at Raghu. He moved away just in time. The wooden table bounced off the couch as it landed upside down on the floor.

I looked around at the family that was never mine. They all returned my look with different expressions – my father with anger, my mother with fear and my brother with triumph. I found my way around the inverted coffee table and headed out the door.

I decided that I had had enough of them. What was the use of wasting my life with people who didn't care about my feelings? They hadn't even deemed it important to tell me about Raghu's marriage being arranged with Vandana.

I headed purposefully in the direction of Block B to the only person I cared about. I was determined to tell Vandana everything about Rail Man. She seemed to be the only person who cared about me and I knew that she would understand why I did it for her. And she would love me for that; I was confident about that.

Vandana and I did not need all these people. Once she agreed to marry me, I would take her away from this hopeless colony and start a new life elsewhere. I was sure it would all happen because Rail Man was a superhero. And at the end of the day, the superheroes always won.

I hurried into Block B and took the flight of stairs, two steps at a time, till I found myself in the dark corridor outside Vandana's door. Without wasting a second, I rang the doorbell. Silence. I rang it again. No one answered. I rang it again and again. But no answer.

I reached for the door handle and felt a huge padlock on the latch. Realization dawned on me that no one was at home. I banged on the door with my fists in frustration and then leaned my head against the door in defeat. Tears rolled down my cheeks as I replayed the last conversation I had had with Vandana.

She said I wouldn't see her after tonight. But I remembered telling her to wait for me. And she hadn't.

I broke down and sobbed. The only person who brought me some hope in my otherwise hopeless life had disappeared forever.

I sensed a door opening and slowly turned my face to see the outline of a neighbour looking in my direction.

"They have moved Babloo. They are never coming back."

I straightened up and sprinted down the stairway. I couldn't believe this was happening. I had never imagined a life without Vandana. I ran out of the colony and headed straight for the tracks.

On the way, I pulled out my black pancake and smeared my face carelessly. I was fed up of being Babloo. Babloo had no future. Now I wanted to be Rail Man and run far away from Babloo, as far as I could.

I found my way to the tracks and ran full speed alongside a passing train. The train slowed down and I overtook it. But I kept running. Only when I reached the edge of Bandra, where the tracks left the ground to cross the bridge over to Dharavi, did I slow down.

The tracks couldn't take me any further in that direction. I realized that my life had turned out the same way. This was a dead end for both my identities. Babloo had no life ahead of him and Rail Man had no motivation to be Rail Man anymore.

I felt the weariness creep into my body. I found a safe spot on the edge, away from the tracks and rested my head on the cool dirt. Within minutes I fell asleep.

## 31

A NUDGE ON MY SHOULDER WOKE ME UP WITH A START. I peered through the darkness but could only see the outlines of three men.

"Are you sure it's him Dada?"

I felt a hand cupping itself around my wristwatch.

"It's him," said another voice.

The hand let go of my wrist. A kick to my side forced my eyes completely open.

"Do you remember me, you *chutiya*?"

I slowly turned my face in the direction of the crude voice. I could only see three figures hovering above me against the bright moonlit sky of the night.

"Get him to his feet."

I felt two pairs of hands pulling me to my feet. I tried to slump back down. Now I could feel pangs of hunger in my stomach. And I was still very sleepy. But the hands forced me to stand up. I was made to face the man who had barked out the order.

"I was in the hospital for a whole month because of you. I was hoping I would find you."

I tried to close my eyes but a hand slapped me awake. I turned to my side and caught the glowing hands of my watch. It was 4 o'clock in the morning. The trains were resting for the night. The tracks were empty.

"Do you remember me?" asked the voice again, more belligerently.

I looked closely at the man. I caught sight of the headband tied around the man's forehead. Now I remembered. It was the same political party activist whom I had got into an altercation with, on the tracks, on the day of Mumbai Bandh.

"He remembers," said the man.

He delivered a tight slap across my face.

"You remember now, don't you? Say something."

I sensed the frustration in the man's voice. He adjusted his headband, briefly revealing a big scar on his forehead.

"Dada," said the other man, directing the leader's attention to my hand.

The leader looked closely at my hand and saw the black colour on my palm. He caught my collar with both hands and pulled me towards him till our faces were just inches away from each other, and he looked carefully at my black painted face.

"Are you the madman who has been running around as Rail Man?" demanded the leader.

I was tired. Now I just wanted to go home and rest. I didn't have the strength to fight. I had had a long night and felt completely drained.

"Look Munna," laughed the leader. "This *chutiya* is Rail Man!"

The other two took a closer look at me.

"Yes, Dada," said the other one. "I think it's him."

The leader put his hand in his pocket and I heard a clicking sound. The moonlight reflected on the steel blade. The leader had taken out a *rampuri* knife.

"Hold him straight," said the leader.

I became alert and knew I had to think fast. I couldn't let the story of Rail Man end this way. With a sudden surge of energy, I forced my body awake and released myself from the now loosened grip of the two men holding me. I pushed the leader with force. He stumbled backwards and tripped, disappearing in the dark.

"*Ghe re!*"

The leader had ordered the men to catch me. By the time they had adjusted themselves to the sudden change of events, I was already running as fast as I could.

From the sound of idle stones being displaced underfoot at regular time intervals, I sensed that they were in pursuit of me. I kept running along the middle of the track. I figured that I would be able to run faster if I kept to a straight line. Also, it was too dark to take chances. Once I came into familiar territory, I would look for a diversion.

Within two minutes, the bright lights of Bandra station came into view. I diverted from the tracks and ran straight up Platform 1. It was empty. I headed through the main ticket counter area onto the road. There were only a few prostitutes brushing up against a constable on duty, on the otherwise sleepy street. I immediately turned in the other direction towards the mosque.

I needed to lose my pursuers before I headed home. I ran around the periphery of the mosque towards the bus depot, disappearing from the view of the main entrance of Bandra Station. I could still hear the thumping of running feet in the distance.

I noticed a taxi parked on the side. As I approached it, I saw that the backdoor was open and there were a pair of legs sticking out. I quietly opened the front door and sat inside, crouching down as low as I could. I tried to breathe slowly so that I wouldn't wake up the cab driver sleeping in the back.

I stayed like that for what seemed like five minutes after which I heard the pairs of running legs pass the taxi. I decided to remain there till it was safe to get out.

As I caught my breath, I felt a firm hand catch hold of my hair and lift me up.

"Who are you? Why are you hiding here?"

I heard the footsteps coming back in the direction of the taxi. I tried to duck back down but my head was pulled up all the way till I was face to face with the cab driver.

"Why is your face painted black?"

I looked at the cab driver in silence. His face was concealed in the shadow.

"You look like that cartoon... Rail Man!"

The man let out a heavy, jovial laugh. I recognized that laugh. The man leaned closer into the light. It was Manjit Singh! The cab driver whom I had shared a table with at National Dhaba!

"It's me!" I said hopefully.

Manjit Singh showed no signs of recognition.

"It's me Babloo...National Dhaba... *rajma* curry..."

He looked at me closely and let go of me.

"Of course I remember you, Babloo! How are you?"

My attention was on the road outside. The leader and his men were now standing in the centre of the road, looking around.

"Why is your face black?" asked Manjit concerned.

He followed the direction of my look and saw the three men looking for me.

"Are you in trouble?"

"Yes," I replied.

He tightened his turban, got out of the car and quickly slid in behind the steering wheel. He turned towards me while he brought the car to life.

"Don't worry Babloo. You're safe with me."

He accelerated the car in second gear and quickly found his way to the main road. The three anxious men caught a quick glimpse of me in the cab when it almost ran them over.

Manjit Singh and I were sitting in his parked taxi outside Santacruz station. A cycle-wallah served us biscuits and coffee from a steel filter that was secured firmly to the back of his bulky Hero cycle. I tore open the sealed packet of biscuits and ate voraciously. Manjit Singh merely sipped from his plastic cup of coffee.

"What happened, Babloo?" he asked in between sips. "Why were those men chasing you?"

I continued eating.

"You can tell me. What happened?"

"I got into a fight," I said.

"How did your face get black?"

I remained silent. I had wanted Vandana to be the first to know about Rail Man. It was to be our secret and I decided not to tell Manjit Singh.

He took out a white handkerchief from his trouser pocket and wiped my face. I didn't like anyone touching me. But it was over in a few seconds before my agitation got the better of me.

"There," said Manjit Singh. "Now you look like a human being."

He let out a huge laugh that came straight from his belly. I simply looked at him.

"Babloo *yaar*!" he exclaimed. "Don't get angry! I was just joking with you."

I finished the last biscuit and crumpled the wrapper in my hands.

"If those men were troubling you, why didn't you go to the police?" asked Manjit Singh curiously.

"No."

"Why not? Those men might trouble you again."

"No."

"*Theekh hai*, Babloo," said Manjit Singh animatedly. "Just be careful. Stay away from that area for some time. Those men might still be looking for you. And Manjit Singh may not be there again to help you."

I had no intention of going to the tracks again. The chapter of Rail Man was closed forever. Rail Man's real mission was justice. But his other purpose was to make Vandana proud of him. And Vandana wasn't there anymore.

Now all I wanted was sleep. I would re-think my life again tomorrow.

"You seem very tired," said Manjit Singh. "My shift is going to start soon. Come, I will drop you home. Where do you live?"

"Railway Colony. Bandra Station."

"I have to go to Khar. I will drop you till there."

We rode in silence. I got off at S.V. Road in Khar. I was grateful to Manjit Singh for saving my life. As a token of appreciation, I invited him to dinner at National Dhaba. We planned to meet there at nine that night.

As I walked down the main road, I saw the city rapidly coming to life. Elderly men were returning from their morning walks. Vegetable vendors were pushing their carts in the direction of the market near Khar Station. Beggars were staking out their territories for the day by the traffic signals. A herd of cows were crossing the street, halting the traffic. Some impatient drivers honked wildly while the religious ones bowed their heads in reverence.

I reached the colony at a quarter to 8 in the morning and passed a few of the colony residents as they were heading out to work, hurriedly. I headed straight home. As I walked up the stairs, I saw the main door wide open. That meant that Papa was just about to leave for work. I decided to take the day off. All I could think about now was sleep.

As I entered the house, Papa appeared and blocked my way. He was still in his pajamas and wore a blank expression on his face.

A uniformed police inspector appeared from behind him. And behind the inspector stood Ma. She had tears in her eyes. I heard a set of hurried footsteps stop behind me in the corridor. I turned around to see four armed police inspectors at the doorway with their guns pointed at me.

"Is this yours?" asked the police inspector.

I looked at the wristwatch that the inspector dangled in front of my face. Papa had moved to the side now.

I felt my wrist. My watch wasn't there. It must have slipped off on the railway tracks during the incident with the leader and his group.

The inspector produced a small plastic bag and took out a black pancake packet from it.

"Is this yours?" he asked.

I remained silent.

"Arrest him," ordered the inspector.

I sensed the men behind me step forward carefully. They pulled my hands behind my back and clasped a pair of handcuffs on them.

As the police led me away from the house, I saw a tear rolling down Papa's cheek. It was the first time I saw him cry.

# 32

THE POLICE INTERROGATED ME IN A SPECIAL ROOM in Bandra Police Station. But I remained silent throughout. They were talking too fast. And I didn't like people shouting at me.

After the hour-long interrogation, I was thrown into a cell. Relieved that I was alone, I quickly lay down on the uneven, dirty ground. The stench from the open pot in the corner was unbearable. I shut my eyes and waited for sleep to rescue me.

But the loud, abrasive sound of the cell door forced my eyes open. I looked up to see a short, uniformed inspector looking down at me with a belt in hand. His moustache seemed to cover his entire mouth. I couldn't see the inspector's lips moving as he spoke.

"*Kya re*, madman," he said condescendingly. "Trying to be a superhero, huh? Trying to make us policemen look stupid, huh?"

The inspector kicked me on the side of my stomach. I felt a shooting pain pierce my body. The inspector went for another kick but was surprised when I caught his leg midway.

"Trying to fight a policeman, huh? Trying to put the law down, huh?"

He raised his belt and I saw it coming down all the way towards my face. I managed to close my eyes just in time. It felt like being slapped by 20 hands at the same time. I made a weak attempt to get up but was held down firmly by the policeman's leg.

He hit me with the belt repeatedly. But I didn't make a sound.

"Shout, you bastard," taunted the inspector, repeatedly.

I remained silent.

After 10 minutes, he retreated to his desk, which faced my cell. For the next hour he kept muttering abuses at me while going about his daily work.

I tried to sleep but the pain didn't let me.

After a few hours, two other inspectors came in and whacked me. And in the evening, when the shift changed, two more enthusiastic inspectors took their turns. I went through it all in a daze. I kept waiting to catch some sleep and then wake up in the familiar surroundings of my bedroom.

At night, no one visited me and I managed to temporaily escape into my safe world of slumber.

I woke up the next morning to the sound of scraping metal. I was relieved to hear the sound of the morning train. But when I turned my eyes from the ceiling to look at the source of the sound, I saw that it came from a steel plate that had been pushed towards me on the ground. The plate had two pieces of bread on it and a cup of tea which had spilled all over the plate soaking the bread.

I looked around and tried to accustom myself to my new environment. I strongly believed that the police had brought me here in error. Rail Man had only fought for justice. He never abused it. I knew that they would eventually realize their oversight and release me. I had never done anyone any harm. Or at least, I had not intended to.

No one bothered me that entire day. Occasionally, people in the busy police station stopped by my cell to take a look at me, as if I was an exhibit for an endangered species in a zoo. But no one spoke to me. A sympathetic constable told me that my parents stood outside the police station all day but the moustached police inspector shooed them away. "Orders from above" is what the inspector told them.

Finally, in the evening, I saw a familiar face in the police station.

It was the MiD-DAY reporter, Shoma Banerjee, accompanied by a man in a black coat and two other women. She was arguing with the moustached police inspector. She flashed her card. The inspector shook his head. The man produced a sheet of paper from his file and showed it to the inspector. The inspector hesitated and then called out to a constable. The constable brought Shoma and company to my cell.

I got up and walked towards the bars of the cell and stood face to face with them. Shoma looked at me closely and smiled.

"So you're Rail Man," she said.

"Yes."

"Thank you," she said.

I looked away from her. I was wondering how the police got to my house, even if the watch was brought to them.

"Babloo," she continued, "don't worry. We'll try to get you out of here as soon as possible. The press is on your side. Very soon the whole city will be on your side. This is Barrister Manu Lalwani. He will fight your case."

I remained silent.

"Barrister Lalwani needs to talk to you. Tell him everything he asks and he will do his best. He is one of the best criminal lawyers in the city."

I didn't understand why I needed a lawyer. What had I done wrong?

Barrister Lalwani proceeded to cross-question me. I answered in monosyllables. I didn't feel like talking to a stranger. Barrister Lalwani made his notes and left while Shoma remained there with the two women.

"Babloo, we're going to do our best to get you out of here. This is Namita Majumdar and Diya Sadrangani. Namita is a senior reporter with the *Times of India*. And Divya works with *Indian Express*. We are going to get your story out there. We will make sure that you have the support of the public. But you need to tell us everything."

I wasn't good with open-ended questions. I never knew where to start so I decided to start from the beginning.

"I was born in Mumbai...," I began.

"No, I mean the origin of Rail Man," interrupted Shoma. I fell silent. I had always been good at figuring things out on my own, but I couldn't figure out how to answer that. Shoma seemed to sense my state of confusion.

"How about we ask you questions and you answer?" she suggested.

I thought about this. This would be easier. But what confused me was that Shoma was the one who had created Rail Man. She should be the one to know how it all started.

Shoma and the women asked me questions slowly, one by one. The two women took notes while Shoma recorded everything on a dictaphone. I answered all the questions in a total daze. I was very tired and my body ached from all the beatings. I didn't remember most of my answers but I did remember asking Shoma how the police got to my residence.

Shoma told me that the people whom I had got into the fight with on the tracks, had noted the license plate number of the cab that I had escaped in. Also, they managed to retrieve the watch I had dropped on the tracks. They used their political connections and immediately got the police to trace the taxi. The police found the taxi at 6 a.m. and interrogated Manjit Singh who told them that I lived in the railway colony. The police then dispatched a special team to my house.

In a way I was relieved. I had been worried that Manjit Singh would be waiting for me at National Dhaba for the dinner that I had promised him. He had helped me and the last thing that I wanted to do was to stand him up. Now he would know why I wouldn't be able to make it.

Shoma and her associates gathered their notes and wrapped up. They promised to do their best to prove my innocence. As far as I was concerned, I was already innocent. But I thanked them anyway.

They left me alone with my thoughts in the bare cell. Each time someone passed, I looked up hopefully. I was secretly hoping that Vandana would come and visit me. But she was far away now.

I sat down in a corner of the cell, tucked my head into my knees and cried. I couldn't imagine my life without Vandana. Without her, I had no one to live for.

The door of the cell creaked upon. The moustached inspector appeared with his belt in hand. I knew that I wouldn't be able to sleep well again that night.

# 33

MY COURT HEARING WAS SET FOR THE VERY NEXT DAY in the fast track court. Apparently, the arrest of Rail Man had garnered a tremendous amount of publicity and the Police Commissioner wanted to close the case as soon as possible.

I was transported to the court under heavy security. The police knew that the media would be there in large numbers and wanted to create a show out of the proceedings.

The distance from the police station to the court was less than a few kilometers. The public had aligned themselves on the road creating traffic jams at regular intervals. By the time we reached the court, we were already an hour late for the appointed hearing.

The same day, before my case hearing, film star Riyaz Khan was being tried in the same court for an incident in which he had allegedly run over a construction worker sleeping on the road.

The police van parked in front of the courthouse. There were crowds of people everywhere. When I emerged from the van, the crowds came to life and raised hand-made banners in support of Rail Man. Some of them had painted their faces black to show their solidarity while others wore T-shirts adorned with imprints of black faces.

Reality hit me and I realized I was in a lot of trouble. But I didn't care about the consequences anymore. After the unfair treatment that was meted out to me in the cell, I knew that there was no such thing as justice anymore. I just wanted to get it all over with.

News reporters surrounded me as policeman shoved me towards the main entrance. The reporters asked me for a comment. I looked at them blankly. They repeatedly asked me questions but I didn't reply. Finally, they gave up and asked me to say anything at all. I looked straight into the camera and saw my miniature reflection in the lens. I looked tired.

"I want to sleep," I said.

I was transported up the stairs, leaving the group of reporters confused. At the entrance to the court, a huge group emerged, trailed by a different set of reporters. At the centre of the group was Riyaz Khan, concealed behind a pair of designer sunglasses. As we were about to cross each other, Riyaz Khan stopped. He removed his sunglasses to reveal his weary eyes and smiled at me giving me a thumbs-up gesture with his hand before moving on. Only a true hero recognizes another true hero, I thought. I felt rejuvenated with this first real sign of encouragement as I was pushed into the room with the high ceiling that would decide my fate.

I had always enjoyed courtroom dramas in films. But being in a real one was a different ball game altogether. The court was crowded beyond capacity. The judge was already seated but the public gathered there showed no respect towards him as they kept talking to each other in loud voices.

I was taken straight to a boxed stand and left alone on the elevated wooden platform with my handcuffs on. Two policemen stood guard behind me. Barrister Lalwani was wearing a black coat and was seated behind a long desk along with other men wearing similar coats. The judge banged his gavel repeatedly but couldn't bring the court to order. Barrister Lalwani and another lawyer stood up and approached the bench. The judge whispered something to them after which they retreated. While the other lawyer took his place behind the long desk, Lalwani remained standing.

It was very humid. I was drenched in sweat almost immediately. I so badly wanted to take a shower, I had been wearing the same clothes for the past two days.

A red, bound copy of the holy *Bhagavad Gita* was held before me. I was asked to repeat an oath, which I did missing out many words. The judge banged his hammer again. The trial had officially begun.

The prosecutor, Barrister Ashok Natekar, related the case to the judge. Due to the loud commotion, he was barely audible but I caught everything he said.

Natekar appealed to the judge to make an example of me and dole out a harsh sentence.

Barrister Lalwani was called to defend his witness.

"Your honour," said Lalwani. "Balwant Srivastav is a victim of circumstances. He had no intention of harming anyone. But to help the victims come out of their dangerous situations, he had to take the course of action that he did. Yes, that could be viewed as taking the law into one's own hands. But he was successful in saving the victims from death. I wish to plead not guilty."

"That's fine," said the judge. "If you thought he was guilty, we wouldn't be here. This is the fast track court, Barrister Lalwani. A decision has to be made today. Please proceed."

I scanned the gathered crowd. I spotted Shoma and her two associates. There were some people from the colony as well. Sitting on the last bench were my parents and Raghu. But Vandana was nowhere around.

"Your honour," continued Lalwani. "I would like to highlight the backgrounds of the alleged victims, who were actually criminals."

Lalwani proceeded to flesh out the criminal backgrounds of the group that had attacked Shoma and the notorious gang that had stabbed Patel. The judge listened to everything silently while reading the reports provided by Lalwani as supporting evidence.

Natekar kept interjecting at regular intervals.

Witnesses were called to the witness stand one by one. My parents, Raghu, Patel, the political activists whom I had encountered on the tracks, Shoma Banerjee, her ex-boyfriend and his gang, Manjit Singh, some colony residents, my colleagues at the office, Sikander, Madan, Mahesh and Pravin. They were each cross examined by both lawyers. Some of them spoke in my favour and some against.

Finally, the judge spoke.

"After listening to both sides, there seems to be some form of mental instability in the accused Balwant Srivastav. The court orders an expedited medical examination of Balwant and the hearing is adjourned to the day after."

He banged the gavel and called for the next case.

After leaving the courthouse, I was transported amidst tight security to KEM Hospital. I was examined by a series of psychologists and doctors. I saw them scribbling on their reports as they questioned me.

They asked me questions to check my social and behavioural skills. I replied to the best of my ability. They wrote down 'Attention Deficit Disorder'.

They asked me about my concentration span. I told them that it was very high. When I thought intently of something, it kept circling in my mind. They wrote down 'Psychosis'.

They asked me many more questions and directed me to draw images in response. I got irritated and pushed the paper away. They wrote down 'Potential Schizophrenia'.

They kept writing and I got fed up and stopped answering. Finally, I was taken back to the jail lock-up. I spent most of the night thinking about Vandana and me sitting on a park bench, talking to each other. She was consoling me, telling me that everything was going to be just fine.

The next day at court passed quickly.

Barrister Lalwani examined the medical reports and forwarded them to the judge. The judge reviewed the reports for 20 minutes. Then he called both the barristers to the bench. He whispered something to them. Barrister Lalwani came up to me and whispered something in my ear. I understood and agreed. Then Lalwani nodded towards the judge. The Judge looked at me sympathetically and turned towards the court to deliver his verdict.

# EPILOGUE

I AWOKE AGAIN TO A METALLIC SOUND. IT WAS broad daylight. The bed next to me was empty. I got out of bed and looked out of the window, searching for the familiarity of the railway tracks. But it had been replaced by a manicured green lawn. I looked around the room to see that the old, peeling walls had been replaced by neatly painted, light green walls. The dusty, brown tiles had been replaced by smooth, clean, white ones.

The metallic sound was the morning bell. And it rang every morning to wake us up and start us on our daily routine.

In an instant, it all came back to me. In court, Barrister Lalwani had whispered to me that the only way out was to plead insanity. He said that I would be able to get away with a few years' sentence in a mental asylum, which was much better than a harsh prison term. I had agreed only because I wanted to go back home faster. That was almost a year ago.

When I first came here, I was scared. I had seen many films which showed mental asylums. The thought of living among crazy people scared me and I felt I had made a mistake by coming here and should have gone to jail instead.

However, over the months I realized that these people were not crazy but victims of circumstances just like me. They were not boring like the people outside. They all had a history, something that made them interesting.

A prime example was my roommate, Kabir Mitha. Kabir could recite by rote, the multiplication table for the number three, all the way to a thousand times three. He could go beyond that but then usually he fell asleep. Then he would wake up again and started from the beginning. 1 times 3 is three. 2 times 3 is 6. 3 times 3 is nine. 4 times 3...

Before coming to this mental asylum in Mumbai, Kabir lived in a posh bungalow in Gurgaon, a suburb close to Delhi. He was in his mid-30s and a financial controller with a big company. One night, a group of armed burglars entered his house. Kabir was upstairs with his eight-year-old daughter. When he saw the figures passing his door, he let out a shout. One of them panicked and fired a gun in his direction. It missed him and got his daughter instead. At the time, Kabir was teaching his daughter the multiplication table for three.

Another genius amongst us was 55-year-old Prof. Mukherjee. A resident of Calcutta, he was a strong contender for a Nobel Prize for something he had researched and developed for 20 years. His only mistake was that he didn't patent his discovery. His colleague stole his invention and made millions by selling it privately, to a company. Prof. Mukherjee couldn't take the shock and since then started delivering his Nobel Prize thanksgiving speech to every person he met.

There were many such tragic, interesting stories but the one they all found most interesting was mine. I was accepted by these people and for the first time in my life I made new friends. They gave me respect and listened to whatever I had to say without judging me. They commended me for my bravery and they all felt that I didn't belong here.

After all these years, this is where I felt a sense of belonging. In no time I settled into the prescribed daily routine. We would start with breakfast and tea at 7 a.m. Then we would exercise in the lawn under the supervision of an instructor. After that we would proceed to lunch, after which we would take our respective medication. The afternoon saw us either in the library or the television room. Then it was evening tea followed by sports time. A few hours later, we assembled for dinner. By 10 at night we were all in bed.

Ma and Papa came to visit me every Sunday. That was the only day visitors were allowed. Raghu never came to see me. I didn't care about his not coming, but I felt nice seeing my parents. They told me sweet things that I had not heard from them in years.

"Everything is going to be alright," "We miss you very much," "We're waiting for you to come home."

These words from them made me feel good and positive. It's amazing what family support can do for a person's morale. They blamed themselves for what happened to me and felt that they should have given me more attention.

I enjoyed spending time with my new friends and we had a lot of fun together. They taught me how to play pranks and how to find things funny. And soon enough, I became less serious and more light-hearted. I laughed often and spoke easily. I stopped staring and learned how to have a conversation, among other things.

There were uniformed attendants on each floor and all of them were very helpful. We saw a harsh side to these attendants only when someone got out of hand. I made friends with a woman attendant called Roma. I told her about Vandana and how much I missed her. Roma said she understood and assured me that time would heal everything and I would learn to forget her.

She was right. With time, I came to terms with the reality that Vandana was gone forever.

The medication did me a lot of good and I slowly stopped hearing that inner voice that had often dominated my mind with Q & A sessions. Over time, my friend disappeared and it was only me who remained. That's when I started getting lonely. My friends tried to cheer me up in many ways. But I missed 'him'.

My friend's disappearance was in a way very helpful. I started speaking in complete sentences. I could translate the exact thoughts in my mind into words. And people said that I was interesting to talk to.

One morning, Roma came to my room and told me that the warden had called me to his office. I had a visitor. I found that strange. Even though there was no calendar around, I knew that it was a Saturday. I was very good at counting days and guessing the time.

I headed to the warden's office wondering how someone was permitted to visit me on a Saturday. I knocked on the door, something new I had learned in this place, and was called inside. The warden was seated behind his desk. Facing him was Shoma, Barrister

Lalwani and a police inspector.

Shoma told me excitedly that she had never given up on me and with the help of the owner of *MiD-DAY*, who was well-connected, had put forth my case to the Chief Minister. The Chief Minister pardoned my sentence and I was free to go!

She searched my face for signs of excitement but found none. I was genuinely lost and sad that I would be leaving my friends. I had finally found my place in the world. I communicated this to Shoma.

"You don't belong here," chided Shoma sweetly. "You belong out there. You are meant to do great things! Don't you get it Babloo? We won! You're free now!"

I guess I should have been happy. But I really wasn't. I had moved on from my previous life. I was safe here. I didn't know what lay in store for me out there.

After collecting my things, I asked the warden if I could bid goodbye to all my friends. He told me that the exercise session had just started and I would have to come back some other day to say my goodbyes.

My parents were waiting outside anxiously and hugged me as soon as they saw me. I hugged them back. My friends had taught me how important it was to emote.

On the drive back, Shoma told me that she would put my story back in the papers and make me a hero again. I thanked her for everything that she had done but requested her not to bring up the topic of Rail Man again and to let people think that he was put away forever. She didn't argue with me and said she understood.

When we reached home, my mother made me wait outside and quickly re-appeared with a *puja thali*. She circled it a couple of times in front of me and then told me to step inside. The house looked different. The furniture in the house was upholstered and the walls were painted. The house looked neat for a change.

My father told me that he was proud of me – words that I had been longing to hear from him all my life. It brought a tear to my eye. We hugged each other and I felt I was not alone anymore.

My mother told me that she had a surprise for me and handed me an envelope. My reading skills had improved and I quickly read the letter. It was from the Chief Minister's office. The letter mentioned that I was to be honoured with a Bravery Award for my efforts in the past. It included a cash award of one lakh rupees. I decided to give the money to my parents.

"So how do you like your surprise?" asked my mother.

"I like it," I replied smiling.

"But how can you like it when you haven't seen it?" asked my mother mischievously.

And then I saw someone come in, and I wondered whether I was dreaming. I pinched myself. I wasn't. Vandana walked into the room followed by her parents. How could she be here? She was in America. Maybe I was dreaming. I pinched myself harder.

"Hey, stop doing that," she smiled. "I'm really here!"

Everyone laughed. I laughed too.

Vandana's parents and my parents had patched up. They had decided to let bygones be bygones.

We sat chatting in the living room till Vandana got up and beckoned me into the balcony. I followed her through the curtained partition and stood next to her, leaning against the railing.

The colony hadn't changed at all. But being back there felt unreal. For some reason, I didn't hate this place anymore. It felt like home.

"So how does it feel to be back?" asked Vandana.

"It feels good," I replied, as I turned to look at her.

I couldn't take my eyes off her. I felt all those feelings coming back.

"Vandana, how come you're here? I thought you were in America. I thought I would never see you again."

"I did go but then decided to come back."

"Come back from America? But you always wanted to live there."

"I came back because of you."

"Me?" I asked surprised.

"Babloo, the last night I was here, the stuff you told me, it made me think. Then I heard about you being Rail Man..."

I had told my parents that I never wanted to hear about Rail Man or my past. Vandana had to know that too.

"Vandana, please don't mention all that. I want to forget about the past. I said many stupid things back then."

"It wasn't stupid, Babloo. Ok yes, running around like a lunatic and beating up all those people was stupid. But that brought out the person you are. You're courageous, brave and you have a good heart."

"Admit it Vandana, it was stupid."

"No Babloo. Being that cartoon character brought out the goodness in you. It showed that you were a man who stood up for what's right. And you did it in the way best known to you."

I kept silent. I was trying to hide my aggravation. I didn't want to hear about my past. She sensed that immediately.

"Babloo," she said, looking me straight in the eye. "Back then, I didn't recognize the person you were. And I came back just to ask you one thing. Did you mean everything you told me on the night I left?"

I remembered what I had said very clearly. I had told her that I loved her.

"I meant it then," I replied. "That was a long time back. Like I told you, I was silly."

"Babloo, I was the one who was silly. Hidden in you was the man I have always hoped to spend the rest of my life with, the kind of person who would always respect and protect me."

"What do you mean Vandana?"

"Babloo, I love you."

I went to pinch myself but she quickly caught my hand and kissed it. She closed the distance between us, as her lips met mine. It was the most divine feeling in the world. It felt like time had stopped. By the way, it was my first kiss.

I think everyone in the living room knew what was going on in the balcony because they suddenly fell silent.

"What do you say to a woman who says that she loves you?" Vandana asked me softly.

"I love you?" I guessed.

"You already said that on the night that I left. What do you say to THIS woman who just said she loves you?"

I knew where this was going.

"Vandana, I have problems," I said. "How can you want to be with a guy like me?"

"Babloo, answer my question. What do you say to this woman who says she loves you?"

"Will you marry me?" This was not a guess.

"I accept," she smiled, and kissed me again, deeply.

I wanted to get a job first and then get married but Vandana didn't want to wait. She said that things would fall in place and that both of us would make it happen. I came to realize that she was a dominating person and that it would be very difficult for me to have my way with her.

The wedding was a low-key affair at a local temple with just both the families in attendance. Raghu stayed away from the wedding for obvious reasons.

After marriage, with the help of the Chief Minister's office, I secured an executive position with a reputed event management company. It was difficult in the beginning, but it was hands-on work which I really enjoyed and my colleagues were very helpful. Vandana secured a job in the creative department of an advertising agency and was happy in her new role.

My dreams of living with Vandana in a house by the sea remained a dream. But that didn't matter so much anymore, because Vandana explained that not all dreams come true.

We stayed at Vandana's house in the colony which Vandana's father had secured with special permission since it had been lying empty as no one had filled his position in the Bandra Station office. But soon, the Railway Housing Board asked us to vacate the place as they needed to accommodate another officer there. I was worried, but Vandana always told me to think positively. She said that things always worked out. And they did.

Patel visited us and offered me the reward money of three lakhs that he had publicly promised Rail Man for saving his life. I refused to take it. He argued but I didn't listen. When he learned of our housing situation, he re-appeared the next day with the keys to an Andheri MHADA flat with its papers. I noticed that he had registered the flat in my name.

He told me that he believed that his life was worth more than the crores that he had earned in his lifetime and he was merely giving me a very small fraction of it. He went on to say that this was something that he had to do for me towards keeping a promise he had made to his Gods, to be carried out in case he survived. I had no choice but to accept it.

It's been a year since my life turned around. Vandana has taken leave from her job because she is six months pregnant with our first child. My company provided me with a car and a chauffeur. My office is in Churchgate, at the other end of town, but I always leave the car home for Vandana to use. I usually travel to work by bus or taxi. Vandana made me promise her that I would never use the train or set foot on the railway tracks again. I hope she doesn't extend it to the Mumbai Metro, the first line of which is under construction.

Vandana's father was transferred back to his Bandra Station office. So every weekend we visit both our parents.

Shoma has risen to the post of Assistant Editor at *MiD-DAY*. She has become good friends with Vandana and we see her very often. Vandana decided that Shoma would be a godmother to our child.

From my parents, I heard that Sikander and his father had been arrested by the Anti-Piracy Bureau for showing a pirated version of an unreleased Hindi film. They were soon let out on bail but all their equipment was confiscated and they were forced to shut down the business.

Raghu lost his job with the stockbroker. Apparently, Raghu's boss was involved in a huge stock market scam and was sentenced to prison. After the incident, Raghu found it difficult to secure a job in the same line of work. Currently he is working in a call center as a tele-marketing executive. He still doesn't talk to me.

But my parents are proud of me and that's all that matters. Even though I told them not to, they sometimes still joke about Rail Man. At first it made me angry and walk out of the room. But then Vandana taught me how to laugh about it with them.

Looking back, Rail Man seemed to be another life altogether. But I will never forget him. Not only did he give me a new lease of life, but he also proved the second prediction of the astrologer to be true.

I have finally found my place in the world. Thank you Rail Man. Thank you Mumbai.

# ACKNOWLEDGMENTS

I am thankful for both the unwitting and the conscious support of many people behind this book. A few names (in no particular order) are:

In Mumbai: Siddharth Haldipur, Sangeet Haldipur, Zia Nath, Gautham K. Sharma, Pratik Thakore, Malini Agarwal, Viola Wadia.

In Delhi: Subhash & Arvinda Arora, Rita Paul, Shishir Gupta.

In USA: Edwin Towle, Mariza Zaragoza, Winifred Arbeiter, Alana Chavez, Joe Magyar, Romi Manchanda.

In Canada: Dionne Bunsha.

I wish to thank Mr. Akash Shah and Mr. R. H. Sharma, along with Lakshmi and Disha and the entire team at Jaico, for investing their expertise in this work of alternative fiction.

And my family and friends, all over, for their blessings.

Above all, I am grateful to Nikki (Natasha), for being my critic, editor, and whose very presence in my life has given me a sense of belonging.

And to little Mia – whose smile infuses me with hope.